# Clash of the Otherworlds
## Book One

# After the Fall

### Elle Casey

All names, places, and events depicted in this book are fictional and products of the author's imagination.

No part of this publication my be reproduced, stored in a retrieval system, converted to another format, or transmitted in any form without explicit, written permission from the publisher of this work. For information regarding redistribution or to contact the author, write to the publisher at the following address:

Elle Casey<br>
PO Box 14367<br>
N Palm Beach, FL 33408

Website: www.ElleCasey.com<br>
Email: info@ellecasey.com

ISBN/EAN-13: 978-1-939455-00-0

Copyright © 2012 Elle Casey<br>
All rights reserved

First Edition

# Dedication

For Elena, the beautiful girl who stole my boy's heart.
I do believe I see more than a little bit of Jayne in you, love.

# Other Books by Elle Casey

War of the Fae: Book One, The Changelings
War of the Fae: Book Two, Call to Arms
War of the Fae: Book Three, Darkness & Light
War of the Fae: Book Four, New World Order

Clash of the Otherworlds: Book 1, After the Fall
Clash of the Otherworlds: Book 2, Between the Realms
Clash of the Otherworlds: Book 3, Portal Guardians

Apocalypsis: Book 1, Kahayatle
Apocalypsis: Book 2, Warpaint
Apocalypsis: Book 3, Exodus
Apocalypsis: Book 4, Haven

My Vampire Summer
My Vampire Fall

Wrecked
Reckless

# Clash of the Otherworlds
## Book One

# After the Fall

Elle Casey

## Chapter One

I RETURNED FROM EATING LUNCH in the dining hall of the Light Fae compound and stood at the entrance of my room, my eyes not really seeing the stone walls and floors or the stark but serviceable wood furniture. Instead, I daydreamed. Reminiscing for a brief moment about the times I had spent inside it, talking and laughing with my friends and contemplating the ways of the fae world with my roommate, Tim, pixieman extraordinaire.

I'd lived here for a couple of months as a newly-made fae elemental - a human girl turned changeling, recruited by the Light Fae to join their cause and save the fae world from certain destruction. Nothing had changed, really. At least not in this room. It looked exactly the same as it had the last time I'd been in it. But everything about *me* was different. I was no longer the girl who had stayed in this small, dark place wondering where I fit in and what my purpose in life would be. *That* had recently been made abundantly and painfully clear.

I sighed, stepping inside and pulling my cloak off my back, throwing it down on the bed. Its shimmering only stopped when the material finally quit moving. I heard a buzzing coming from the hallway and sighed. *And here he is, Mr. Sassypants, himself.*

"Jayne!" yelled the tiny voice that belonged to my roommate. "Aren't you packed yet?"

"No, I just got here," I said, irritated at the unspoken admonishment carried with his words. He knew I'd been hung up talking to well-wishers, and was just harassing me because it was his favorite thing in the entire world to do. I had wondered earlier if having his wife and son around would change anything about him, but so far, no such luck; he was still a pain in my ass. Of course, it hadn't even been a full day since they'd been reunited - or in the case of his son, introduced - so there was still hope.

"Well, you'd better hurry up," he said slyly. "Your boyfriend's waiting for you."

I tried to control the red heat of embarrassment that climbed up my neck to burn my cheeks and ears, but it was impossible.

Tim came flying over from behind me and got right up in my face. "Are you scared? Do you need me to tell you about the birds and the bees? Do you want to know where babies come from?"

I tried to catch him but he flew out of my reach. He was tricky like that. *Little bastard.*

His maniacal laughter bubbled out of him. "I am *so* happy right now, you have no idea."

"Trust me, I'm getting the idea. Did Abby pixilate you, or what?"

"Is that code for something?" asked Tim, waggling his eyebrows at me while biting the tip of his tongue.

He was almost near enough for me to grab. I tried to act harmless while at the same time willing him silently to come closer. I had some serious onion breath from lunch, and I had no qualms about suffocating him with it.

"No, it's not code, perv. I'm wondering if she zapped your big

## Clash of the Otherworlds: Book One

butt with some pixie dust or whatever. I'm not used to seeing you so ... frisky."

"This is the *new* me, Jayne. The new Tim. The new and improved Tim. Twenty-five percent more Tim, free. Tim the terrific. Tim the fabulous. Tim the ..."

"Tim the wingless pixie, if he doesn't shut the hell up for two minutes so I can talk to him about something that matters."

Tim frowned, silently scolding me while he flew over to his bed. Once there, he sat down and crossed his legs, lacing his fingers together over his knees. "I'm all ears. Let's talk about important stuff. I'm ready. Let's do this. Fire away. Let 'er rip."

I glared at him.

He gave me an arrogant sniff and then pantomimed zipping his lips, locking them closed, and throwing away the key.

"What I wanted to know is whether you're coming with me or if you have your own place now. With Abby or whatever." I didn't want to admit that I wasn't looking forward to losing him as a roommate. *Yes*, he was annoying a lot of the time. *Yes*, he had intestinal problems and wasn't shy about sharing. But he'd been incredibly loyal to me since I'd saved him from bell jar imprisonment months ago, and we'd become sort of a team. Tim hadn't replaced Tony as the best friend of my heart, but he was special, nonetheless - kind of like a bonus best friend, in a way.

Tim started bobbing his head all over and gesturing with his hands as if he were answering me but with his mouth closed. I could tell by the goofy look on his face that he was totally killing himself with his comedy routine.

I decided to play along. "Yes, that's what I thought. Okay, so I'll tell Dardennes that you want to room with Leck, then. That should be fun. You can fart in his face while he sleeps, and he can melt your brain and drink it out of your ear for breakfast. Cool." I turned as if to leave and transmit the message, but I didn't get far before Tim was all up in my grill again. He could fly really fast when properly motivated.

"No! That's not what I said!"

"Oh, it's not?" I asked innocently.

"No, you know it wasn't. Why are you being such a party-pooper, anyway? Of course I'm still rooming with you. As long as you don't mind my lady friend and the fruit of my loins joining us."

"Fruit of your loins? *Gah*, do you happen to have a barf bag I could use?"

"I'll have you know that the fruit of my loins? ... It's passionfruit, baby. *Passionfruit.*"

"More like fruit loops," I mumbled as I walked over to the dresser.

"What was that?"

"Oh, nothing. Come on. We have to pack." I was already feeling a little bit better. Teasing Tim always did that for me.

Once the Light and Dark Fae councils had come together and voted to have all of the fae join forces and become one big, happy family, they determined that in order for the integration to have any chance of success, the fae would need to learn to live together. Starting today. Tim and I weren't the only ones getting our lives turned upside down.

"Do you know where our new room is?" I asked.

"Yeah. It's nice. It has a big window and a garden."

"Get-the-fuck-out."

"No, I'm serious. A terrace and everything. Abby's already there getting flowers put in."

"Flowers?" My brain wasn't computing. *I'm going from a tiny*

## Clash of the Otherworlds: Book One

*windowless cell to a garden terrace room?*

"Yeah. Pixie chicks loooove flowers. They're only truly happy when they're covered in pollen. Abby looks good in pollen too, I have to admit."

*"Huh.* Learn something new every day." I opened up the top drawer of my dresser and grabbed all the tunics out and threw them on the bed. "So, what's the deal with the room? How'd we score such a sweet pad?" I opened up the next drawer and pulled the jeans from inside, adding them to my pile.

"You're kidding, right? You're our Mother. Of course they're not going to put you in a changeling room. Don't be ridiculous."

I could hear Tim's feeling-pretty-proud-of-himself tone, which told me more than his words had. Ever since I'd been officially recognized as the long-awaited Mother of the fae species, Tim had taken on the self-appointed title of His Pixieness and all the royal attitude to go with it. It didn't matter one bit that the title was his own invention and meant absolutely nothing to anyone but him.

"What about Ben? Where's he staying?" I asked with feigned casualness, almost afraid to hear Tim's answer. *Please don't let it be with me.*

Ben had been my arch enemy for months, especially when I had thought he was trying to steal my best friend Tony away from me while I was here learning about being fae and Tony was still in Florida living a regular human life. Eventually, I came to realize that I had been wrong about Ben. He was flawed and had done some stupid shit in his zeal to save his people, but he wasn't the evil monster I had once thought he was.

I could hardly hold Ben's mistakes against him, since I'd made plenty of my own, but that didn't mean I was ready to have him overwhelming my life. And I knew he was the type of guy who could do that very easily. He was an elemental too, like me; but he was tied to Fire and Wind, where I was tied to Earth and Water. He was pretty friggin intense, and he'd already told me how attractive he thought I was. It made me nervous just thinking about it.

My emotions where he was concerned were tied up in knots. I wanted to distance myself from him to make it easier to figure things out, but the kiss we'd shared during our binding ceremony made that impossible. Even when he was far, he was still close because I couldn't stop thinking about him. Somehow, he'd made the loss of Chase, my guardian angel and former number one object of lust, easier to bear. I sighed heavily, wondering if my future was going to be any easier to figure out than my past.

"He's staying in the room attached to ours. There's a door connecting them, so don't worry; when you guys want to get busy, you can just go in his room and you'll have complete privacy."

I snorted. "Please. You don't need to worry about that, trust me."

"I don't know, Jayne. I saw the lip lock, you know. That binding ceremony got pretty hot for a few seconds there, and it wasn't just Ben's element firing it up, either."

The heat began to rise in my face again. My chest was probably getting blotchy, too. My traitor emotions were giving me away, once again. "I was caught up in the moment, okay? I know we're ... bound or whatever. But that doesn't mean we're married or anything."

"Um, yeah. It kind of does," replied Tim as he began taking things out of his drawers and putting them on top of his dresser in a stack. "You're stuck together for life. Like thousands of years. You're the Mother, he's the Father. I suggest you get to more of that kissing stuff and not try so hard to resist the inevitable."

## Clash of the Otherworlds: Book One

"*Pfft.* You're one to talk. Your poor wife's been waiting for you to see reason for what? A year? Slaving over there in the Dark Fae lab, trying to come up with a cure for pixelation so you guys could be a family again and live in harmony with other fae instead of being sent to a pixie colony ... "

Tim frowned at me. "Low blow, Jayne. Even for you."

I tried not to feel guilty, but I wasn't entirely successful. I knew Tim felt terrible about the misunderstanding that had kept him separated from his wife and caused him to miss the birth of his baby boy. Apparently, pixie births were a super huge deal too, since they were so rare.

"Whatever. Just so we're clear - I'm not going to go jump into bed with Ben just because he's hot and we were bound in front of the whole friggin world. I don't just sleep with any guy like that."

"I'll keep that in mind," said a deep voice from the doorway.

*Fuckbuckets.* I didn't want to turn around. Maybe if I never made eye contact with him again after this, my shame could never be fully consummated.

"Oh, hey, Ben!" said Tim. "Nice to see you there. Standing right behind Jayne this whole time. Come to collect your bride?" Tim giggled and then stuck his tongue out at me.

I knew Ben couldn't hear Tim, so I amplified for him. "Tim wants to know what you're doing here."

I heard footsteps coming towards me and then his voice again. "I came to see if you needed any help."

I felt his presence at my side. He practically vibrated, he had so much energy coming off of him. *Has he always been like this and I've just never noticed it before?* I caught a whiff of something nice. *Cologne, maybe. The woods. Fire. Ben.*

I turned to face him, taking a step back to put some distance between us. "Hey. What's up?" I tried to smile but my face was spasming in its nervousness, so I quit.

Ben looked me straight in the eyes, neither smiling nor frowning, and it made my heart race a little faster than it already was. I had to fight the urge to fan my face with the socks I was holding in my hand. I broke eye contact with him, acting interested in the top of my dresser.

"Nothing much," he responded. "I got my stuff moved into my room; and since we're neighbors, I thought I'd come over here to see if you needed me for anything. I'm good at carrying stuff."

I tried not to look over at his biceps, I really did; but it was impossible not to. He had some mighty fine specimens. They weren't as big as Chase's, but I definitely wasn't complaining.

The bleakness descended with a speed that took even me by surprise. The brief thoughts I'd just had of Chase instantaneously brought back the memory of him opening up his huge white wings and taking off to disappear into the clouds above us, after my bond with Ben had been officially recognized by the Spirit. The last thing I saw, after Chase told me he would watch over me forever and wait for me in the Overworld until the day I died, were the tears that ran down his face. Any happy thoughts I might have been having about Ben standing next to me in my room went right out the door.

"Did I say something wrong?" asked Ben, concern marring his devastatingly handsome features.

"No." I stepped back to the dresser and opened up the last drawer, pulling out the towels and few other odds and ends that remained of my possessions.

Ben put his hand on my shoulder. "I'm sorry about Chase," he said, turning me back towards him and searching my face, doggedly refusing to let me look away.

I could feel the tears coming, so I jerked myself out of his grasp and went to the bed, grabbing my backpack out from under it to stuff my things inside. "Don't worry about it. It's not your fault."

"I know it's not; but I know how close you were to him and how much he meant to you. He was your daemon. Your protector."

"No, he wasn't. He was *never* my daemon or anyone else's for that matter." My voice held the bitterness that my heart couldn't let go. There was nothing I wouldn't give to have Ben's words be true. "He was an angel who wasn't even supposed to be here. It's not your fault he had to go back to the Overworld, I know that. I'm not going to dwell on it, and I don't want to talk about it anymore." *Because I don't want to cry in front of you.* And I didn't like the way it made me feel so empty inside.

"Okay. I'm not going to make you talk about it now. But later? ... I can't promise I won't bring it up again." He walked over and took my now full and zipped backpack off the bed. "Anything else? Toothbrush? Favorite pillow?"

"Everything I want and need is packed. Except that pixie over there. You can just shove him in your back pocket or something."

"As if," said Tim, buzzing out the door. He yelled over his shoulder, "Don't forget my furniture!"

I walked over and grabbed the tiny bed, dresser and side table off the top of my chest of drawers, putting all of them in the small front pockets of the pack that Ben held for me.

"Come on," he said, slinging the backpack over his shoulder, "I'll show you to your new room."

I followed him out the door and down the hall, not even glancing in my rear view. *Moving forward, never back. That's my new motto.*

I didn't see anyone I knew along the way. My friends were all busy moving, too. Everyone was starting a new chapter in their lives today, but none of them had lost as much as I had, and none of them had the mantle of responsibility lying heavily over their shoulders like me. Except for Ben. He was in the same boat I was - Father to the Fae and barely eighteen himself.

I scarcely noticed the doors and halls we passed along our way. I had heard that the Light and Dark Fae witches had worked together from the moment the bonding ceremony was over to connect the two compounds and create one giant living space for all of us, hidden by magic in the trees of the Green Forest of Ardennes, France. I knew that former Light Fae were being mixed in with former Dark Fae so that there wouldn't be a segregation of old habits causing friction in our midst. I wondered if I'd be able to find my way around this new, confusing place.

Ben stopped in front of a set of double doors.

They immediately struck me as strange. The only other room in the whole compound I knew that had doors like this was the assembly hall - and it was huge inside.

"Welcome to your new home," said Ben, pushing them open.

*What the hell?* I stood there, speechless. My eyes scanned the large space, left to right, from ceiling to floor. I couldn't figure out how this room could even be possible. I turned to look at Ben but his expression was guarded. It was impossible to tell if he was happy or sad, curious or scared. He seemed ... expectant. As if waiting for my reaction.

I had no idea what I should say or even what I should be feeling. But who could blame me? I was standing in the entrance of a room that looked a hell of a lot like an indoor Garden of Eden.

## Chapter Two

TIM CAME BUZZING UP TO my face with his son in hand.

"Do you like it?" Tim asked, a huge grin on his face. "Abby's been on those flowers all night and day. Make sure you tell her they look nice."

"Nice!" yelled his son, Willy, just before sticking his finger up into his tiny nose.

I bit the inside of my cheeks to keep from laughing out loud. Tim's son was the most adorable thing I'd ever seen in my life. He was a third Tim's size, making him about as big as a large bumble bee and just as chunky. Apparently, he didn't miss many meals.

"*Ew*, gross!" exclaimed Tim, reaching down and pulling his son's finger out of his nose. He took a breath and schooled his features to look encouraging. "That's right, Willy, the flowers are nice. Go tell your momma. And tell her Papa says she's hot stuff."

The little pixie went buzzing off, looking as if he were stumbling in the air and possibly drunk. "Hot stuff! Momma is hot stuff!"

"I think he needs a little work on that flying business," I said, watching the little guy disappear around a group of plants in a far doorway, leading to a terrace.

"He's only a baby, Jayne. Give him a break," said Tim, buzzing over to land on my shoulder. "I had no idea how fascinated they were with the inside of their noses, though. I hope that's normal," he said, sounding concerned.

"I'm sure it is," I mumbled, stepping farther into the room, my eyes skimming over the rock walls that had trees growing right out of them somehow. Flowers were coming out of the floor on the edges of the room. For the first time since entering the compound, I felt like I was actually living in the forest and not some hidden ancient military bunker. I looked up and saw that the ceiling was a mass of branches and leaves, so thick, it was impossible to tell if there was sky above it or more stone.

"How long before he can fly straight?" I asked, moving on from Tim's concerns about his son's booger-picking problems, since I didn't want to spoil my appetite for dinner any more than Willy already had.

"Several years. It takes lots of practice to be at my level," said Tim. "I make it look easy, I know. It's a burden to be so awesome at being awesome that you make everyone else look bad." He sighed.

"Yeah. Poor you," I said. "Where do you want me to put your furniture?"

"Abby has a spot all picked out for us. Follow me."

I looked at Ben. "Can I have the backpack? I need to go put Tim's stuff away."

Ben slid the pack off his shoulder. "Want me to stick around? Need me for anything else?"

I shook my head. "No. I'll see you at dinner." I started to walk away, but he caught me by the arm, halting my exit. I looked down at his hand and then back up at his face.

"You know, you don't have to feel weird around me."

## Clash of the Otherworlds: Book One

"Okaaay," I said. As if him telling me that could possibly make it any easier for this to seem normal.

"I'm not going to bite you, you know."

"I know. I'm not worried about that. Anymore."

He smiled, letting my arm go. "Good. Why don't you come over and see my room when you're done with Tim?"

I shrugged. "Where is it?"

He pointed to the archway that was across the foyer area where we were standing. "Just through there. I'll leave the door unlocked from my side."

"Maybe I'll see you later," I said, not wanting to commit to anything where he was concerned.

Ben reached up as if to touch my arm again, but I shied away. His hand dropped to his side and he gave me a half-smile, before walking away and leaving me standing alone in the entrance to my room.

"Are you coming?!" came Tim's voice from around the corner. "I can feel myself getting older in here!"

I rolled my eyes. I'd thought before that Tim was bossy, but now that he had a wife and child to impress, he was getting positively annoying. I wondered how we were going to work everything out, with his whole family living with us. I hadn't had time to talk to Abby much yet. I really didn't know what she was like at all.

*No better time than the present*, I said to myself. I walked through the hallway and around the corner, following the direction I'd seen Tim and Willy fly.

# Chapter Three

MY EYES WIDENED AT THE room that appeared before me. It had actual living room furniture in it, like a house. It was nothing like my former cell. There was a couch and two sitting chairs with a coffee table in between them, and a sunroom and terrace off to the side. Fancy carpets were placed in both rooms, making them seem homey, but in an elegant kind of way. An arched door set into the stone of the far-right wall looked as if it might lead to a bedroom.

Tim and his son were hovering over a table out in the sunroom that was up against a tree and stone wall. "Out here, Jayne!" said Tim. "This is where we want our stuff. On this."

I walked over, reaching into the backpack's front pocket to pull his things out. His new home was a round tabletop, covered in plants and flowers, with a space in the center that had been left clear. It looked like a tiny jungle campsite. "You want it right here? In the middle of all this junk?"

"Shhh!" admonished Tim, looking furtively, left and right. "It's not junk! It's our Eden, dummy. Now put the things in there before Abby gets back and hears you."

"Junk!" shouted Willy, his finger in his nose again.

Tim pulled Willy's finger out. "No. Not junk. Pretty, pretty.

Like your momma. Pretty."

"Pretty momma! Junk!"

Tim rolled his eyes and then glared at me. "Can you please watch your mouth around him? Damn kid copies everything he hears."

"Damn kid! Damn kid! Damn kid copies everything!" shouted Willy, breaking free of his father's grasp and flying off in a drunken fit of spins and dips. He disappeared into the garden, singing a tune whose lyrics included things about a damn pretty momma living in the junk.

I snorted.

"Do *not* laugh at that, Jayne. It's not funny."

"Sure it is," I said, chuckling as I pulled out his bed and set it down in the space between the plants. "I think he's going to be keeping you very busy." I put Tim's dresser and side table down next, adjusting it beside the tiny bed. "And that's my politically correct way of saying he's going to be a total pain in your ass."

"Tell me about it. Abby better get back here soon. That kid is wearing me out."

"Your days as a childless bachelor are over, I guess. Life was so easy back then ..."

"Yeah," said Tim, sighing. He flew up and let himself drop onto his bed from above, landing on his back with his hands folded behind his head. "But I don't mind. I'd rather be a dad and a husband than a bachelor."

"That's sweet," I said.

"Besides, all the boobs around here are too big anyway."

I was about to reply, but Abby beat me to it, coming through the entrance to the sunroom from the garden, saying, "Speaking of boobs, Tim, would you mind tracking your son down, please? He's harassing the bees, and I'm never going to convince them to help us pollinate this garden if he keeps doing that."

Tim got up and bounced on the bed a few times before launching himself into the air with a fancy twist. "A father's work is never done." He flew away, out into the garden, yelling, "Wiiillyyyyyy! Come to Paaapaaaa!"

It was the first time Abby and I had been alone since I'd met her earlier in the day, just after my binding ceremony with Ben. I was nervous. Her husband had been my roommate for months, and even though he was no bigger than the palm of my hand, we had a pretty close relationship for fae of two different races. It made me feel weird that we'd lived together while he was married to her.

"Oh, that looks nice," said Abby flying over to check out the furniture in her little jungle, zipping around to view it from several angles.

"Do you want me to move any of it?" I asked.

"No, this will be just fine." She looked at me and smiled. "I hope you're okay with us sharing your space. We can always go out into the garden if you'd prefer. Pixie babies can be very noisy sometimes. And nosey. They're naturally very curious."

I shook my head quickly. "No. Not at all. You guys can go wherever you want. Shoot, I'm used to Tim sleeping just a few feet away and snoring like a sawmill, so this will seem far." I smiled and then stopped, immediately feeling weird again.

We both stared at each other for a few moments before Abby finally broke the silence.

"I can see why Tim likes you so much."

"Oh yeah?"

"Yes. You're kind and thoughtful. And Tim has always been

drawn to those who are a little ... different."

"Different." I wasn't sure if I was being complimented or insulted very politely.

Abby flew up in front of me. "I didn't mean that in a bad way. I meant it in a good way. You are not like the other changelings or the humans I have known. You're ... stronger, maybe. More opinionated. Like Tim, actually."

I couldn't fault her for her perception. "Well, I've been called that before. Maybe not kind and thoughtful, but yeah, definitely opinionated."

Abby flew down into her new bedroom, adjusting the quilt on top of the bed and fluffing the pillow I had thrown down. "You've made it possible for Tim and me to live here in this compound with our son. That would never have happened before you intervened in his captivity. We will be forever grateful to you for that." She looked up at me, her hands folded in front of her. She was so pretty with her curly red hair and freckles. I wished she were bigger so I could hug her without smashing her to bits.

"You would have accomplished that on your own, with your work in the Dark Fae clinic. I guess you found the cure for pixelation, huh? Chase seemed normal before he left." He'd had a nasty run-in with Tim who threw some pixie dust on him and had him laughing and dancing like a lunatic until the Dark Fae healers were finally able to get him under control with their antidote.

"Yes, we finally did find the right formulation. But you helped us overcome the prejudices and misconceptions between our race and the others. Really, this is an important time in our history for us."

"I'm surprised more pixies aren't here now, if that's true," I said.

"Oh, there will be. Believe me. Word is spreading."

I tried to smile, but it probably wasn't quite coming across that way. All I could think about were the accidental pixelations that were going to happen all over the place and what a mess it would be.

"I can see that disturbs you, and I can understand your reticence. There's a reason we've been relegated to pixie colonies for thousands of years. Some of our race have been perhaps a bit too ... enthusiastic about sharing their dust."

"No, I'm cool with it. In theory."

"We will definitely have to put some rules in place. It's been a long time since we fae have lived together like this." She looked around her jungle and then flew up to gaze around the room. "I can't tell you how long I've dreamed of it - living free among other fae." She lifted her hand up to her face and wiped away a tear, placing her fingers on her lips and keeping them there.

I panicked, thinking about freaking Abby out, then Tim out, and then the baby, too. A mass of crying pixies couldn't possibly be good. "Don't cry, Abby. It's okay. I'm ... uhhh ... happy too! We're all just one big happy family here, right? Don't worry about it. Everything will work out fine with the other pixies coming."

Tim appeared from out in the garden, dragging his son along with him. "What'd you say to her, Jayne? Why is she crying?"

Abby waved him away and sniffed hard. "I'm fine, I'm fine."

"I didn't say anything," I protested. "She's getting all verklempt over living here, right, Abby?"

Abby nodded. "Tim, honey, please. Leave the poor girl alone. I'm just so happy to be here. I get this way sometimes, as you might recall."

Tim nodded, taking his wife in his arms. "I know, babe. I

gotcha, ya big fat crybaby. Rest your weary head on my wonderfully broad shoulders and forget all your troubles."

I snorted, knowing for a fact that Tim was paranoid about his shoulders being too narrow. Thank goodness his wife was okay with being called a big fat whatever. If he were my husband, that would have earned him at least a gut punch.

He frowned at me over Abby's back. "Don't you have somewhere to be, Jayne?"

"No. I don't think so."

"Council meeting? Before dinner?"

*"What?* I didn't hear anything about a meeting."

"Didn't I tell you?" he asked innocently.

"No, you neglected to mention that," I said, frowning at him.

"Oh. My bad. It's in five minutes."

"What?!" I yelled, looking around desperately for my cloak. I shook my head clearing it, grabbing for the backpack at my feet. I hadn't even unpacked yet. I pulled the shimmering turquoise material out and threw it over my shoulders. "Where's the meeting?"

"Oooooh, Poppy, look at the pretty dreeeesssss," said Willy, stumbling over in the air towards me, his eyes fixed on my shoulder, his hands outstretched.

"No, no, Baby Bee, leave Jayne alone," said his mother, flying over to intercept him.

He saw her coming and made an evasive maneuver to the side, intent on getting to me without her interference. She almost had him, but then he farted, giving himself a little burst of power that sent him zooming out of her grasp. He came right for me, clearly out of control, and bounced off the front of my chest. It must have knocked him a little unconscious because he started to fall, and his wings weren't working. I held out my cupped hands and caught him halfway to the ground.

He landed on his back, his arms and legs spread wide, blinking his eyes a few times in stunned silence.

"Willy!" shrieked his mother, flying over to my hand.

"Whooooaaaaa, that was awwwwwesome," said Willy, grinning from ear-to-ear. "I wanna do that again!" He scrambled to get up, his tiny butt crack showing when his pants came down partway in the back.

"No, sir you are *not* going to do that again. Are you trying to give me a heart attack?" asked Abby, landing in my palm and taking her son by the hand. "Come with Momma. We're going to go play in the roses. Would you like to do that? We can balance on the thorns."

Willy pouted. "Wanna bounce off the lella-mental."

"You can't bounce off the elemental right now. She's late for a meeting," I heard her say as they lifted up and flew away through the door to the garden.

*Holy shit is this kid gonna be a handful or what.* I was starting to question the idea of living with a family of pixies when Tim came up and landed on my shoulder.

"Good catch, there, Lellamental. Saved my boy from a solid bounce, that's for sure. Ready to go?"

"You're going to the meeting with me?"

"I'm gonna try."

"Doesn't Abby need you?"

"Nah. We're takin' turns watching Willy. It's her turn today. Mine's tomorrow. Or next week."

I laughed. "Nice."

"Yeah. Come on. Seriously ... get me out of here," he

whispered, "before they come back."

I shook my head as I walked out the door. "You're gonna get yourself in some serious trouble if she ever hears you saying that."

"So what else is new."

"True. So true," I said, closing the door behind me, stepping out into the hall at precisely the same moment as Ben.

## Chapter Four

"READY FOR THE MEETING?" BEN asked, throwing his cloak over his shoulders. Reds and blues shimmered inside the blackness of the material. It reminded me of the sky outside our atmosphere - a picture taken of another galaxy, maybe.

"I guess. How come you didn't mention it?"

"Sorry, I thought you knew." He led the way down the hall, turning back several times to look at me, as if urging me to come and walk by his side.

I gave up on the idea of staying away from him and joined him there, walking next to him as we chatted. It felt weird to be striding down the hall looking like a couple, but I forced myself to stay with him, even when we came across other people who smiled knowingly at us.

"I'm never in the loop in this place," I complained. "Even Tim knows more about what's going on than I do."

"That's because he spies on everyone all the time," said Ben.

"Hey!" protested Tim from my shoulder. "I'm no spy! I just happen to be in the right place at the right time. Often."

"Tim doesn't appreciate the accusation," I said, smiling.

"It wasn't an accusation. It was admiration. He's very good at it."

I knew for a fact without even seeing Tim that he was preening right now. I glanced at Ben out of the corner of my eye and saw him smiling. He knew exactly what he was doing, flattering Tim like that. *Why you sneaky little dog.* I nudged him ever so slightly with my elbow, and he continued to smile, looking straight ahead. I liked the idea of messing with Tim, tag-team style. Maybe this wouldn't be so bad all the time, having to hang out with Ben.

"I am known in certain circles for being an expert in the area of surveillance. True fact. I don't mean to brag, but you know ... awesome is as awesome does."

"You're not going to be allowed in, you know that, right?" asked Ben.

"They won't even know I'm there," said Tim deviously, moving to hide in my hair.

"He says they won't even know he's there."

"Okay. But don't say that I didn't warn you."

Tim stuck his head out. "What? Is there a spell? There's a spell, isn't there?"

I translated for Tim again. "He wants to know if there are spells on the meeting."

"Yep."

"Damn those witches!"

"Why'd you tell him?" I asked. "That would have been fun to see him get zapped."

Tim climbed out of my hair and flew up in front of me. "Sometimes I wonder whose side you're on, Jayne."

His hands were on his hips as he scolded me, and he once again reminded me of my father. *So lame.* I tried to snatch him out of the air, but he got away from me.

"Don't embarrass me in there!" he yelled as he disappeared down the hall.

I shook my head at his teasing talents. He always knew exactly which buttons to press to get me going. Now all I could think about was making a stupid mistake.

"Don't let him bother you," said Ben, reading my thoughts or facial expression somehow.

"He has a point. I do screw shit up a lot."

"Well, that's normal for a changeling. You'll get better over time."

"I need a manual."

"That's what you have me for," he said, stopping at a door and opening it for me.

"You're my manual?"

"I'm whatever you want me to be," he said, staring down at me, making me feel funny in my special places.

I quickly stepped into the room, hoping the breeze created by my fast walking towards a seat would cool my face off before I sat down. All Ben had to do was say one little hardly suggestive thing, and I was all embarrassed again. I seriously needed to get a handle on myself. I might be a virgin, but that didn't mean I was totally inept around guys. Not normally, anyway. But something about Ben made me feel like a fluttering idiot whenever we were alone.

I took a seat at the far end of the table, while Ben stopped to talk to several other fae who had beat us to the meeting. They were Dark Fae I had only seen once at our binding ceremony, both witches. My mind wandered to the one Dark Fae witch I did know - Samantha. Supposedly, she and I shared the same grandmother, Maggie. Actually, Maggie was more like a great grandmother times ten or something, she was so old and so many generations back. I still wasn't sure that I believed that story, but Maggie was a real stickler for the truth. I couldn't imagine her lying about it, as strange as it seemed. The fact that Samantha had tried to kill me a couple times and seemed hell-bent on hating me made the idea of being related to her almost laughable. I shouldn't have been surprised, though; my own parents hadn't seemed to like me much, either.

I refused to consider memories of my mom right then, because she'd died in such a horrible way, being tortured by a demon. I didn't want to cry in front of all these people. Surely, they'd revoke my cloak then. Not that I'd mind, but I was pretty sure it would be a huge disappointment to a lot of fae who were counting on me to be mature and do the right thing by them. I sighed, thinking how light the cloak was when the mantle of responsibility it represented was so damn heavy.

"What's the big sigh for?" asked the fae to my right. I looked over and saw a werewolf sitting next to me. I assumed he was a wolf because he was totally built and had very hairy arms; plus, he was sitting next to a guy I knew to be a Light Fae werewolf.

I shrugged. "Just thinking about how much work it is to be on the council."

"Eh, it's no big deal, really. You just talk to your people and bring their ideas and decisions to the table with you."

"What do you do now, though? Now that you have two werewolf members at the table, I mean?"

He smiled. "Well, in theory we're supposed to be all the same people. But some of our brothers and sisters aren't quite ready to do the group-hug thing, so we're still talking to people individually - he to his and me to mine. Then we have a quick meeting together before we come here to get on the same page."

I smiled back. "Naughy, naughty. We're all supposed to be on the same team now."

"Yeah, I know. It'll happen eventually." He held out his hand. "My name's Aidan by the way. Nice to meet you, Jayne."

"You already know me, I guess." I gave him a half-hearted smile. "Exactly how much of my reputation has preceded me?"

He laughed. "I'd have to be living under a rock not to know who you are at this point. But that's a good thing; don't let it get you nervous. I've only heard good things, so no pressure."

"Yeah, right." I rolled my eyes.

"Want to hear a story that will make you feel better?" he said, whispering conspiratorially.

"Sure," I whispered back, leaning closer to him.

"My first council meeting? I got so freaked out, I shifted," he rapped his knuckles on the wood table, "right there at my seat." He chuckled, looking at me for my reaction.

"You shifted? What do you mean? I don't get it."

"I shifted. I changed. You know ... I went from man to wolf?"

"Oh. Damn. That sounds scary, actually. Did you eat anyone?"

"Eat anyone? No. And not scary; more like humiliating. Not only did I lose my pants, but there I was, showing everyone I was supposed to be impressing that I had the control of a two-year-old." He shook his head at the memory. "I still haven't lived that one down."

"Well, that's one way to liven up a meeting, I guess."

"I'm good for that. You'll see." He winked at me, promising future mischief.

I liked him already. Anyone who managed colossal screw-ups

at council meetings had to be someone I could hang with, even if he was Dark Fae.

Ben came to the seat on my other side, just as the meeting was starting, nodding at Aidan. "Hey, Shifty. How's it hangin?" he asked, smirking and pulling his cloak out from under him as he sat down.

"See? What'd I tell ya?" said Aidan, winking at me before shooting scowls in Ben's direction.

I couldn't help but giggle. I was reading all kinds of things into Ben's greeting which was probably what I was supposed to be doing, but it felt bad to be doing it in a place we were supposed to be so serious and mature.

I tried to get my mind off Aidan's missing pants by examining the group around the table. Maléna and Dardennes sat at the head of the table, Céline at Dardennes' right. I recognized all the Light Fae council members, but knew only a couple of the Dark Fae. They had two green elves, which we had none of here. Otherwise, we were pretty evenly-represented. It was curious to me that there were no gray elves here, though, Light or Dark.

"Thank you, council members, for gathering here today. On behalf of the Light and Dark Fae, Maléna and I welcome you."

Maléna the silver elf nodded her head, gesturing for Dardennes to continue. They had once been an item, when Dardennes was Dark Fae, before he got booted out and sent over to the Light Fae.

"We've asked you here for several reasons. First, to move forward with our plans to integrate the fae here in the compound; and second, to discuss the current status of the situation which brought us together in the first place." He looked over at Ben and me, making me squirm under the attention.

## Clash of the Otherworlds: Book One

Ben was much cooler than I was. He nodded his head, looking first at the silver elves at the head of the table and then at all the other faces around us. I was feeling wimpy at the moment, though, so I focused on him instead of the strangers. Ben never looked at me, but he reached under the table and found my hand, squeezing it. I returned the gesture for a second and then pulled my hand away, lacing my fingers together in my lap. I didn't want anyone to get the impression that I needed to hold onto him to feel confident, even if it might be true at this particular moment.

"The rooming situation seems to be well in hand. Everyone here is empowered to settle any disputes that arise, but please feel free to come to Maléna or myself if you feel as though our intervention is required."

Maléna spoke next. "Is there anything that needs our attention now in this regard?"

A dwarf raised his hand. "We've had some problems in our section."

"What kind of problems?" she asked.

"Some axes got away from a few hands. Some facial hair was removed."

A few fae gasped. I looked around, trying to figure out what that meant. *Is it code for cutting someone's face off or something?*

"That is serious," said Dardennes. "How do you recommend we move forward?"

"We've already taken the wrongdoers into custody. They're spending some time in the lower levels, ruminating on their transgressions. And we've given the standard punishment - eye for an eye."

Aidan winced, whispering, "Harsh," under his breath.

I wished I had pen and paper. I needed to write a list of all the questions I would have for later. First on that list would be: *What's the big deal with facial hair and do they actually take eyeballs as punishment?* I knew the expression, but Aidan's response and similar ones from the others caused me to question whether it might be a literal thing with these fae.

"Sounds as if you have matters taken care of," said Dardennes, visibly relaxing.

"Yes. But it bears keeping in mind that some will need to be reminded of our common goals and the consequences for not following the edicts of our combined council."

"Well-said," added Niles, nodding his head in respect. The dwarf speaking smoothed his beard down onto his chest and made a small bow in Niles' direction.

It looked to me as if the guy had everything he needed to keep the Light Fae dwarves in line, because if Niles were on his side, the rest of them would be. He was the hardest hard-ass of them all.

"Moving on then, to probably more pressing matters," said Dardennes, signaling for Maléna to take over.

"Yes. Regarding the matter brought to our attention by the Overworld creature, Chase ... our first order of business must be to find the breach where the Underworld creatures are entering our realm."

"He's not a creature," I burst out, unable to stay silent about it like I probably should have.

Maléna narrowed her eyes at me. "He most certainly is."

My nostrils flared in contained anger. "No, he is not. He's an angel. There's a difference."

"Not to us, there isn't," she said, staring me down. "Any being who is not from here, who does not *belong* here, is a *creature* by definition."

## Clash of the Otherworlds: Book One

I didn't want to argue with her and seem like a petulant child in the middle of the meeting, so I just shot my thoughts really hard in her direction. *He's not a creature, you stupid bitch. He's a guardian angel and nothing you say will change that!*

"I'd keep that comment to myself if I were you," said a girl's voice in my head.

I screwed up my brows in confusion, rolling my eyes up into my brain, as if I'd be able to find the answers to my questions up there. *Did I just think that to myself?*

"No, you did not. But please, stop making that face. Everyone's going to think you're missing a screw."

*You mean, they'll think I have a screw loose,* I corrected.

"Loose ... missing ... same thing. Stop it. Seriously. You look like a lunatic."

I schooled my features to seem normal again, acting as if I were shrugging off Maléna's insults. Her voice faded into the background as I continued my internal conversation.

*Who are you?*

"A friend. Just pay attention to what she's saying. It's important."

And then the voice disappeared. I searched the faces of those around me but couldn't tell who was talking in my head; and whoever it was, she refused to respond to any more of my questions. Maléna's voice came back into focus.

"It's obviously somewhere in the Green Forest, within the trees. Orcs have been sighted near both compounds. We were informed by Céline that a demon was present in Florida at the home of Jayne." She barely glanced at me before continuing. "There is apparently a plot of some sort to impregnate Jayne to spawn some sort of *creature* with the power to bring about the end of our world." She stared at me, her chin lifted ever-so-slightly, daring me to contradict her about the creature thing, I guess.

But I was in total agreement with her on this one. Any child conceived with a beast like the one that killed my mother and tried to steal my virginity would definitely qualify as a creature in my book.

"Does anyone else know of this legend or foretelling?" asked one of the witches.

"We have heard nothing of it," said Red, the Light Fae witch I knew from our council. He was the one who had nominated me to be here, wearing this cloak. Part of me hated him for that, while the other part couldn't help but have a soft spot for the old geezer. He tried so hard to stay annoyed with me, it was almost entertaining. He made it look so easy.

"Has anyone talked to the old witch of the wood?" asked Aidan.

"She won't speak with us," said Celeste, another witch from the Light Fae council.

*"They're talking about Maggie,"* said the voice in my head.

*Oh, so you're back. Who are you?*

The voice sighed. *"You could go talk to Maggie. She likes you. Not so much with these other fae."*

"Are you guys talking about Maggie?" I asked no one in particular.

"Yes, we are," said Maléna. "What do you know of her?"

"She and I go way back," I said, laughing to myself about the irony of that statement. This wasn't one of those figurative things, since she really was an ancestor of my mother's. "I could talk to her if you want."

Maléna looked to Dardennes who nodded. She turned back to me and said, "Yes. It's worth it to try at least. What's the worst that could happen, right?" She smiled, but there was no warmth there, almost as if she were hoping Maggie would unleash on me.

"Well, she could turn me into a toad ... spell me to throw myself into a fire ... root my feet into the ground, making me stand in the forest until I starved to death."

Maléna just smiled, lifting an eyebrow briefly before continuing. "Anton, please let her know what exactly she should be discussing with the witch. I don't want her going off-plan and revealing things she shouldn't."

I tried not to let Maléna's tone or words make me feel small and stupid, but it was difficult. But then Ben's hand touched mine, and a shot of heat came through and rushed into my chest, making me feel strong and ... fiery. A quick glance in his direction told me he'd pulled some of his Fire element into himself and shared it with me. His cloak was glowing a little with it. I wondered if he even knew.

"I think we need to have a rule at the meetings," said a green elf at the end of the table. "No bringing Elements into the room."

I felt like I'd been caught being bad or breaking the rules. I looked guiltily over at Dardennes and Céline, ready to apologize and swear I'd never let it happen again. It hadn't even been *me* doing it, but it just as easily could have been; I didn't have the best control in the world.

Ben startled me by speaking first, and loudly. "Neither you nor this council is in any position to tell me what I can and cannot do with the Elements I command. And the same goes for Jayne. *We do not answer to you.*" The rest of his statement remained unsaid, but that didn't matter. It was floating in the air above all our heads: *You answer to us.*

I stared at his face. It was dark with anger and power, the

likes of which I hadn't seen there since we took down the demon at my mom's house and sent its soul back to the Underworld. I was both afraid and intrigued by Ben's reaction. He seemed to have a much stronger opinion than I did about what our place in this world was.

I expected the fae around the table to start yelling and protesting Ben's show of arrogance and power, but none of them said a word. Some of them shrugged it off, a couple looked down at the table hiding their expressions, and others seemed slightly surprised. The only one who looked angry was Maléna. Her sister, Céline, stared up at her with trepidation.

Maléna spoke first. "You answer to this council, just as everyone else here." Her voice held a note of authority that matched Ben's.

Dardennes looked as if he were about to step in, with his hands held up and his best peace-maker grin on, but he was cut off by Ben's sharp response.

"You are mistaken, Maléna. Jayne and I answer to *no one* but one another. This council answers to *us*. Spirit has recognized our union; our positions as the Mother and Father have been recognized in the Overworld and the Underworld. Your recognition is of no consequence to who and what we are."

"You have been in contact with the Underworld? Well, isn't that interesting," she responded, acting as if he'd just revealed some big secret he shouldn't have.

"As have Céline and Jayne and several other Light Fae who met the demon called Torrie."

"What does he mean?" asked a green elf. "What has the Underworld done to acknowledge our elementals' positions?"

Céline responded calmly. "Torrie was very clear that Jayne

was to be the Mother to the creature that would somehow make it possible to open the Here and Now to the other realms." She looked at me apologetically, pity in her eyes. She and I both shared some very unhappy memories where Torrie was concerned.

I looked at Maléna to gauge her reaction. Torrie had held a torch for her, back when he was a member of the Here and Now and before he'd been banished to the Underworld. Nothing in her expression belied her feelings about him, though. She looked as cold and calculating as ever.

"Since none of us know the legend to which Torrie referred, there's no reason or basis for us to assume that anything Ben has claimed is a valid conclusion."

I shook my head. She was going to cling to this you're-not-the-boss-of-me thing, and I could already tell that it was a mistake to piss Ben off like this. He was definitely used to getting his way, and while he'd been willing to follow Maléna's lead in the past, apparently he wasn't anymore.

"You risk much by denying who I am," was all he said.

Our connection was humming. I could feel Earth and Water straining to join with his Fire and Wind. It was almost an effort to keep them apart right now. My cloak swirled with their power, and I wasn't doing any of it consciously. I wasn't sure if it was Ben's anger that was causing it or what, but I had to force myself to stop looking at Maléna and focus inward to keep myself under control.

*"Just focus. Breathe in and out. You'll get it,"* came the voice again.

*Listen,* I thought to the voice, *if you're not going to identify yourself, then just stay the hell away from me, okay? I don't have the patience for your stupid games.*

*"I cannot reveal myself to you, and I ask that you not share my*

*existence with anyone else right now."*

Oh, like I'm supposed to trust a voice in my head? Are you kidding me? I'm not that stupid. I'm probably going insane. You're probably, like, the Devil in there. Pretty soon you're going to be telling me to eat a pixie or something.

"All in due time. Trust me. And I would never tell you to eat a pixie. I hear they're bitter, and they have almost no meat on their bones. They're like pheasants."

No. Not possible. I'm telling.

"What if I told you something ... something that could help you? Could I earn your trust enough to have you keep our connection quiet for a little longer?"

I shrugged before I caught myself. I looked around the table to see if anyone noticed, but they were all too busy shifting around uncomfortably, staring at Ben and Maléna, wondering if a gauntlet were being thrown down, putting them in the middle of a wind storm of epic proportions.

*Maybe,* I responded. *Depends what it is.*

"Okay. But if I tell you something you agree is helpful to you, you in turn will agree to keep our secret."

*I get to tell one person. One fae,* I countered.

"No. No deal."

*Just one. Tim. The pixie.*

The voice didn't answer right away.

*Come on. I can't keep a secret from everyone. I'm not built that way. If you won't let me tell anyone, I'll break and tell the world. It's a character flaw I have.*

"Fine. You can tell Tim the pixie so long as you make him swear on his life he will not reveal your secret. Pixies cannot break this vow."

*Done. Now out with it. I'm sick of the suspense.*

# Clash of the Otherworlds: Book One

*"You have another weapon at your disposal that you can use to fight the creatures of the Underworld."*

I frowned. This didn't seem like some big secret to me.

*Of course we have other weapons. The Dark Fae probably brought in a few hundred with them when they moved in.*

*"I'm not talking about other fae. I'm talking about you. And this is a weapon that no other fae can manage, other than you. And Ben, in a manner of speaking."*

I swear the voice laughed then, and I wasn't sure whether it was a good laugh or a devious one, which made me a little nervous. *So what's the weapon?*

*"Another time. Now listen to the conversation going on around you. You're could miss something good."*

I felt the voice leave. I hadn't sensed it entering, but I definitely now noticed the void where it had once been. *Dammit. Who are you?* I received no response, but didn't expect to. The owner of it was somewhere else, and Dardennes was speaking in raised tones now, enough to pull me out of my head.

"The Light Fae recognize the position of both Ben and Jayne as the Father and Mother. There is no need to rehash that argument or situation here today. Certainly, Maléna, if you wish to challenge their positions in our community, that is your right." He gave the group a knowing half-smile. "I wouldn't necessarily recommend that, but if you so wish, I would be happy to preside over an official, sanctioned challenge. I'm sure Ben and Jayne would be happy to accommodate your wishes." He raised an eyebrow at us.

"Absolutely," said Ben, staring Maléna down.

"Uhhh ... yeah. I guess," I said, not feeling nearly as confident in my ability to take that mean bitch out as Ben apparently did.

"Set it up," she said to Dardennes, never taking her eyes from

Ben.

*Oh great. Something to look forward to. A death match.* I could sense Aidan looking at me, so I glanced over and caught him smiling with barely contained laughter. I kicked him to get him to quit it. Pretty soon he was going to get dragged into the fight, if Maléna saw him cracking up over her getting her panties in a bunch.

"Moving on then," said Dardennes, clearing his voice, remaining completely professional. "Jayne, you are going to speak to Maggie for us. We ask that you determine, if you can, the legend to which Torrie referred and possibly the location from which the orcs and demon have entered our realm."

"And how they're doing it," added a witch. "It's not just a doorway. There has to be some magic involved."

"Quite right," said Dardennes, nodding his head. He looked around the table. "Anyone else?"

"Maybe she could ask her to do some scrying," suggested a green elf.

Several of the witches hissed and glared at him, moving around in an agitated way.

"Hush your mouth, green elf!" growled Red. "Do not encourage such deviant behavior!"

My eyes widened. *Deviant behavior? What the hell is scrying and why does a green elf want me to do it with Maggie?* I shivered involuntarily, wondering what the heck it could be. Whatever it was, no one here liked it, especially the witches.

"No. I'm sorry, ..." Dardennes looked at the green elf expectantly. "Forgive me ... I don't yet know everyone's name..."

"Thaddeus."

"Thank you, Thaddeus. No, Thaddeus, I don't think that is

such a good idea. Scrying has long been frowned upon by our Light Fae witches, and it appears the Dark Fae witches agree. I believe this is a stone we should leave *unturned*."

Thaddeus shrugged. "Why leave stones unturned? We're fighting battles with demons here."

I was with Thaddeus, unless it involved me doing something nasty with Maggie. I raised my hand.

Everyone else ignored me, since taking turns speaking wasn't really a fae thing, but Dardennes had learned that this generally meant I wanted to say something, so he gestured in my direction. "Jayne?"

"What's scrying?"

Maléna snorted and rolled her eyes, immediately making me want to slap her. She was so smug, I was almost looking forward to this challenge match now. But I knew I was going to have to go into total Rocky mode and train-up so I could whoop her ass sideways. She would be no easy win. I gritted my teeth together to keep from saying anything.

Ben leaned down and said quietly, "Scrying is looking into the future, basically."

"Whoa," I said, my voice filled with awe, "Maggie can do that?"

"Yes," said Ben, turning his attention back to Dardennes.

"Any other suggestions?" the silver elf asked.

No one said anything, probably too worried about sounding stupid like Thaddeus and me. He didn't look affected by it, but if I were him, I'd feel like an amateur. They all acted like scrying was a seriously bad idea.

Dardennes nodded at me. "You have your work cut out for you then, Jayne. Good luck. Please come to my office when you have accomplished your mission."

I didn't know what to say to that, so I just nodded back. I snuck a glance at Ben, wondering if he'd go with me. I kind of wanted to go alone, so I could ask her about this fortune-telling stuff, and if he were there, he'd probably stop me. *For sure I have to go alone or with just Tim.* I started formulating the plan in my mind as the group continued on with other business.

By the time I'd snapped out of it, we were taking a vote.

I leaned over to whisper in Aidan's ear. "What are we voting on?"

He covered up his laugh with a cough. He leaned towards me and said, "Yes for adjourning the meeting; no for coming up with more plans for world peace."

I threw my hand up with the rest of the yeses.

"It's unanimous," said Dardennes. "The meeting is adjourned. You will be notified of our next meeting by courier."

We all stood to leave, the sounds of scraping noises on the stone made by our chairs grating my ears.

"So, how'd you like it?" asked Aidan. "Our first council meeting as one big happy family."

"It was pretty good, I guess. I didn't put anyone into a coma, so that's always a good day for me."

He laughed. "I heard about you and that stuff. I think I'd like to try that sometime ... getting lost in the Green for a while."

"You're nuts. It turns people into crying babies."

"Sounds like good drugs to me," he said gamely.

Ben leaned in. "You have to be careful of those weres. They're total adrenaline junkies."

"Look who's talking," said Aidan good-naturedly. "First meeting and you've got a challenge going with Maléna. Good work on that, by the way." He gestured with his head over at Maléna, his distain clear.

"Not on Team Maléna?" I asked.

"Not exactly," he said quietly. More loudly he said, "The wolf has no quarrel with the silver elf."

He reminded me of the werewolves who had no quarrel with the siren of our lake, Naida. They'd said the same thing to me about her once.

"Who *do* the wolves have a quarrel with?" I asked.

He shrugged. "Demons named Torrie, for one."

I totally wanted to hug him for that. A smile burst across my face as I battled to keep my hands down at my sides and not around his shoulders.

"What's wrong?" he asked, smiling, a little mystified.

"Oh, what the hell," I said, before flinging my arms around him. "I love that the wolf has a quarrel with a demon named Torrie."

He put his arms around my waist and squeezed me back for a second before stepping away. "Good," he said nodding. We held hands for a couple seconds before I let go and turned to join Ben near the door. "See ya," I said over my shoulder.

"Yeah. See ya around," Aidan said, turning to speak to his wolf friend next to him.

I caught up to Ben at the door. He was staring at me saying nothing. I could see the muscle of his jaw twitching.

"What's wrong?" I asked.

"Nothing," he said, instantly dropping the brooding look and smiling at me. "Come on. I wanted to show you my room. Ready to see it?"

I shrugged. "Ready enough."

I walked out the door and was immediately accosted by Tim, buzzing so close to my face I feared a pixie wiener-to-the-nose incident. I quickly leaned my head back as far as I could to avoid the potential disaster.

"Tell me everything that happened in there and do not leave a single thing out. My electronics totally didn't work. I'm so disappointed in me." He sighed, sounding pitiful.

"Let's go see Ben's place first," I said, walking next to my Dark Fae counterpart, trying to ignore his arm that occasionally brushed up against mine. "Then you and I can do some girl-chat after."

"Oh, goodies. And then you can help me with Baby Bee's flying lessons."

"How can I possibly help anyone with flying lessons?" I asked. "I can barely walk without tripping."

"You'll make a good backboard," he said, flying out in front of us. "Especially with your boobs and all."

"Great," I said shaking my head, picturing poor Willy doing face-plants into my private parts.

"What?" asked Ben.

"You don't want to know," I said, walking down the hallway, not paying attention to where we were going.

My mind wandered to the voice I'd heard in my head during the meeting. I wondered who it belonged to and if Tim would know how to find her. If she knew about a weapon I could use, I needed to get my hands on it before this match with Maléna, and in enough time that I could learn how to use the damn thing.

## Chapter Five

WE ARRIVED AT BEN'S ROOM a few minutes later. Unlike mine, it had only a single entry door. He pushed it open and gestured for me to go in ahead of him. I walked by him, trying to ignore the Ben-smell that snuck up into my nose. It was nearly intoxicating, the way it made me instantly think of him as a guy - one I'd kissed pretty passionately not that long ago.

I stepped over the threshold and was immediately struck by how masculine the room felt. It was dark, much darker than mine; and the greenery was at a bare minimum. No pixies would be making their homes here. This was more a place for bugganes - classy ones, though, if there was such a thing.

The walls had tapestries woven of strange thread that seemed to wink with dark amber and colors of the rainbow in deep hues. They had battle scenes on them, with many creatures I knew and others I'd never seen. I stepped closer to one that was done in blacks and purples with some turquoise mixed in, noticing the theme of this one was dragons. I was reaching up to touch one of them, fascinated with how fierce they looked, when Ben's voice caused me to jerk my hand back.

"Careful. Beautiful, aren't they?"

"Yes," I said softly, mesmerized by the artwork and now wondering what I needed to be careful of. Maybe they were ancient and would fall apart at the slightest touch, but they sure looked sturdy enough.

"Would you like something to drink?" he asked.

I turned around to see what he was offering. He was standing near a table that had a decanter, a small silver bowl with a lid and crystal glasses around it.

"What is that?" The liquid in the crystal container was a light green color for the most part, but the cuts of the decanter made it look different shades, catching some of the darkness of the room to make parts of it seem almost black.

"This is absinthe here," he said pointing to the liquid I'd been eyeing with mistrust. "But I have other things as well. Juice, water, ...." He looked at me expectantly.

"I'll have some water, thanks." I had no idea what absinthe was, but it looked enough like a buggane martini that I knew it wasn't going to be my thing, at least, not in the middle of the afternoon. I continued my perusal of his room while he poured me a drink from a bottle inside the cabinet the glasses were resting on.

A seating area of chairs and a couch dominated the space I was standing in. The wood was done in a dark stain and each piece was heavy. This furniture was nothing like the type in the conversation area in Dardennes' office - those looked delicate and classy. This stuff looked like things from an ancient castle. The materials on the seats and backs were silk and crushed velvet, except for one chair that was done in a deep, blood-red leather. Intricately-patterned, thick, persian-style carpets were scattered around the space. There was an arch-shaped door on the left side of the room, leading presumably to a bedroom. I still hadn't seen my own bedroom, and no way was I going to wander over and look in his. I was afraid he might take it as a sign of interest - interest that I still wasn't sure I had, regardless of how stimulating I might have found our one and only kiss.

"Here you go," he said, walking over and handing me a glass of water.

I took a sip. It was cool and refreshing, making me want to guzzle it down, but I resisted, wanting to be able to make it last. I was feeling weird around Ben and needed to keep something there to hold in my hand as a prop, if nothing else. I felt on the defense around him, but I wasn't sure if it was nervousness stemming from the binding ceremony or the fact that I still wasn't sure who he was or even who *I* was anymore. Life had changed so much in the last twenty-four hours, I was having a hard time adjusting or something.

"Did you design this room yourself?" I asked, taking a few steps back from him before wandering over to the tapestry with the dragons again. There were four of the magical beasts on this one. They all had a mix of colors to their scales, but each had one that was dominant. From left to right, there was one purple, one silver, one red, and one black. My eyes lingered on the black one, wondering if I had his fang in the holster at my leg. I reached down absently to touch it, wondering if the slight warmth I felt there was my imagination.

"Yes. I prefer darker colors. I find them soothing."

I nodded. "It's nice. A little medieval, but nice."

"It is from my time," he said.

I turned to look at him. He was staring at one of the dragons - the red one.

"What do you mean ... from your time?"

He looked at me, his eyes penetrating into mine. "I am a changeling too, but I was changed a long time ago." He turned his gaze back to the tapestry. "When I was your age, this was the style."

"So that makes you, like ... a few hundred years old."

"Give or take," he said, noncommittally.

"You don't seem a day over three hundred," I said, forcing myself to keep a straight face.

"Thank you. I think."

"You're welcome."

He was staring at me now instead of the tapestry, making me feel nervous again.

I cleared my throat and walked around him to get closer to the artwork, moving along the wall and following the flow of the design in the threads. "This is amazing. It looks almost ... magical," I said, admiring the way the picture seemed to wink at me with its lights.

"It is."

I stopped, turning my head sharply to look at him, to see if he was kidding.

His expression held no trace of humor.

"In what way?" I asked, itching to touch it but now a little afraid.

"In ways we don't need to talk about right now," he said, walking over and taking me by the hand, leading me to the couch. "Come sit. Let's talk about us."

My heart leaped into my throat and my hands immediately began to sweat. "Us? You mean, you and me?" I said, my voice coming out sounding slightly choked.

He sat on the couch and pulled me down next to him, letting my hand go. "Don't panic. I'm not going to jump you." He smiled humorlessly.

I didn't trust myself to speak, so I took a sip of my water instead. I looked at him over the rim of my glass, remembering how I'd despised him and wanted him dead as recently as yesterday and as far back as all the months before that - since the first time I'd laid eyes on him, practically. He was like a different person now, though. I wondered how that could even be possible. *Who had changed? Him or me?* I pulled the glass away from my face and swallowed.

"I told you already, Jayne," he said, looking at me earnestly. "You are the one calling the shots here. I'll be whatever you need me to be for you, okay? No pressure."

"How come everyone keeps saying that to me?" I asked, smiling crookedly. "The no pressure thing."

"Because. You put too much of it on yourself. It blocks your power and sometimes sends it awry. You just need to learn to relax and go with the flow of our realm."

"You make it sound so easy."

"It can be, once you learn how to let go."

"Letting go?" I asked. "Like you do? Just let the world do what it does and not interfere?"

He smiled, nodding his head. "Okay, so I've not yet learned to master the art of letting go completely."

"Or at all," I suggested.

"Now you're being too harsh. I do let go whenever I can; and I can help you learn how to do it too, if you want."

I shrugged. "If it'll make it easier to live with the screw-ups, I'm all for it."

"Not only will it make that easier, but it'll make the screw-ups less frequent and less ... epic."

I cocked my head. "Are you suggesting I've had epic screw-ups?"

"Not at all."

Tim's voice broke into our conversation from beyond the door. "Yoooo hoooo! Anyone want to help a pixie out over here? Can't fit under, can't fly through!"

"Go away!" I said loudly.

Ben jumped in surprise, leaning back a little with his hands up, looking confused. "Wow, what'd I say?"

I laughed, shaking my head and getting up, waving him off. "No, not you. Tim. He's at the door." I walked over to open it.

"I really need to get one of those hearing spells from the witches," mumbled Ben, following behind me.

I grabbed the handle and pulled, but the door wouldn't budge. I frowned, wondering if I'd missed a lock somewhere. I moved my hand out of the way, but didn't see any kind of buttons or hooks or anything that could be securing the door. I tried once more, but it definitely wasn't moving. I tried to force the panic away, but my brain couldn't stop thinking about how I was trapped in the room with Ben.

"Here ... let me help you," he said, taking the handle and easily pulling the door in.

Tim flew through the opening, exclaiming as he went. "Whoa, nice place. A little heavy on the doom and gloom, but I like it." Tim stopped in the middle of the room, doing a slow hovering circle before he stopped, facing me, his hands on his hips. "It's *exactly* what I'd expect from the Lord of Darkness Himself." He grinned from ear to ear.

"What'd he say?" asked Ben, shutting the door.

"He said he likes your place. That it suits you." Ben eyed me suspiciously, so I gave him my most innocent look.

"Thanks," he said, looking over at Tim.

Tim came over to me, doing some midair rolls as he talked. "So, what's happening in here? Were you guys making out? Sucking face? Snogging? Lighting each other's fires? Gettin' busy?"

I closed my eyes, sighing loudly before answering. "We were talking about ..." I looked at Ben, not quite remembering what we'd been discussing. My eyes kept going back to the dragon tapestry. We hadn't really been talking about it, but it was far more interesting to me than anything else right now for some reason.

"We were talking about Jayne's powers and me helping her to use them better - to feel more confident - and for her to learn how to go with the flow."

"Oh, that's good," said Tim. "I'm sure the green elves will be happy to learn they will be coma-free from now on."

I sighed.

"What'd he say?"

"His usual. He's begging our forgiveness for the fallout we're suffering."

"Fallout?"

"From his intestinal issues."

Tim buzzed up in front of Ben, gesturing and yammering on and on about personal boundaries and so on.

Ben heard none of it. He just looked at me and said, "Maybe I don't want one of those hearing spells, after all."

I shook my head. "Trust me. Pixies are better seen and not heard."

We shared a smile, knowing we were both pissing Tim off to no end. I was feeling more cheerful and confident already. Maybe working with Ben wouldn't be all that bad.

"Jayne, I sure hope you don't really mean that," said Tim, buzzing over to land on top of the decanter of absinthe, "because I have some juicy news for you. But hey, if you'd rather just see this pixie and not hear him, I'll understand." He pretended to be admiring his fingernails, squinting his eyes in careful examination, first holding his hand in an upside down fist below his face and then opening his hand and extending his arm out to view his manicure from a distance, palm facing out.

"What'd you hear?" I asked, coming to sit down in the leather chair next to him, facing the dragons.

"I'm not sure if we should be sharing with you-know-who," he replied, trying not to look at Ben but stealing glances in his direction anyway. He couldn't have been more obvious.

"What's going on?" asked Ben. "Secrets?"

"Maybe. He's trying to tempt me into begging for information right now."

"Take my advice," said Tim. "You should beg. Go ahead, I'm ready. Lay it on me. I suggest knees being involved."

I had nothing better to do to pass the time before dinner, and being alone with Ben made me uncomfortable, so I begged - but not on my knees. The chair was way too comfortable, and the day I went on my knees for a pixie would be one for the record books for sure.

"Please," I said in a bored voice, "oh handsomest pixie of all pixiedom, please tell me what you heard."

"You can do better than that," Tim said, dropping his hand and looking at me, finally.

I cleared my throat, speaking now in a disaffected monotone. "Oh, Tim, you godlike, fearsome, hot-sexiest pixie of all of faedom, please tell me what you heard."

"You're getting warmer."

I stood up and took a step towards him, fixing him with a devious smile. "Tell me the fucking secret or I'll rip your damn wings off."

"Hey! Watch the language, lady! You represent the ruling class now. You need to clean up your act if you want to get any action out of me."

I laughed. "The ruling class?"

Tim smiled. "Yeah. You know. Boss of the elements and all."

"Well, I didn't ask for the ruling class bit, and I'm pretty sure no one's going to listen to me if I try to boss them around anyway, so screw it. Now tell me what you're hiding, or your wings are going bye-bye."

Tim folded his appendages in very tightly to himself. "You'd have to catch me first."

He probably thought he had it in the bag, but Ben had different ideas. A wind came rushing into the room from I have no idea where, grabbing onto Tim and spinning him so fast, it turned him into a pixie dust devil. One second he was sitting on the flat decanter top, and the next he was like a deranged ballerina, spinning in place at such a high rate of speed, I could no longer see anything but a fuzzy, pixie-shaped blur, squealing at the top of his lungs.

"Aaahhhhyyyeeeeee!! Oookaaaayyyyyy!! Stop pleeaaaasse!!"

I put my hand on Ben's arm. "I think he's ready to give up."

"Good," said Ben, closing his eyes once slowly, the wind disappearing as quickly as it had arrived. He opened his lids back up. "I don't like seeing you beg. You shouldn't have to beg anyone." I couldn't tell whether it was the sexual tension or anger that had him smoldering, but neither was welcome right now as far as I was concerned.

"He was only playing around," I said, trying to bank the fire I saw just behind Ben's gaze. "And I can take care of my own problems, thanks."

He shrugged. "Your problems are my problems now, too."

"No, they're not," I said, getting testy.

"Yes, they are; whether you like it or not, agree or not. We are one. You need to get used to that."

"I don't need to do *anything* I don't want to do," I insisted, getting seriously cranky now. I looked down at the glass of water in my hand that was half-full, sorely tempted to toss it on him to cool him off a little. He was bossier than I generally liked my guys to be, and I was extra pissed now that I was tied to him. One minute he was cool and interesting, and the next just ... not. His attractiveness and ugliness flipping back and forth were giving me emotional whiplash.

Ben continued lecturing me. "Need and want are two different things entirely. What you need may not be what you want, but that is immaterial." He glanced down at my glass and then up at my face again. "And you can douse me with what's in there, but I'm not a wicked witch that will melt away."

"I was kind of hoping it would cool you down, actually," I said, looking back over at Tim. He'd finally come to a rest, draped over the top of the decanter on his back, his arms and legs flopped over the edges. The side of his face that I could see was the same green color as the liquid in the container. I stepped over and put my water glass down, gently picking my friend up and setting him in my palm where he lay spread-eagle, nearly unconscious. His wings looked a little tattered, but still useable, hopefully.

# Clash of the Otherworlds: Book One

"It was nice talking to you, but Tim and I have to go," I said, walking to the door that led to the hallway, ignoring the one that connected our two rooms. It seemed too intimate to use that one for some reason. I didn't even want to look at it.

"Where are you going?" asked Ben, not moving.

"None of your damn business," I said, grasping the handle and yanking. Again, it refused to open. I pulled on it over and over, harder each time, trying to get it to budge, but it stayed firmly closed. "What the hell is wrong with this friggin door?"

Ben walked over and reached across me to take the handle.

I hurriedly pulled my hand away to avoid touching him.

He easily freed the door from its latch, and it swung open to reveal the hallway beyond.

I frowned. "How in the hell did you do that? Where's the lock?" I leaned back to look at the handle again, trying to see what I'd missed.

"There is no lock. It's spelled. Only the person who belongs in the room can open it."

"Whaaat?" I exclaimed, not even sure I believed him. I looked again at the latch, wondering if there was some tiny trigger there that he was pressing.

"How'd you get in and out of *my* room, then?"

He shrugged. "I guess I belong there."

I put one hand on my hip, the other holding Tim out in front of me. "How can you possibly belong in my room when I don't belong in yours?"

"Maybe because I've accepted that's where I belong and you haven't yet, I don't know. I'm not the witch who put the spell on these rooms."

"Well, who is?" I demanded. "Because I have a few words to

share with him or her."

"I'm not so sure that's something you want to do, actually."

"Oh, believe me. I *am* sure."

"Fine. Go talk to Samantha, then."

I stopped the rant that was about to fly out of my mouth. *Samantha*. I really, really didn't want to see her, Ben was right about that - not that I'd admit it to him. After she'd tried to kill me a couple times, succeeded in murdering one of my friends, and made my life just miserable in general, I'd decided we would have to be enemies for life. Then Maggie the old hag witch went and told me that Samantha and I are related - cousins or something - getting a huge kick out of it, probably, since she knew how much I disliked her. At least, I thought it was Samantha she'd been talking about. I couldn't think of anyone else it could be.

To say my emotions concerning this chick were confused would be an understatement. Aside from an absent father I had no desire to see ever again, Samantha and Maggie were my only living relatives that I knew of. And we shared being fae, which was the strongest link I'd ever had to anything in my life. So I both hated Samantha and wanted to get to know her better, which was kind of sick in a way. All of this messed up emotion had the final result of me wanting to walk up to her and punch her in the face, so I decided it was probably better if I avoided confronting her on the door issue for now.

"Figures," I said. "Leave it to Samantha to do something stupid and annoying like this." I stepped out of the room. "Come on, Tim. Let's get out of here. This place stinks like witches."

"Yeah," said Tim's voice, weak and trembling. "Like witches and demons."

"Yeah," I said, smiling. "It sure does."

"It's a good spell," said Ben as I walked out. "She's very skilled."

"*Pfft*. Whatever," I said, entering my room and shutting the door to his last comment.

# Chapter Six

I WALKED WITH TIM OVER to the archway on our right, just on the other side of my sitting room, and pushed open the door. I was happy to see that it moved without any problems.

It led to my new bedroom which was about three times the size of my last one. The bed was bigger also - big enough for two. Not that I needed that kind of room, since Chase was gone, and it would be a cold day in hell before Ben was ever sharing a mattress with me, especially if he kept acting like he had today. There was a double dresser for my clothes now instead of a single-sized one, with a decanter of water or some clear liquid on top and three glasses next to it, along with a small silver tray for me to put chocolate ball tokens on for my brownie housekeeper. A large armoire was in the corner with a chair next to it, and two bedside tables on either side of the bed finished off the furnishings.

I walked over and put Tim on my comforter, sitting down next to him. "Are you okay, Tim? You look kind of green." His color was better than it had been, but he definitely still looked sick. He hadn't opened his eyes yet, either.

"Has the world stopped spinning yet?"

"Yes. And you're in my bedroom now without Ben around, so

you can wake up and say whatever you want."

Tim opened his left eye. "I think I'm gonna ralph."

"Please, not on my bed," I said, looking around. I jumped up and ran over to the dresser, grabbing one of the glasses. I went back over to Tim and held it down near his face. "If you're gonna spew, spew in this."

He opened his other eye. "I think you'd better just bring me out into the garden. Put me in a rose. I'll feel better in a jiff."

I picked him up and carried him out of my room and into the garden. Abby met us at the entrance, buzzing around Tim anxiously.

"What happened? Is he okay?" Then she looked closer at him. "Why are you green? Did you try that quintuple barrel roll with a triple-twist again? I told you that's too much. You're spinning your equilibrium off." She looked at me, concern marring her features. "Tim is always trying to push the envelope. *Always*. I wish he would just settle down like other pixie husbands sometimes."

"He's pretty good at the barrel rolls, actually," I said. "What happened was not really his fault, though. Ben spun him around in a miniature tornado. He's motion sick, I think."

Abby smiled tolerantly. "Pixies don't get motion sick. We're built for flying in extreme conditions, so long as we don't try to do too many acrobatics." She turned back to Tim, ready to let him have it again.

"Seriously. It was Ben," I said, getting annoyed at her for brushing off my explanation. "He threw him into wind spinning at about three hundred miles per hour. I don't care how well-built pixies are for aerodynamics; that'd make anyone sick."

Tim held up an arm. "Ladies, ladies. No need to argue. There's enough Tim to go around for everyone."

I smiled. This was the surest sign he was feeling better - an elevated sense of his own sexiness.

Abby sighed. "He does like to get himself into trouble, doesn't he? I never realized that about him before, but ever since he's met you, he can't seem to avoid it."

I wasn't sure whether I was hearing censure in her voice or not, but I decided it didn't matter. Tim was fun and happy when he was getting into mischief, and I was sure it had nothing to do with me - except for the fact that I didn't really chastise him for it. If that was encouraging it, then I was going to be on Abby's shit-list probably; but that sure wasn't going to change anything for me.

"He wants me to put him in a rose," I said, walking towards one with bright red flowers.

"No, not that one," said Abby, buzzing over to my right. "Put him in this yellow one over here. He needs something a bit sweeter than the red can offer him right now."

I shrugged, changing course and stopping in front of the flower Abby was nearest. "Here?" I asked.

"Yes. Please."

I tipped my palm over the flower until Tim fell into it. He went face-first into the center, his arms and legs lying over the edges because they didn't fit all the way in, even though it was a pretty big bloom. I giggled at the vision he made, splayed out across the flower, his face hidden from view but his butt on full display. One wing was lying flat and the other was sticking up. His hair looked like he'd put his finger in an electric socket. I wanted to leave him to his mess, but if I walked away and stopped supporting the flower, he'd for sure fall out onto the gravel path, so I stayed.

"How long do we have to do this?" I asked, taking a moment

to look around the garden, my hand supporting the base of the flower where the petals were secured. I couldn't help but think that this place was magical - as in, literally, there was some serious hocus-pocus going on here. Blooms of every color and shape were bursting out in full glory. The air was crisp, so it felt like I should be seeing dead things and red leaves, but this place looked more like a garden in Spring.

"Wow," I said, my mouth on auto pilot. "This place is like ... a magic garden or something. The Garden of Eden." I could feel the power of the Earth element humming under my feet. The Green was strong out here and seemed as if it were waiting anxiously for me to connect. I resisted, though, not wanting to use the power unless I had to. I knew my future was going to be full of learning how to manage it, so for now, I just wanted to be me - just Jayne - in the garden.

"I do my best," said Abby, her voice full of modesty.

I looked down at her and caught her blushing. "Do you use magic?"

"Noooo, don't be silly. I just talk to the flowers and my garden partners, and we do everything we can to make it work." She hesitated. "Well, okay, we did have a witch put up a little acceleration spell to get everything ready for you and Ben to move in, but the spells don't do much without us working together. It was a one-time thing and won't need to be repeated."

"Garden partners?"

"Yes, of course. I could never do this all on my own."

"Who's helping?" I could imagine one of the dirty gnomes I knew running around in here with clippers, and it made me nervous for my ankles and eyesight. I examined the spaces between the plants, looking for signs of Scottish tartans hidden among the leaves. The gnomes were prone to wearing very short kilts with nothing on underneath, which tended to make me want to gouge my eyeballs out when I made the mistake of looking at the ass-end of one of them when they were bending over.

"Bees, worms, ladybugs, snails ... you name it. We're all here for the garden." She smiled, looking around her.

"Well, whatever you're doing, keep on doing it," I said, giving her the props she deserved. "This is the most peaceful place I've been in since ... ever." Even my mom's garden didn't come close to this one. "I feel like never leaving, actually," I said, my eyes moving from flower to flower as I lost myself in the colors and lazy, dancing motes of pollen and fuzzy seed pods floating on the light breeze. I felt my cheeks getting warm and a slight tingle moving over my skin. A giggle rose up into my throat unbidden, making me smile like a loon. My lips moved up in a huge grin, but I couldn't put my finger on what was so funny. But then, I found that I didn't care, either. This place was taking over ... me.

"Get her out of here," said Tim weakly, his voice muffled in the flower petals. "She's gonna get mesmerized, and we'll never get her out."

"Oh, you're right," said Abby, buzzing up near my face. "Mother! Listen to me! You have to leave the garden *right now!*"

My hand slipped away from Tim and fell to my side, my strength suddenly waning. The pixie lady was flitting back and forth in front of my face like an irritating fly, so I tried to brush her away, my arm as heavy as lead. "You're annoying. Beat it," I said absently, trying to focus on the pinky pink of a flower a few feet away from Tim. It kept going in and out of focus for some reason. I took a step towards it, but it moved back. I got another step closer, but the bush stayed just out of my reach. I frowned, trying to make sense of what was happening, but my brain wouldn't focus.

I turned around and around, the colors of the flowers and trees swirling together into a beautiful blur. I held my arms out, delighting in the dizzying madness, no longer caring about the thing that had been bothering me. All my problems and worries seemed to float out and away from me, up into the air and out of the garden. I looked up at the sky and felt myself falling backwards, while my heart and mind flew up into the ether. I knew I must have landed on my back, but I felt no pain and no jarring as my body was cushioned in the leaves, branches, and vines of a nearby tree. It was almost like falling underwater.

I was zooming away from the earth now, going to the heavens to be with Chase, not caring for a second about the friends and family I was leaving behind. I could see my guardian angel's face, looking at me, intent and not smiling as was his way. His strong arms hung by his sides and his wings remained folded behind him, but I could see them over his shoulders and down by his legs. I'd never seen a man look so beautiful as he did in that moment. The closer I got, the higher my heart soared. He'd only been gone for a day, but I missed him so much. We were going to be together again, and it was all I wanted. I got closer and closer, and only when I was nearly to him, did I see that one of his wings had blood on it.

A splash of cold water shocked me out of my dream.

The vision of Chase disappeared and was replaced by Tony's face above me, a worried expression telling me I'd messed something up again. I was lying on the ground in the garden, sticks jabbing me uncomfortably in the back.

"What the hell?" I asked, totally confused. "Tony, where did you come from?" I turned my head to the left and right, seeing plant stems and dirt near my face.

## Clash of the Otherworlds: Book One

"Welcome back," he said, holding out his hand for me to take.

I grabbed it and used it to stand, brushing myself off absently, looking at the three pixies hovering in front of me.

"Papa, she's awake!" said a very disappointed-sounding Willy, pouting. "You said I could look in her nose, but she got up."

"Well, you should have done it when I said you could instead of talking about it. Now it's too late," said Tim, smiling at me. "Welcome back, Jayne. Thought we'd lost you for a second there."

"Samantha needs to get in here and put a grounding spell over this place or we *will* lose her," scolded Abby, looking at me critically. "Why didn't she do that before? She knew this could happen." Abby flew away, muttering to herself.

I gave up on removing all the soil from my clothes and looked from one friend to the other. "Does anyone want to tell me what the heck just happened here?" It sounded like I had Samantha to thank for my garden-tripping. *Surprise, surprise.*

Tony guided me gently out of the plants and into my sitting area, pushing me down onto a chair.

"I found you in the Gray. You were wandering around looking for Chase, I think."

I dropped my gaze to my lap. "I wasn't looking for him, but I did find him."

"Well, I suggest you not try to not look for him again," said Tony. "How did you get in there anyway?"

I shrugged and mumbled, "I have no idea."

Tim flew over to join us. "You saw Chase? How's he look?"

"Awesome, of course." I sighed, looking up at my pixie friend, noticing he was back to normal, his color pink again and his smile in full force.

"Jayne, seriously. You need to let him go," said Tony. "He's dealing with some heavy-duty stuff right now. You're a distraction he can't afford."

My head snapped over to Tony. "What? How could you possibly know that?" The blood that I'd seen on Chase's wing was nagging at me. It couldn't possibly be a good sign of anything.

Tony glanced to the side, almost guiltily. I could practically see him trying to come up with a lie.

Tim started up with his singsong voice. "Someone's got a secret ... someone's got a secret ..."

"Don't even try it, Tony. Tell me the truth. You and I don't play those games, right?" *Please don't turn into one of the fae I cannot trust. You and Tim are my last hope. And even Tim's a bit iffy, the little bastard.*

He sighed. "No, we don't play games. I just don't know if it's such a good idea to share what I know with you right now. You have enough on your plate, and things are in flux. I could tell you something that's true now, and it could be untrue the next day. Things are just ... weird."

"Weird, my ass. Tell me. All of it." I was determined to get to the bottom of all this stuff, starting with Tony's secrets and then Tim's. Chase had told me we were through until the day I died, but since I never really listened to anyone anyway, I figured I should leave that option open - especially now that I'd seen him again. My heart spasmed painfully with the recent memory of his beautiful face.

## Chapter Seven

TONY SAT DOWN ON THE couch opposite me, and Tim rested on my shoulder, his arm gripping onto a lock of my hair. I tried not to wince as he moved around, tugging on it. Abby had stayed in the garden with her son - the mischievous little wannabe nostril explorer.

"I've been spending a lot of time in the Gray, becoming better at finding my way around and getting in and out quickly. We think this is how the creatures from the Underworld are getting through to our realm."

"How is that possible? I mean, I thought it was a place you could only get to from here - in the Here and Now."

"That's what everyone thought. But it's kind of like the waiting room between realms, so since there is a way for a spirit to leave the Gray and enter either the Overworld or the Underworld, I guess it makes sense that with the right amount of magic, someone could reverse the doors or keep them open somehow and go the other direction, too."

I thought about that for a few moments. The terribleness of it was nearly unfathomable. Tim must have gotten nervous too, because he farted on my shoulder.

I sighed heavily. This was not good - neither Tim's gas nor the idea of demons coming into our world through the Gray. Like Torrie, for example. The former silver elf was known by the still-living silver elves in this fae compound, and he was not only disgusting and evil, but he was also very hard to kill. It had only been the combined forces of all of the elements being managed by Ben and me that had finally sent him back to the Underworld. It was where he deserved to be sent, after having beaten my mother to death and after having planned to rape me in order to conceive some evil half-demon child who would make it possible for Torrie and all of his buddies to enter the Here and Now and end the world as we know it.

I shook my head. "If there's a door in the Gray that's open somewhere, we should be seeing a lot more of those things over here."

"We have no idea how many there are here, first of all. There could be many, hiding and waiting to strike. And we also don't know if there's some sort of time issue involved with the door or anything like that."

"Time issue?" I asked.

"Some of the gray elves have hypothesized that the demons are only able to get through during certain times."

"Like, times of day?"

"Maybe. Or the week, or the year, or ..." Tony shook his head. "We really just don't know yet. That's why I'm spending so much time in the Gray, trying to get answers."

"You're like a Gray detective or something," I said, proud that my best friend was playing such an important role in our new world, even if it was all kind of screwed up right now.

"Yeah. Something like that. It's not easy getting those spirits in there to talk."

"How come?"

"They don't care about the things we care about, so they don't focus on details. And they aren't motivated to help me, either."

I didn't really want to ask my next question because it gave me the heebie-jeebies a little, but I had to. "How do you motivate them, then?"

"It depends on the spirit. I try to find the one thing that's important to them and then work with that."

I frowned, wondering how far Tony had gone to help our friends. "Give me an example."

Tony squirmed a little in his seat. "I can't really think of anything right now, off the top of my head."

"Bullshit. Tell me now." I knew right away when Tony was avoiding something. He absolutely could not tell a lie without broadcasting it to the world.

Tony sighed. "You know, Jayne, you don't need to know everything that's going on with me all the time."

My mouth dropped open in shock before my righteous indignation came blazing up to save me. "Say *what?!* Since *when* do I not need to know your every last personal detail?"

"Well ..."

"No, seriously. When did that happen? Because I didn't get the memo, Tones." I gestured between the two of us. "We share shit. We're soulmates. We don't keep secrets."

Tony smiled. "You feel pretty strongly about this, I see."

"You bet your sweet freckled ass I do. Now spill it. I want to know what you've been up to and what kind of crazy shit they've talked you into doing."

"No one's talked me into doing anything. Everything I've

done has been my own idea."

"Well, what is it then? Stop stalling." I fixed him with my staredown, knowing he'd never be able to resist me now.

"You can lose the lunatic expression, Jayne. It doesn't scare me; it makes me want to laugh."

I kept my gaze as penetrating as possible, not moving a muscle. "No, it doesn't. Right now you're worried I'm going to send you into a coma, and you're lining up all your stories and facts so you can tell me every last one of them."

A small smile played on Tony's lips. "Are you trying to hypnotize me or something? Because it's not working."

"Tony!" I yelled, dropping my staredown and throwing my hands up. "Come *on!* Stop messing around!"

"Whoa, Nelly!" yelled Tim, swinging around on my hair. "Simmer down, there, mule. Give the boy a chance to speak."

I reached up to knock Tim off my hair, but he swung out of my reach, giggling his tiny ass off.

Tony smiled. "Fine, okay. Don't get your panties in a twist, I'll tell you. It's not that big a deal."

I folded my arms across my chest. "I'll be the judge of that."

Tony sighed. "Okay. Well, for example, earlier today I talked to a spirit in there who remembered Torrie coming through. Only it was him going the other way, back to the Underworld, not him coming in."

"Well, Torrie would have come in months ago, right? That's when he took over my step-father's body and started working on my mother."

"Exactly. Finding a spirit who is still there now, and who was also there back then, is difficult on a couple levels."

"As in ...?"

# Clash of the Otherworlds: Book One

"Plead the fifth!" Tim yelled, jumping off my shoulder and buzzing in front of Tony's face. "Plead the fifth! You're going down in flames! Mayday! Mayday! Mayday!"

Tony smiled at Tim's antics. "What's he saying?"

I leaned over to swat at Tim again. "Go away, big ugly bug. No one's interested in your intestinal problems." One of these days I was going to find out how Tim knew so much about American culture; and I was more motivated than ever, now that he was talking about the Constitution, for shit's sake.

"He's talking about ... intestinal problems?" asked Tony, leaning away from Tim, staring at him suspiciously.

Tim buzzed back over to me. "Stop talking about my intestines! And I'm trying to save your friendship here, Lellamental, so back off!"

I caught Tim in midair, much to his consternation. He pushed against the top of my fist, struggling to try and free himself. I blew my stinky lunch-breath into his face as I spoke, delighting in his wilting expression and flagging energy.

"Listen up, pixieman. The grownups are talking now. Time for you to go play in the garden." I drew my hand back behind my shoulder and launched him towards the open glass doors that led out towards the flowers, releasing him from my fist at the apex of the throw, knowing he'd recover in mid-flight and right himself but only after being far away from me. It would give me at least five seconds of peace and possibly another ten seconds of Tim working himself into a snit before I'd have to deal with him again. And that might be just long enough to get Tony talking.

"You were saying?" I asked, ignoring the sound of Tim's screaming as he flew through the air, tumbling ass over wings.

Tony's gaze was following my pixie projectile, so I snapped

my fingers near his face. "Hey! I'm over here. The story?"

Tony shook his head, getting himself back on track. "Yeah. Ummm ... okay. So ... as I was saying, it's difficult because first of all, fae and humans usually move on to either the Overworld or the Underworld pretty soon after dying. They just use the Gray as a transition zone of sorts. And for those who end up staying - the ones who can't or won't move on - they start to get so disconnected from what we'd consider reality, they're very difficult to communicate with. They're almost in their own worlds, locked inside themselves, if that makes any sense."

Tim came buzzing back, remaining ominously silent, giving me the stink-eye before sitting down all prim and proper-like on the edge of a nearby chair, crossing his legs and folding his hands over his knee.

Tony spared him a concerned glance and then turned back to me. "I met a woman in there today who looked like a warrior of some sort, so I just talked to her about her last battle and that kind of woke her up a little ... or a lot ... at least, enough to get her focused on the spirit world so I could ask her some questions."

"Did she help you? Who was she?"

"Not really. Like I said, they're in their own worlds in there, so they ignore a lot of what's going on. But I asked her if she could try and ... keep her eyes open for us, or whatever. And no, I have no idea who she is or was. They lose their Here and Now identities or names pretty quickly. That stuff isn't important there."

"How did you know she was a warrior?" I asked.

Tony gave me a small smile. "She reminded me a lot of you, actually."

"Me?" I asked, confused.

"Yeah. The way she stood, her posture. The way she held

herself. She was a take-no-baloney kind of spirit, just like you. Plus, she wore weapons and armor."

I couldn't help but smile. "Thank you, Tony. I like being described as a take-no-baloney type person."

"I could think of another description," said Tim in a haughty voice, not changing his polite and cultured stance.

"Save it, pixieman," I said.

Tony leaned forward, whispering. "Is he talking about his stomach thing again?"

Tim zoomed up to hover in front of Tony's face, his hands on his hips. "Listen up, Luke Gray Walker ... I don't talk about your pimples *or* your mighty unibrow, so you shouldn't be talking about my *farts!*"

I burst out laughing, shooing Tim away, but a lot more gently this time.

Apparently he didn't like being a pixie-baseball. He flew backwards from the room and into the garden, giving us the finger as he went out.

"Oops," said Tony, ducking his head down into his shoulders a little, grimacing. "I guess I offended him."

"He's easy to offend, don't worry about it. Tell me more about what you've found out. And about Chase, too."

"There's not much to tell. I've only had a day or so to look around and ask questions. Chase is working on his end to try and help us, but I don't communicate with him. I just get a feel for his presence in the Gray - traces of him, I guess you could say. But we're going to find the spot where those demons are getting through and find a way to close it up, with or without the Overworld's help."

"*You're* going to do that?"

"I'll find the hole, but it'll be someone else's job to close it up. That's beyond my capabilities."

"So, who, then? A witch?"

"Probably," he said. I could tell he was not saying something the way he was looking at me, as if judging my reaction.

"Any particular witch?"

"A strong one," he said, still staring at me.

I sighed heavily. "Don't tell me, let me guess. Samantha?"

"Maybe," said Tony, visibly relaxing. "Does that make you upset?"

"Yes, of course it does. I can't get away from that bitch. First she kills our friend, then she causes all kinds of problems trying to start a war between the fae, and now she's in here putting spells all over shit and pissing me off all over again. Wouldn't you be upset? Aren't you? Honestly, Tony ... sometimes your ability to forgive anything is annoying as hell."

"You've been the beneficiary of that forgiveness, you know."

I picked up a pillow off the couch and threw it at his head. "Shut up. That's different."

He caught the pillow after it bounced off his face. "Yeah, yeah, I know. We're soulmates."

"Exactly. So unconditional love and forgiveness is my right."

"But not so much for anyone else," he finished.

I smiled. "Yes. Now we're on the same page. *Finally.*"

He tossed the pillow back onto the couch, out of my reach. "Anyway, it's almost dinnertime, and I'm starving." He stood. "Are you coming?"

"Hell to the yes. I'm hungry too, and no friggin way am I going into dinner with Ben."

Tony frowned at me. "What's going on with you guys? I

thought after the ceremony that ... I don't know ... you'd find a way to at least be friends."

I moved towards the door, looking back to see if the pixies were coming. Abby and Tim were floating above their jungle room, looking down at something. I stood at the entrance, waiting for them to notice us leaving, answering Tony without looking at him. "I can tolerate him. That's about all I'll commit to right now."

"That's not very romantic-sounding," said Tony, stopping at my side.

"Yo, pixies! Are you coming?!" I yelled.

Both of them waved their hands at me, like they were slapping me over and over in midair.

"I think their baby is sleeping," said Tony in a quiet voice near my ear, staring over at them with me.

"Oh, shit. I hope I didn't wake him up. He's a pain in the butt sometimes."

Tim came over to join us, blowing his wife a kiss on the way. "Let's ride, feeps. Willy's napping and Abby said to go."

"Feeps?" I asked.

"Yeah. Fae-peeps. Feeps." He shook his head and rolled his eyes like I was the dumb one.

"Tim, how do you know all these slang words like *peeps?*" I asked.

"He knows peeps?" asked Tony.

"I heard it once in the forest. Come on, before that kid wakes up."

I stifled a laugh. "That *kid* is your *son*, goof."

"Yeah, whatever. Come on. There's a strawberry on that buffet that's got my name on it."

I looked at Tony. "Yeah. Tim has lots of secrets. He's going to tell them all to me one day. The first one I want to know is how much time he's actually spent with humans, because he knows way too much about our culture to be learning it from here."

"The mysteries never cease in the Green Forest," said Tony.

"You aren't kidding," I agreed, pulling the door to the room open, relieved that it moved so easily. *I guess I still belong here.*

# Chapter Eight

THE THREE OF US MADE our way down the hallway to the dining room. Tony and I wore moccasins that made no noise on the stone floors, and I felt the need to speak in low tones so my voice wouldn't echo off the carved rock walls.

"Tim, you haven't told me your secret yet."

"What secret?"

"Stop messing around. You said something in front of Ben, so I know you know something. Have you been snooping around again?"

"First of all, I'm not sure I'm inclined to discuss any of my insider information with someone who thinks a pixie-toss is an enjoyable way to spend her free time. And secondly, if I had a secret - and I'm not saying I do - I wouldn't want to be sharing it with your wrathe soulmate standing next to you. He would tell all the rest of them, and then I'd lose my advantage. Not that I have one. I'm just saying ... "

I sighed.

"What's the matter?" asked Tony, his gaze following Tim's flight path out in front of us.

"He's being coy. Don't worry ... I'll get it out of him." After I heard whatever it was Tim thought he knew, I would decide whether Tony was on the need-to-know list. I was pretty sure the advantage that Tim referred to was his super snooper setup. He claimed to be very good with electronics and things that acted like electronics, such as witch-casted listening spells. If he had somehow convinced a witch to cast for him and was getting good intel from fae by listening in and spying, I might not necessarily want to clue anyone into that little nugget of information. Having Tim as a friend and roommate was like having an extra set of tiny ears all over the fae compound; and I could use all the help I could get, trying to ferret out who was on my side and who might be trying to make my life more difficult - fae like Samantha, for instance.

We reached the dining hall and entered through a heavy wooden door, the noise from over a hundred fae gathered for a meal hitting us all at once.

"Wow. There are a lot fae in here," said Tony, scanning the room. "I kind of miss the days when it was just the Light Fae."

"Tell me about it," I agreed. I nudged him in the shoulder, gesturing towards a table in the far corner. "Look, there's Finn and Becky. Let's go sit with them."

We walked through the mass of crowded tables and over to our changeling friends. We'd been semi-homeless teenagers living in Miami together for a couple days before entering the fae-challenge that had been disguised as a physical fitness clinical trial thing. Our dormant fae blood had been awakened after completing the nightmare test in the Green Forest, and now we were all in the same boat - trying to figure out the limits of the powers we had as members of our different races.

I walked up to the table, and Becky jumped out of her seat to give me a warm hug. I always felt like I was going to crush her tiny frame when we embraced.

"How's my favorite water sprite?" I asked over her shoulder.

"Excellent. Better than excellent," she said, pulling away and shooting me one of her super-sized grins. She was almost never without one.

I looked down and caught Finn's face going red. I nudged him in the shoulder. "What's up, green elf? Been hanging out at the lake lately, maybe?" His crush on Becky was finally out in the open, but he was never one to share much beyond that.

Finn stood up and grabbed me into a rough embrace. "Hush, girl. Just gimme a hug."

I squeezed him hard, winking at Becky behind him. She blushed in response. The two of them were perfect for each other.

Finn sat back down, ignoring Becky and me in favor of his dinner.

"What do you get when you cross a water sprite and a green elf?" asked Tim, snickering already at the answer I knew I was going to hear whether I liked it or not.

"I don't know. Tell me," I said.

"A frog!"

I laughed a little, despite the fact that I didn't really get the joke. Tim was enjoying himself too much to not appreciate it for that reason alone.

"You don't get it, do you?" he asked, dropping his smile.

"No, not really."

"Water sprite? Green elf? ... Fishy-face girl, green guy hopping around the forest all the time trying to shoot the wings off flies?"

I nodded slowly. "Yeah. Okay, I get it."

"But you're not laughing."

"Technically, it's really not that funny."

"What's not that funny?" asked Becky.

"You don't want to know," I said, looking around our table. "Where is everyone else?"

Finn spoke up as he tore a hunk of bread from his roll, poised to pop it into his mouth. "Spike's with them succubus twins somewhere - I saw 'em earlier. And Scrum's comin'. He had a couple buddies practicin' their bear hug thing on Theresa and Felicia, and they got a little messed up. They're at the clinic." He threw the bread into his mouth from a few inches away and chewed slowly, just like he talked.

I raised my eyebrows at his comment. I had tangled with the twin succubi before and knew they were tough as nails, even though they looked like a couple of model-gorgeous cheerleaders. Anyone on the wrong end of their bad moods would be in serious trouble if he didn't know how to manage them. They could suck the life out of a fae in a matter of minutes, and all their victim would do is gaze lovingly up at them and thank them for taking their life energy. I knew from personal experience that it wasn't the most unpleasant experience in the world.

"Are they okay?" asked Tony, pulling out a chair and sitting in it.

Finn talked around his food. "Yeah, they'll be alright. Just need a little R-n-R is all." His gaze landed on something on the other side of the room. "There he is now. You can ask him yourself." Finn left off the conversation to stab a few vegetables on his plate and shove them in his mouth alongside the bread.

I shook my head at the amount of food he was able to eat at once. He reminded me of Chase, which brought my attention over to the table of daemons that were sitting close by. They were

## Clash of the Otherworlds: Book One

guardians of various important and somewhat vulnerable fae, like Chase had been for me during his temporary, undercover stay in our realm. Scrum was my protector now that Chase was gone, but I hadn't seen him all day. Now I knew why.

"Let's get some food," Tony said, standing. "Save our seats?" he asked Becky before receiving her nod and walking away.

I joined him at the buffet, taking a plate and putting fruit on it for Tim and a few meats and salad on it for me. "So what's up with the training schedule?" I asked Tony, feeling as though I were talking to his back because he kept moving away from me. "You're still in charge of setting that up for the changelings, right?"

"Yeah. Everyone has their stuff ready to go. They've been notified."

"Well, what's my schedule? No one's told me."

Tony shrugged, suddenly looking very interested in the salad toppings. "You're, ummm ... not on the regular schedule," he said, reaching for a pair of tongs to put some olives on his plate.

"Oh, yeah?" I said. "What am I supposed to do everyday, then?"

"Go to council meetings, train ..." The rest of what he said disappeared over his shoulder as he turned and moved quickly down the buffet line.

"I missed that last part. What'd you say? I'm supposed to train? Where? With who?"

Tony cleared his throat but didn't turn to look at me when he answered. "With Ben. You're scheduled to train with Ben, wherever he thinks is appropriate."

"For how long?" I asked, the slow burn of anger starting in my gut.

"Indefinitely," said Tony, his head dropping a little.

"And whose idea was this?" I was getting more upset by the minute. I knew Ben could help me, but I felt like I was continually having him shoved down my throat; and I didn't appreciate that one bit, especially when he'd so recently been overbearing and arrogant enough to make me want to slap him.

"The combined councils are responsible," Tony said, turning to face me finally. "I'm sorry, Jayne. I know it bothers you, but there's nothing I can do, nor would I want to. He's the only one who can help you learn how to control your elements, and he can protect you when you're not in the compound. It frees up at least one daemon to do other things."

I sighed heavily in defeat, knowing being angry at Tony or the world wasn't going to change anything. This was my new life, suck as it might. It wasn't his fault I'd gone and gotten myself tied to a turd. "I'm not mad at you. Or the council. I'm mad at ... fate, I guess." I shuffled away from the buffet and back to the table, any spring I might have had to my step gone. I felt like a deflated balloon, and all I wanted to do was go take a long nap and never get up.

Tim came over and sat on my shoulder. "Why the frown, clown? What's got you down?"

I sat in my seat, quietly eating my bland food for a few seconds before responding. "I guess I'm training with Ben the arrogant assbag for the rest of all eternity. What are *you* guys doing tomorrow?" I asked my friends, trying not to sound bitter but probably not succeeding.

No one said anything, but I noticed all of their gazes went to a spot above my head and behind me.

My face flushed as I realized what was going on. "He's behind me, isn't he?" I asked Becky quietly.

She nodded her head silently, still looking up at him.

"Hello, Ben," I said, not even turning to acknowledge him. *You arrogant assbag.*

"Hello, Jayne. I came to get you."

I put my fork down and lifted my head, frowning but still not turning to look at him. "I just sat down and started eating."

"Good. We can eat our meal together, then."

I turned to face him, my torso twisted halfway around. "I'm fine here, actually. But thanks." *Arrogant assbag a-hole.*

Tony kicked me under the table, probably vibing my feelings again like he did when I least wanted him to. *Stupid empath ... go away!*

Ben lifted an eyebrow at me and then purposefully looked over at a table in the front of the room. "You are expected to share your meals with me over there."

I followed his gaze to find a table set only for two, off by itself and noticeably separate from all the others.

"Mmmm, no thanks." I turned back around and began eating again.

In my peripheral vision, I could see Becky's eyes bugging out, and Finn was shifting around in his seat uncomfortably. I kicked them both under the table.

Tony cleared his throat before saying, "Jayne, why don't you go sit there? We'll come join you after we're finished."

My anger started to boil up, threatening to spill over. I slammed my fork down next to my plate. "Why don't *you* go sit over there, Tony, since you and Ben are such good buddies now." I glared at him, throwing my emotions at him silently but as strongly as I could.

He flinched, and then looked up at Ben. "Why don't you join

us over here, Ben?" he suggested.

"There's no more room here," I growled, staring at the table now, methodically chewing a now tasteless hunk of meat.

"Jayne," said Becky softly, "be nice. He can sit here. We can make room."

"Here," I said, jumping up and pushing my seat back with my legs, letting my napkin drop to the floor. "I'll make it easy for you." I stepped away from the table, gesturing towards my empty chair. "Have my spot. I've lost my appetite anyway." I took at look at all of their shocked expressions and then stormed out of the room before anyone had a chance to respond. I'd had enough of everyone pandering to Ben and his bossiness and wanted nothing but to get the hell away from all of them. *Friggin traitors.* It made me feel just a tad bit connected to Maléna, fighting Ben's assumed authority like this, and that did nothing to make me feel better.

## Chapter Nine

STUPID JERKS. ALWAYS BOWING DOWN to Ben and his bullshit. Well, they can do what they want, but I am not going to eat every meal with his stupid ass and I am not going to pretend like he's this nice guy everyone has to love and I am not going to be his friggin life mate.

*There.* I'd said it. The thing that had bothered me from the first second I'd heard we were to be permanently bound together, the thing that I had tried to ignore for the good of everyone else ... it had finally come to the surface to be officially recognized by me - only way too late for me to do anything about it but bitch.

"I do not want to be tied to this guy for the rest of my life! He's arrogant and bossy and annoying as hell!" I yelled out into the empty hallway. I had no destination in mind and wasn't picturing any door to the compound, so I knew I'd be wandering this corridor forever until I did; the damn witch spell would make sure of that.

*"Feel like talking about it?"* asked the mystery girl's voice in my head.

"Oh, so you're back?" I said into the air around me. "Great. You want to lecture me too? Fine. That's awesome. The voices in my head are giving me shit me now, right along with my best friends. I should just go into that friggin garden and never come out." It was tempting, too. Getting lost in the colors and the smells had been so peaceful. It was like a dangerous drug, and I was seriously considering overdosing on it right now. Every anchor I thought I had keeping me firmly tied to this place and its people felt like it was dragging me down somewhere I didn't want to be - into a dark abyss very much like the one I thought I'd left behind in the human world, where everyone else decided what was best for me and disregarded what I wanted.

"Who are you talking to?" asked Tim, flying up from behind me.

"Myself. What are you doing here?"

"*Pfft.* Like you even have to ask. That Ben guy is a total gnome-butt. He makes me lose my appetite, too."

I smiled, more than glad for the loyalty. "Me too. But you may want to abandon ship right now, because I'm going to go see Maggie." The decision had come to me the instant Tim's voice had hit my ears.

"Are you serious? Why would you want to do that?"

"Council business." I strode down the hallway, imagining the door with the small gargoyle head on it so the spell that kept the corridor going on forever would allow me to reach my destination.

"Hmmm, what to do, what to do ... ? Risk life and limb to hear possibly earth-shattering secrets or stay safe and warm in bed?"

"With the booger-eating pixie baby," I added.

"Excellent point. I'll risk it. What are we going to talk to her about?" He landed on my shoulder, grabbing a hunk of hair to keep himself steady.

I laughed at Tim's lame-ass parenting, even though I probably should have scolded him. "They think she might know something about how the demon got over here. And someone on the council mentioned scrying."

Tim's sharp intake of breath told me how he felt even before he spoke. "Baaaaad idea, Jayne. Super bad. Like pixelation-of-the-entire-compound bad. Like making booger-eaters with Ben bad. Don't do it."

"I don't get why it's so awful, but you're not the only one who thinks so, so I'm not saying I'm going to ask her to do it."

"You know I'm all for bucking the system and thumbing my nose at the Man, but not this time. Not for scrying. No good comes from seeing the future."

"Why? I don't get that at all. I mean, couldn't it help us fix our problems before they happen?" We'd reached the gargoyle door, and I pushed it open to step out into the meadow that would connect us to the part of the forest where Maggie lived in a tree called the Ancient One. Already I felt its presence in the Green; it was always there waiting for me to reach in and connect.

"Everything we do is linked and interrelated. You mess up one of those links in that chain of fae and time and places and humans, and it can set off a series of catastrophes that are impossible to stop or control. We live in a symphony, Jayne. Can't you hear it? Imagine what would happen to that symphony if one of the instruments started playing the wrong notes."

"I'm not sure if I believe that," I said, pushing through the thigh-high grasses. The chill of an early autumn had set in, making me wish I'd put on a heavier cloak. My tunic and jeans weren't enough at this time of day, after the sun had gone down, to keep me warm. I rubbed my upper arms quickly, trying to build up some friction as I moved closer to the edge of the forest.

"I know you feel the Oneness, Jayne. Don't pretend you don't."

"The Oneness?"

"Yeah. The connection. How all of us are linked together. What you do, what they do ... it's all part of one big whole ... thing. The Oneness."

"All I feel a connection to are my elements, Earth and Water. And my friends. That's it."

"Bull-dookie. You've said it before - all of the living beings are connected in the Green. How can you say that and not realize what you're actually feeling?"

I thought about it for a minute as we entered the trees. The air wasn't moving as much here, so the wind-chill left; but it was replaced with a dampness that was ever-present in this part of the forest, bringing its own special kind of shiver to my bones. I never felt like I really knew everything about this place. Like, there were creatures here watching me that I couldn't see, but could somehow feel.

"I don't know. I don't want to try and put it all together today. It's like solving world peace or something; it strains my brain too much."

"*Meh.* Fae brains aren't meant to comprehend it any more than human ones are. Just take my word for it. You don't want to see the future. You would end up making a decision you wouldn't normally make knowing outcomes and then different outcomes would come out, and we'd all be out in the cold."

"Stop, Tim. You're giving me a headache."

"Undo your ponytail. I need to hide."

I reached back and pulled out the elastic holding my hair back. "She's going to know you're there. She can smell you or whatever."

"I prefer to be harder to get to," he said, climbing into my hair, giving me goosebumps with his movements.

"Listen," I said, coming to a stop in a particularly dark part of the forest, "I have something to tell you, and I'm not sure I should do it in front of Maggie."

"What?"

"I don't know how to say it without sounding crazy."

"Nothing you say could make me think that about you, Jayne."

"I've been hearing a voice in my head lately."

"Except that. Time to medicate."

"Shut up, I'm not kidding. There's seriously someone in there, and she's not me and she's not my conscience."

"But you know it's a girl," said Tim, leaving my hair to fly out in front of my face. He searched my eyes as he hovered there, his wings a blur. "You *look* sane ..." He frowned, zooming in to look at my pupils or something.

I backed up and waved him away. "I'm completely sane, and I'm not imagining it. She's as clear as day in there, and she's come twice now."

"When?"

"At the council meeting and in the hallway just now. Right before you came."

Tim flew behind me.

I turned to see him backtracking a few feet, staring off into the darkness towards the compound door.

"What are you looking for?"

"Someone following us and messing with your head, that's what."

I shook my head. "It's not someone physically here. She wouldn't have been able to get into the council meeting. Even you can't do that."

Tim came back to join me. "You have a point. If I can't get into one of those, no fae could. And believe me, I've tried."

"So who is she, and how is she in my head?" I asked.

"You're asking me? How the heck would I know? I'm not crazy."

I sighed. "I hope you're kidding, because insanity would be just the thing I need to add to my already busy schedule."

Tim got back onto my shoulder and climbed into my hair again. "Ask Maggie. She might know."

"She knows everything," I said bitterly. She always managed to irritate me with that skill, too. She either kept secrets I needed to know, or told me things I wished she wouldn't. And no matter what the situation, she seemed to enjoy the torture it brought me.

We passed the last few trees that ringed the circle around the Ancient One, bringing it into view. The arched door in the base of its massive trunk was the entrance to Maggie's home, and its branches reached out above our heads and into the surrounding area for twenty yards in either direction. It was massive. A ley line ran beneath it, amplifying the power of any nearby fae using magic or the elements. Maggie was the one who had taught me how to tap into it, which had saved my bacon on a couple of occasions. I was begrudgingly grateful to her for that.

I approached the tree-door and knocked three times. She got cranky if I did more or less than that, and since I was here to ask her for information, I figured I'd save the four-knock greeting for another day. I did so love to mess with her when the timing was right.

"Who's there?!" came the loud cranky voice from inside.

"It's me, Grandma Maggie. You're long-lost granddaughter."

The door opened a crack, exposing her one good eye. "Don't call me that. It makes me feel old."

"You are old, Maggie. Like a couple thousand years old."

"You're only as old as you feel, which makes me only two hundred." She wheezed out a juicy, gargling cough before recovering enough to continue. "What do you want?" she barked. "I'm busy."

"Busy doing what?"

"Wouldn't you like to know!" she shouted, cackling at some private joke.

"Actually, no ... strike that question. I just want to talk to you on behalf of the fae councils."

The door swung in, and she shuffled away, saying nothing.

"Do you have any idea how much I hate going in there?" whispered Tim. I could feel him shaking.

"About half as much as I do," I said. I would never forget the day I was here with Tim when we traded his wings for an antidote to Chase's spelled arrow illness he'd received protecting me.

"Talk to me about hating this place after you've been dismembered," said Tim.

"Yeah, okay. You've got me there. You hate it more." I shut the door behind me and waited just inside the entrance. Her place was small enough that I could see almost everything from where I was standing, except for a back room that always had a door closing it off from the rest of the main room where her kitchen and sitting area were.

Maggie was hunched over her big black cooking pot, and one of her huge dirty rats was lumbering around the table top it was sitting on. It pooped as it went and Maggie jumped with glee, picking up the turd and adding it to her brew.

My stomach churned. "Oh, God, that's nasty," I said under my breath.

"What?" whispered Tim. "I missed it. What's happening?"

"She just put a rat turd in her stew."

"Oh, that's a baaaaad sign. We need to leave." Tim yanked my hair hard. "Go, Jayne! *Leave!*"

I felt the panic rising up into my chest. "Why? What's she making?"

"Do you really need to ask that?" whisper-screeched Tim. "What good could possibly come from a rat turd in a witch's spell?!"

"You have a point," I whispered, slowly backing towards the door.

"Leaving so soon?" Maggie asked, cackling to herself and then hawking up another loogie.

"I suddenly remembered something I have to do," I said, feeling for the door handle behind me. "It's very urgent. Urgent council business."

*"Humph.* You can ask me about the voice in your head later, then," she said, shuffling around her table and entering the room next to the kitchen, leaving the door slightly ajar behind her.

My feet refused to go any farther. *"Shit."*

"What? What are you doing? Run for it! ... Rat turd alert! Rat turd alert!"

"I can't! I need to talk to her about the voice."

"Voice schmoice. We'll get you some medication or a spell. I'll personally clean your ears out for you - it's probably just wax build-up or something. Please, let's just go." He was pulling my hair until my eyes watered.

I reached back and flicked him on the butt. "Stop it. You can go if you want, but I'm staying."

"Open the door," he said, buzzing up into the air next to my face. "I'm gone like the wind, baby. You're on your own."

I turned around and pulled on the handle, opening it enough to let him out. He buzzed through, moving so fast he was nearly a blur.

"See you later! I hope!" he yelled, disappearing in the distance.

I shook my head, shutting the door behind him. *So much for loyalty.*

Maggie came back out, her eyes focused on her pot. "Decided to stay, eh?"

"Yep. Go ahead with your rat turd brew. I have questions that need answers, and I don't trust anyone else with my secrets right now."

"Truth!" she screeched, making me jump. She played lie detector every time I was with her, but she still always surprised me with her intensity over the whole thing.

"So, I've been hearing this voice in my head. How do you know about it, and who is she? Is it me?"

Maggie looked up at me, one eyeball cloudy and the other black. "What do you think? Does she sound like you?"

"No. She sounds like someone I've never met. I *hope* she's someone I've never met, otherwise I might have to check myself into the clinic."

"Ha! Those quacks can't help you."

I didn't doubt her on this fact. She'd had to bail them out before with antidotes, and the Dark Fae healers seemed to be a lot more advanced than the Light Fae ones when it came to treating pixelation problems; but even that had taken thousands and thousands of years to figure out.

"So who is she? And why is she in my brain now? And how did you know she was there?"

Maggie shook her head, adding a pinch of something from a

nearby jar to her brew that caused a small explosion to come out of the top of her pot and envelope her in smoke. She choked out her answer, waving the offensive-smelling blackness out of her face. "Tears in the veil. All kinds of unmentionables are getting through. Many more are trying."

She wheezed out a few more coughs, the last one I was pretty sure bringing up part of a lung. I tried to tamp down the nausea that threatened to make itself known in the form of the tiny bit of dinner I'd eaten before abandoning my meal.

"Unmentionables?" I asked, trying to get Maggie back on track. She had picked up a big spoon and was stirring the stuff in her pot around. The stink that was wafting over to me made me reach over and crack the door open.

"Shut that door!" she yelled at me.

I slammed it closed. "Geez, chill, Granny. It friggin stinks like burned rat shit in here."

"I need that odor here or the spell won't work, ignorant girl. Now go over there and sit down before you blow up my tree."

My eyes widened at the idea of inadvertently making a nuclear bomb just by cracking a door open. Maggie worked with some seriously dangerous shit, apparently.

I probably should have high-tailed it out of there like Tim had, but instead I followed her instructions, gingerly stepping over to sit on the lumpy chair in the corner. At least I was as far away from her as I could get and still be inside the tree.

"Whatcha makin'?" I asked, not sure I even wanted to know but somehow sickly curious about how an escaped stink could alter a spell and turn it into something explosive.

"Demon bait."

I nodded my head slowly, letting that little nugget of

awfulness roll around a little bit before responding.

"Uh-huh. Yeah. So you're baiting a demon toooo .... ?" I lifted my eyebrows at her, hoping for an answer that wouldn't make me nauseous with fear.

"To capture it, of course. Stop asking me stupid questions. I don't have time for your nonsense today."

I frowned, deciding to change tactics. "So, the council asked me to come here and ask you how the demons are getting into our realm and what we can do to stop it. And also how they know about some sort of legend that says my baby will make it possible for the demons to come all the time."

She slammed her spoon down on the wooden table and fixed me with a one-eyed glare. "The council, eh? The *council* would like to know?!"

I gritted my teeth and pulled my lips back in a fake smile, not sure if I should laugh or be scared at her instant fury. "Uh, yeah?"

She picked up the spoon and pointed it at my face, limping over to stand at the edge of her table nearest me. "You can tell that council of yours to sit around their meeting and turn their heads to the *left* and the *right*. Their answers are *there!* Right in front of their ignorant noses!" Her arm dropped to her side, and she turned to go back to her stew, grumbling and muttering to herself things I couldn't discern.

"So what are you saying? Do we have a mole?"

"A mole ... *ha!*" she responded, stirring and muttering again, staring down into her pot, her eyes blinking rapidly at the smoke that entered them.

"*Ha*, as in, yes we have a mole, or *ha*, as in, you're a stupid asshole, Jayne?"

She looked up at me and slowly withdrew her spoon from her

brew, carefully placing it down on the table. She leaned over and grabbed her rat by its back, lifting it towards her face and gathering it there by her mouth with both hands, kissing its side and staring at me over its dirty body. She spoke into its fur.

"Do you hear her, Melvin? She wants to know if they have a mole in their midst." She laughed and her rat lifted its head, sniffing the air and then looking over at me.

*If that thing fucking laughs, I'm outta here*, was all I could think. But its beady eyes just looked around, as if searching for something. Its nose stopped moving when it got over the pot. It wiggled its head up and down twice before it started squirming, back-pedaling its little legs, trying to get away with everything it had.

*Oh, that cannot be good if the disgusting rat doesn't even like it.* I stood and moved slowly towards the door. Maggie was always a little strange - or a lot strange. But she had never seemed unhinged to me until now.

Maggie casually swept her arms out to her sides, flinging her rat onto the nearby shelf in the process, her eyes never leaving mine.

Melvin landed on his feet and scurried away, hiding behind the cloudy and dusty glass jars that were lined up like dirty fat soldiers.

"Okay, well, I can see you're busy today, so I'll just come back another time. The council says hi and thanks for all your help." I was at the door, my fingers scrabbling for the handle when she said one word that stopped me in my tracks.

"Shayla."

I'd heard that name once before. A gray elf named Gregale had mentioned her when he'd told me about my weapon's history. I looked down at the black dragon fang that was strapped to my leg. I called it Blackie, mostly because it reminded me of my old badass-tempered dog of the same name and because I'm not all that creative with my nicknames; and this thing was potent enough that it seemed to *need* a name. At the time I had assigned the moniker Blackie to it, I had no idea that it already had a name - the Dark of Blackthorn. And it had once been in the mouth of the Dark Fae dragon who was known simply as The Dark.

"Shayla. She's one of my ancestors, isn't she?"

"Yes. She's the one who slayed the dragon whose fang you carry with you today."

"And you're saying she's the one in my head? Talking to me? Even though she's been dead for like a thousand years?"

"Yes."

"How is that even possible?" Recognition dawned, causing me to sigh in defeat. "I've lost it, haven't I?" I let go of the door handle that I'd finally connected with and leaned my back against the wood, sliding down to land on my butt. I stared at the floor as I thought Maggie's words through.

"Dammit!" I exclaimed, hitting my fist on the floor. "I wanted to stay sane for this! I mean, okay, being nuts might make some things easier. I'll be able to do whatever I want and never be held accountable ..." I was talking to myself now, mentally tallying the pros and cons. "I guess there's a certain amount of freedom in leaving sanity and reason behind. I can just wander around the compound, hanging out, taking naps in the garden, floating up into the ether and visiting with Chase ..."

Maggie rudely interrupted me. "No! You stay *out* of the Overworld and the Gray. You have no business there!"

She had moved over to stand near me now, seeming intent on communicating, finally.

"Why?" I asked, looking up at her face so I wouldn't give myself too much time to contemplate her awful shoes that had holes in the toes, perfect for exposing her blackened, long and jagged toenails. "If I wasn't meant to be there, don't you think I'd be cut off from it?"

"You should be, and that's the problem. As I said ... the veil has tears in it. We must repair it before it is too late." She walked back to her brew and began stirring again. "Get off the floor. Come over here and help me with this."

I shook my head. "No thanks. I'm cool over here, away from the rat shit soup."

"I'm not asking. Get over here, or I'll cast a spell on you that amplifies your smelling capacity tenfold."

I shrugged. "What's that gonna do? I can already smell your crap from here without it."

"I believe your pixie has issues that would make this particular spell quite torturous for you."

I jumped up and ran over. "Holy shit, Maggie. You're threatening me with level-ten pixie fartage? That's just cruel."

She shrugged. "I do what I must. Here." She handed me her spoon. "Keep stirring, and don't stop, no matter what happens. We must keep it moving."

## Chapter Ten

MAGGIE LEFT ME IN THE kitchen stirring the pot alone while she entered the attached room. I yelled so she'd hear me.

"How did you know Shayla was in my head?"

"She's not in your head!" responded Maggie from the other room. Her voice was muffled, making her sound like she was in a closet.

"Well, that's where I hear her," I yelled back. I continued speaking in a quieter voice, "Shayla? Are you there now?"

"She can't hear you in here," said Maggie, coming back into the kitchen carrying a wooden box in her hand. She laid it gently down on the table before taking the spoon from me and continuing the stirring.

I stood on my tiptoes and started to lean in so I could take a look into her pot, but she pinched my arm, causing me to flinch and fall backwards onto my heels.

"*Ow!* That *hurt*, you old bag!"

"Keep away from the vapor. I am fresh out of gecko testicles and without them you would perish."

I grimaced. "Fresh out? As in, you had some yesterday, but you don't today?"

"Yes."

I swallowed hard. "You have a seriously strange appetite, Maggie."

Maggie cackled but said nothing to dissuade me from thinking she actually ate lizard balls for breakfast. The bitterness of stomach acid burned my throat, and my salivary glands were working overtime. I swallowed three more times, trying to get a grip on myself.

"Open the box. Put the contents in, but only when I tell you to," she said, gesturing towards the thing she'd taken out of the other room.

I stepped over and picked it up, my hands trembling with fear and nausea. I cleared my throat before speaking. "What's in here?" I almost dropped it when I thought I felt something moving inside, scratching at the wood.

She glanced at me and lifted an eyebrow. "You really want to know?"

I shook my head fast. *"No!* No, don't tell me. I was only kidding. Keep your nasty secrets. What I don't know won't hurt me, right?" I smiled at her weakly, but all she did was shrug her shoulders. I rolled my eyes. *What did I expect? Reassurances from a lunatic witch? Don't hold your breath, Jayne.*

I stood next to Maggie, holding the box up near the edge of the pot, keeping my face way back. "So how do you know about Shayla talking to me?"

"I am hearing a lot of talk from the other realms. Too much chatter. The spirits are restless and others are waking."

"Others?"

"The Forsaken."

I gritted my teeth together, my jaw muscles bulging and

loosening with the rhythm of my panic. Every minute spent with Maggie was another chink in the armor of my sanity. I could almost feel it falling away, piece by piece.

I opened my mouth wide, trying to stretch my aching jaw out before responding. "Spirits? Others? The Forsaken? Demons? Gecko balls? ... Maggie ...," I pleaded, "could you please stop doing this to me? Seriously, I think I'm losing my mind." I wasn't even kidding anymore.

Maggie was staring at the open pot, her stirring going faster now. She had sweat glistening on her forehead, some of her greasy hair sticking to it. "Open the box," she said, barely above a whisper.

I fumbled with the latch. It was tiny and loose, refusing to cooperate with my shaking fingers.

"Quickly! Open it!" she hissed.

"I'm trying!" I said, practically crying I was so freaked out. I couldn't think of anything worse than fucking up a demon bait spell.

The box opened just as Maggie was about to hit me with her free hand, and she screeched, "Put it in!"

"The box?!"

"No, you fool, the thing *in* the box!"

I flipped up the lid and started screaming as soon as I saw what was inside.

Maggie grabbed the box from me and dumped it upside down over the pot, the contents falling into the brew. A chorus of unholy shrieks followed shortly thereafter - some of them coming from me, and some of them coming from the creature who'd just become part of a rat turd demon bait spell.

"Oh my god, Maggie! You just *killed* that thing whatever it was!"

A loud explosion came from the pot, throwing both of us backwards and onto the floor in a heap.

Maggie's nasty-ass, dirty robes tangled around my legs and her disgusting, rotten breath was blowing in my face. I thought I was going to die from it until I realized there was a much bigger threat to my survival than Maggie's gingivitis that I had to deal with, and it was standing in the middle of the room now.

And I also realized in that moment that there actually *was* something worse than fucking up a demon bait brew: it was getting the brew exactly right, and successfully luring a demon into a house you were trapped inside.

## Chapter Eleven

I PULLED THE GREEN UP into me without thinking, tapping into the ley line so fast and without any finesse at all, that it sent my Element into a frenzy. I hadn't connected in a while, so it was eager to be with me again, and with the amplification of the extra Earth magic running beneath Maggie's house, it made for a very potent combination.

Maggie and I were now surrounded by a thick green bubble of protective power, keeping us in and the demon out. The elemental shield hummed and crackled with the energy, making my ears pop with the uneven pressures going higher and lower in the atmosphere immediately surrounding us.

We both sat up, a little groggy from the bomb's percussion and our rapid descent to the hard ground that I could tell already was going to be responsible for several bruises on my backside. I rubbed it gingerly as I stood.

I kept my eyes on the demon the entire time. It stood in the center of Maggie's living room, turning around slowly, taking everything in. I was calling it a demon in my head because Maggie had said this brew was for demon baiting. But if I had seen him out in the forest, I would have called him just a regular fae guy. And not a bad-looking one, either.

"Who is that?" I asked in a whisper.

"How am I supposed to know?" asked Maggie, straightening her robes around her middle.

I glanced at her, praying her robes wouldn't open up to reveal anything, knowing it would scar me for life to see her two-thousand-year-old boobs hanging down to her knees.

A sudden movement from the demon brought my attention fully back to him. He had walked up to the edge of my bubble to tap on it, getting himself a nasty shock in return. He yanked his hand back and shook it a few times, trying to get the pain to go away. Once he'd recovered enough, he stepped close again, being sure not to make contact with the energy. His eyes moved first to Maggie and then to me. He stared and stared, not moving a muscle.

"*Fuck*, Maggie ... he's staring at me!" I whisper-yelled. "What should I do?"

"Don't stare back!" she hissed, whacking me in the arm.

I flinched away from his gaze, rubbing my newly bruised bicep muscle. "Damn, Maggie, have you been lifting weights or something? That hurt." I looked back at the guy for a second and then again at Maggie. "What kind of demon is he?"

"He's a vampire. I think."

"A *vampire?!*" I squeaked, unable to keep from looking at him again. He was dressed all in black, just like my incubus friend, Spike. "Vampires are demons?" I could already tell my lack of education concerning the whole Underworld structure was going to be a problem, because this situation made absolutely no sense to me.

"Demon is a generic term. It covers all manner of Underworld inhabitants. Stop *looking* at him!" she yelled, hitting me again.

I stepped sideways to get out of her range, jumping in fright when the vampire spoke.

"Who are you? Where am I?" He had an accent - British maybe.

"You first," I said, ignoring Maggie's attempts to shut me up.

"I am Garrett. I have resided in the Underworld for ... a long time. Am I no longer there, then?" He looked around the room again, stopping when his gaze reached the window. He turned and walked over to it, peering outside. "I am in the Dark Forest of the Here and Now, am I not?" He spun around and strode back over to the bubble, stopping just in front of me. His body language oozed high energy intensity. He reminded me of Spike so much it prompted the memory of something he'd said once - that one day he could end up being a vampire in the Underworld if things didn't go as he hoped in the Here and Now.

I took a step back, even though I knew this vampire couldn't get to me. His eyes blazed red, no swirling blackness to them at all. I had always thought Spike's eyes were a little freaky that way, but now I decided I much preferred a little black mixed in. It made them look less ... demonic.

Maggie answered his question. "You are in the Green Forest, in my home. I have called you here to answer my questions and to do my bidding. Do you accept these tasks?"

Garrett straightened his shoulders and took two slow steps over to be in front of Maggie. His posture could only be described as rigid.

I watched him warily, worried about the devious expression that had gradually appeared as he glided along the edge of our power shield. "Ahhh, so you want to make a deal with a demon, is that it? I wondered what you were about. And with whom do I have the honor of dealing?"

"I am known as Maggie. And this is Jayne," she said, gesturing to me. "She is of no consequence to our interactions. I will send her away."

Garrett looked over at me, lifting an eyebrow. "Of no consequence? I am afraid I do not agree. It is she who holds this energy around you, is it not?" He didn't look at Maggie, but continued to examine me from my head to my feet and back again.

I glanced nervously at Maggie.

She frowned, sticking her pursed lips out but saying nothing.

He shrugged delicately, bringing my attention back to him. "No need to respond. I already know the answer to my query. She nearly vibrates with the power, doesn't she?" He licked his bottom lip, making me feel faint in the process. "No. I think I would prefer that she remain in my presence."

When I first saw him I thought he was old like Valentine. Maybe it was the way he moved, so confidently and almost arrogantly, like royalty. But then as he spoke and I watched him closer, I realized he was much younger than that - probably in his early twenties; but he spoke like I imagined someone from the seventeen hundreds would have.

"Drop the power shield and we will converse like civilized fae, hmmm?" he said to me softly.

"You cannot mesmerize her, Garrett. She is impervious to your charms," said Maggie, snorting at him. "And while you are in my home, you cannot harm me or anyone else, so you can wipe that smug expression from your face right now." She looked over at me. "Drop the shield, Jayne. We don't need it."

I looked back and forth between Garrett and her, not sure I

trusted her knowledge of demon power. He looked way too happy at the prospect of being able to get at us.

"Are you sure?"

"Yes, I'm sure. I would actually like to see him try. It would be very entertaining." She smiled, showing off her three remaining front teeth.

"I'm trusting you on this, Maggie."

She shrugged, moving up to the edge of the bubble, preparing for it to disappear.

I closed my eyes to shut out the visions of this scary guy in front of me, showing the Green that I wanted it to go back where it had come from, picturing it leaving my surroundings and going back into the earth. It left, but not willingly; I could feel it trying to cling, even as it went.

As soon as it was down, Garrett stepped in close to me, grabbing my hand and pulling it up to his face.

I was too shocked to move, my feet rooted to the floor and my mouth hanging open in a silent, unspoken cuss word of surprise.

He whispered his next words, closing his eyes as he pressed my palm to his cheek. "I cannot tell you how long it has been since I have felt the warmth of a living creature's skin on my own."

His face was cold - colder than the ambient temperature of the room. Before I had time to figure out how it was that someone living in hell could have cold skin, he opened his eyes again, and I was struck by how strange it was to see such bright red eyes that looked like fiery heat coming from such a cold-blooded creature.

I pulled my hand away, breaking the stare between us. "Keep your grubby dick-beater demon fingers to yourself," I said, stepping back to get some breathing room.

"That, I will," he said, smiling vaguely, "for now." He turned his gaze to Maggie. "So, witch ... you have questions. Perhaps I have answers. Let us strike a bargain then, shall we?" He clasped his hands together behind his back and tilted his head almost politely, waiting for her answer.

She grunted and nodded, gesturing to the seating area near the one window she had in the room. They both moved to sit and I followed, choosing a footstool as my place to rest. I set it down near the front door, several feet away from them, so I could make a quick getaway if necessary.

Once everyone was comfortable, Maggie spoke. "I have summoned you here for your help. I am not foolish enough to think you will give it for nothing in return. Name your price, but be reasonable. If you upset me, I will send you back with less than nothing."

"And you have so much to give," he said, his gaze sliding over to me meaningfully.

"Jayne is not on the auction block. Try again," she said.

He shrugged. "All I ask is for a little taste. I would make it worth your while. I know about that information which you seek. And time is of the essence, my dear Maggie. Make no mistake. Events are unrolling as we speak."

"What's he talking about, a taste? As in blood? Sucking *my* blood?" I asked, sickly fascinated with the awfulness of it. No way was this guy getting his fangs anywhere near me.

And just as I thought that, I saw them. *Holy gecko balls, he's got fangs.* More like really sharp canines, but there was no doubt they could puncture my skin with little effort.

He smiled at me, the tip of his tongue flicking the pointed end of one of them as he winked.

I shook my head in horror, the hair on the back of my neck

standing up and a shiver moving down my spine.

"You could not manage it. But feel free to take some of mine." She held out her arm, pulling up her robe's sleeve as she did. Her purple-veined, boney arm looked about as appetizing as I imagined a buggane's butt would be.

He curled his lip in distaste. "No, thank you. You are too kind."

She smiled evilly. "What's the matter? Too sweet for you?"

He put his bent finger to his lips and cleared his throat, hiding a grimace, I think. "A-*hem*, yes, quite right, quite right." He dropped his hand and looked over at me. "No, only she will do. I have decided. If you do not agree, you may send me back. I shall take my information about Torrie with me." He winked at me again, lowering his hand to rest his forearm on the arm of the chair. His legs opened wider and he slouched down in the seat ever-so-slightly, suddenly giving me the impression of a cocky teenager. His other hand stroked his thigh towards his knee, and he flicked his head, causing a lock of hair to fall down over his forehead.

I narrowed my eyes at him, wondering why he looked so familiar and ... current. Before he'd reminded me of how I'd pictured Sherlock Holmes or one of those old-time fancy English guys to look. Now he looked like ....

"Noooo ... !" I whispered, staring at him, taking in the high cheekbones, olive coloring and red eyes. Had they been green, they would have made him look almost exactly like someone I knew only too well. The closer and longer I examined him, the more the resemblance came into focus.

He smiled at me lazily, cocking up an eyebrow and gently biting his bottom lip before saying, "See something you like?" He could have stood up and said, *Want to go have some kinky sex?* and his message wouldn't have been any clearer. This guy was seriously hot and bothered, and it was all about the blood he wanted a taste of. From me.

I looked quickly over at Maggie who was frowning at him. "Maggie, is this guy related to ... you-know-who?"

"I do not know who he *was* related to or what his position in the Underworld is now. I merely summoned a being who had a connection to this mess in the Here and Now. So whoever he is, he knows something. The question is, how much? And is it worth bothering to find out?" She stood up slowly, using the arms of the chairs to steady herself. She stared at him for a few moments before declaring, "I think not!" And then she shuffled off towards the kitchen.

Garrett sat up straight, losing his come-hither look and shoving his bangs back over the top of his head. "Wait!"

Maggie didn't even look back. She just waved him off, muttering, "Melvin, where are you, my sweet? I need some droppings. Come to Momma."

I looked at Maggie and then at Garrett in alarm. Maggie had made her decision, but Garrett knew something good, I was sure of it. He knew about Torrie, and Torrie was no minor player in this crapstorm. He was at the dead center of it.

Garrett caught my panicked look and gave me his full attention, speaking hurriedly. "I'll tell you what you want to know. All you have to do is give me a sip of your blood. Just a sip, that's all I'll take!"

"Be quiet!" yelled Maggie from her kitchen. "You had your chance. You're going back with less than nothing, just as I've promised." She cackled with glee.

Garrett launched himself from his chair and threw himself

down on his knees at my feet, taking both of my hands in his and pulling them to his chest.

I had no time to react or think about what he was doing before his face was right in front of mine.

"Please, Jayne. I'm *begging* you. I could just *take* your blood right now, but I'm asking your permission. Please spare me. I can help you."

"She's not listening to you, demon. Save your empty, soulless breath." Maggie's cooking implements made clanging and banging sounds as she rushed to put together her potion.

"Why do you look like Ben?" I whispered, freaking out so bad I was unable to put more volume to my words.

"Ben? Ben who?"

"Ben the elemental." I searched his eyes.

I thought a saw a flicker of recognition there, but then he said, "I have no idea. Perhaps we have some distant relation. If he is special to you, then I appeal to that emotion. Spare me from that purgatory. Let me taste your lifeblood."

"Why were you in the Underworld and not the Overworld?" I asked, not knowing what I should do yet. I was stalling for time, looking for something that might tip my decision one way or another.

"I made some terrible mistakes. Several terrible mistakes, actually, and a lifetime in the Underworld was my punishment. I was soon to be reborn into the Here and Now anyway, so this is hardly any interference in the Order of Things at all. A trifling, really. Please, Jayne." He leaned in, staring me in the eyes and whispering, "She's nearly done with her potion and then so will I be. I beg of you. I am but your humble servant." He squeezed my hands and at the same time, pulled them to him, forcing me to come close so he could kiss me once, gently on the mouth.

I didn't resist, struck speechless by what he was saying and his resemblance to Ben. Even his kiss what like being with a ghost.

He put my hand on his heart, where I felt no beat at all. "I will be forever in your debt. Just. One. Sip."

I did the calculation in my head in less than a second. *Vampire demon who knows what Torrie's up to who also promises to owe me for life.* "Do it," I said, clamping down hard on my jaw, waiting for the pain to start.

## Chapter Twelve

HIS TEETH WERE ON MY wrist as soon as the last word was out of my mouth.

I wasn't sure what I had expected, but this wasn't it. The pain was sharp, and his bite stung like the bejeezus. I kept waiting for it to get all sensual and pleasant like it was in the movies, but that never happened. Before I could complain about getting ripped off, he pulled his mouth away from me, first licking the bite mark and then some crimson drops from his lips. He used his thumb to press down hard where he'd bitten me and lifted my arm up above my head.

"What are you doing?" I asked, looking up at my hand, trying not to whimper over the pain.

"Stopping the blood, helping it coagulate. I cannot have you bleeding to death on me, now, can I?" He smiled and my stomach turned over at the blood in his teeth.

He closed his mouth quickly. "My apologies. How do you feel?"

"Queasy. Confused. Curious. Cranky. Sad. Pick your adjective."

He smiled, almost guiltily. "I do regret my hasty approach and hurried blood letting. Our dear friend Maggie left me with little choice."

I turned my head and realized that she hadn't even noticed anything happening. She was humming over her brew, stirring fast, the smoke coming up from the pot and obscuring her vision.

"I'm not sure what will happen to you if she finishes that, and I need to talk to you," I whispered. "She has one last ingredient to add if it's like the last brew, and then it'll be finished."

"What was the ingredient, do you remember?"

I grimaced. "Are you kidding me? I'll never forget it."

"What was it? Tell me. Perhaps if I know what it is she is brewing, I will be in a better position to know what we can do to thwart her efforts."

I didn't know about thwarting Maggie's efforts, since sending a demon back to where it belonged sounded like a good plan to me in theory, but I couldn't let her do it just yet. Not when I was this close to getting some answers.

"She had a wooden box with a small creature in it."

"What kind of creature?" he urged. He pulled my hand back down and quickly licked the small rivers of blood that had escaped his thumb to run down my arm, all the while leaving his finger on my wound.

I watched with barely concealed disgust, wondering how much damage demon spit would do to my fair skin. "It looked like a tiny version of Torrie, actually."

Garrett squeezed my hand tight enough to make me squeak. "Sorry ... but did you say she had a miniature version of Torrie? The demon?"

I nodded.

His eyes slowly moved over to Maggie, almost as if he were

afraid to look at her now. "Who *is* this witch?"

I leaned in close to him, while looking at her still muttering over her pot. "She's my grandmother," I said even quieter.

He turned to look at me at the same time I moved to look at him, putting us nose-to-nose. "We need to get out of here," he whispered.

"Jayne!" barked Maggie from across the room, making me jump. "Come stir this for me!"

I stood and pulled Garrett up with me, causing him to drop his thumb from my wrist. I didn't bother to look at it, pressing it up against my stomach, hoping my tunic would stop the bleeding.

"Sure, Maggie. I'll be right there." I looked at Garrett briefly and then pulled him along a few steps towards Maggie, holding his hand in mine.

When we were even with the door, I yelled, "Run!" while throwing up a green shield between her and us.

"Great spirits alive ... you've done it again!" he said, staring at the green, crackling energy.

I dropped his hand and shoved him towards the entrance, grabbing the handle of the door and pulling on it with all my might. It wouldn't budge.

"Maggie," I yelled over my shoulder, "let us go!"

"You have no idea what you're doing, Jayne. Put this wall down and bring that vampire over here."

I felt for the Ancient One in my connection, pulling its essence towards me. The door was part of its corporeal body, and I knew there was no way Maggie could hold me in here without the tree's approval. I let it know that I needed to get outside and felt the answering acquiescence. The door swung free of its locking spell.

Garrett seemed too in awe of the magic and show of elemental force going on around him to react appropriately, so I grabbed his tunic sleeve and yanked him out the door with me.

Once outside of Maggie's house, he snapped out of his trance and realized our dilemma, running so fast it was difficult for me to keep up. He wasn't going quite as fast as the incubi and succubi normally did, otherwise I would have lost him in a second, but he was going fast enough that I thought I'd seen the last of him. I had to stop a moment once we were in the trees a bit to release the Green from holding Maggie, calling it into me rather than letting it dissipate back into the earth. I wouldn't put it past her to fling some kind of pixie-fart-smelling spell at my back, so I made sure to have a film of energy around me to repel anything nasty like that.

"Slow down!" I yelled at Garrett's fading back. "I can't run that fast!"

Thankfully, he stopped and waited for me to catch up. "Come here, Jayne. It will be faster for both of us." He swept me up in his arms and began running again, the trees and branches whipping by so fast, they were just a blur.

"Holy shiiiiiiiit, Gaaaarrett! What are you doing?!" I yelled at first, freaking out about feeling like I'd been captured. But I stopped when I realized it was a pretty decent way to travel. I just hoped he had good enough vision with the fading sunlight that he didn't run smack into a tree and knock us both unconscious.

"Just hang on. You'll be fine."

"Where exactly are you going?" I asked after a few seconds.

"Away from that place."

"Take a left," I said, pointing him in the direction of the Infinity Meadow. It was the safest place I knew of, especially since my mother had been buried there and a huge oak had grown up over her grave in a great show of magic and the forces of nature coming together in harmony for a singular purpose. I was probably dead wrong, but it seemed like only good could happen there - like evil couldn't touch it. Despite the fact that it had been the scene of my bonding ceremony with Ben, it was still a place I felt where I could be at peace and think.

We arrived in less than ten minutes at a more relaxed pace, which made my stomach much happier. Garrett set me down on my feet when we arrived at the edge of the grassy meadow. The flowers were still in bloom here, but they were on their last legs. I picked a few of the dried-out husks as we walked side-by-side over to the tree, plucking the petals off and letting them drop to the ground. I was trying to work out in my mind what questions I wanted to ask him and what I was going to do with him once we were done. *Maybe I can bring him back to Maggie and she'll send him off, no harm no foul. Oooor maybe she'll bust my ass and let him eat me. Hmmmm, what to do, what to do...*

When we got to the base of the tree, I sat down, gesturing for Garrett to join me. He smoothed his hands down his tunic and pants a couple of times before sitting with his back against the tree. I was in front of him, facing the spot just over his left shoulder where my mom had been laid to rest.

"This place is special to you," said Garrett, watching me closely.

"Yes. My mother is buried just over there." I pointed and then threw the petal I'd been holding in my hand in the general direction.

"What race was she?"

"She wasn't fae. She was human. I'm a changeling."

He nodded slowly. "I had heard this realm had begun to bring the changelings in greater numbers." He smiled humorlessly. "You hear things there, in the Underworld ... but it's impossible to know what is truth and what is merely hope."

"It's true. The Light and Dark Fae were both doing it."

"And now?"

I shrugged. "Now they're living and working together to try and figure out what to do about you guys coming here."

He raised his eyebrows. "You mean to say that the Light and Dark are no more? That they live as one?"

I nodded. "That's the idea. It just started today, actually, so it's not totally done."

"Wow. Desperation is the word of the day, I see."

I huffed out a frustrated breath. "You have *no* idea."

He tilted his head to the side. "You remind me of someone."

"You remind me of someone, too. Ben, like I said." I studied his reaction but couldn't tell if he suddenly looked nervous or if I was just imagining it. Even if he was nervous, it didn't necessarily mean it was because of Ben. Neither of us knew what the heck was happening here or what the fallout for sneaking him into the Here and Now might be. At least, I didn't.

"I knew a warrior once. She was a silver elf," he said.

The voice came back into my head without any notice, startling me with its sudden arrival.

*"Ask him how his heart is holding up."*

I frowned. *What?* I asked the voice in my head - Shayla, if Maggie was correct.

*"You heard me. Ask him how his heart is holding up."*

I cleared my throat, deciding that prodding him a little might help my cause or at least give me a direction to go in for my own questions. "So, Garrett. How's your heart holding up?"

His face blanched, and that was saying a lot because he was

about as pale to begin with as Spike. All of the incubi and succubi seemed to share that same almost undead complexion. His hand drifted up to his chest and rubbed his muscle there - the one directly over his heart.

"What did you just say?" he whispered.

"I said, how's your heart holding up?"

"It's ... uhhh ... holding up just fine, thank you for asking." His brow furrowed as he stared at me.

*"Ask him how he likes your weapon. Ask him if he wants to give it a go."*

*You're crazy. I'm not going to do that.*

*"Come on. It'll be fun!"*

Shayla was obviously trying to torture the guy; but they had some sort of connection, and since she knew what it was and I didn't, I figured she'd know better than me how to re-forge it.

"So, Garrett. Do you like my weapon?" I pulled Blackie out of its sheath and held it out in front of me. "Would you like to give it a go?"

Garret threw himself over to the side and then flipped over, scrambling to his feet, looking left, right, and then at me, suspicion darkening his eyes. "Who are you?!" he growled.

I laid Blackie across my legs, leaning back on my hands, smiling. "I think the question is, who are you? And how do you know my ancestor, Shayla the dragon-slayer?"

## Chapter Thirteen

GARRETT STOOD SEVERAL PACES AWAY from me, off to the side of the large oak tree that cast a shadow over my mother's grave, his face a mask of suspicion. "You ... you've said things ... things you couldn't possibly know to say ..."

I frowned. "All I did was ask you about your heart and if you wanted to give the Dark a go. What's the big deal?"

Garrett looked around us, speaking out into the air. "Shayla! I know you are here, you minx! Come out and stop toying with me like this. It tisn't proper."

Shayla giggled. *"Don't you love how he's insisting we be proper, when he's a summoned demon and I'm a ... well, right now, a voice in your head?"*

"Yeah, it's a laugh riot," I said sarcastically.

"What is a laugh riot?" Garrett asked, taking one more step away from me.

"I was talking to Shayla, not you."

He spun left and then right. "She's here?! Where?" His arms were out at his sides now, ready for the attack he seemed certain would come.

I stood up slowly, brushing myself off, giving up on the idea of a relaxing evening under the tree getting to know one another's secrets. "I have no idea where she is technically, but her voice is in my head."

Garrett stood up straighter, letting his hands fall to his sides. "Come again?"

"I said, her voice is in my head. But her body? I have no idea where that part of her is."

"So she is talking to you? Right now?"

"Not at this exact moment but she told me what to say to you just now."

*"Tattletale."*

I sighed.

"Did she just say something?"

"She called me a tattletale."

"Can she hear me talking to you?"

I nodded. "I think so."

Garrett drew himself up, his posture rigid with formality. "Shayla, show yourself. Stop hiding behind this young girl like a coward."

*"Tell him I said that I owe no presence to an hourly promise breaker."*

I sighed. "This is the last one, Shayla. Then you can either come out and play yourself, or suffer in my head right along with me. I'm done being your messenger girl." I looked at Garrett. "Sorry for this, Garrett, but she said she owes no presence to an hourly promise breaker, whatever that means."

His mouth thinned, and he spoke in clipped tones. "She slings insults using the weapons issuing from Shakespeare's own pen. How cruel she always was and appears to still be." He closed his eyes and took a deep breath, in and out, before hanging his head, making him look defeated.

"I hope you're happy, Shayla. He's sad now."

"I am not sad," he said, his head snapping up. "I feel very sorry for her. She never believed me, or *in* me, and for an eon has blamed me for something that was never my fault." He turned his attention to the air around us. "It must be a singular torture, dear Shayla, to be wrong for such a long and wasted time."

*"Call me to you, Jayne. I need to face him."*

*What do you mean? How do I do that?*

*"Speak these words: Shayla Blackthorn, guardian to me and others of mine, come to me. I am in need."*

I wondered how much trouble I was going to be in pulling an angel out of the Gray, but only for about two seconds before repeating her words. "Shayla Blackthorn, guardian to me and others of mine, come to me. I am in need."

My eyes were immediately drawn to a glow that began off to my left, casting a light over the quickly darkening night and the especially black place under the branches of the mighty oak.

I stepped back a few paces, not quite trusting what I was seeing and not sure it wasn't more bad news to add to my already messed up I've-brought-a-demon-to-visit-from-the-Underworld evening, which was only slightly worse than my I-married-an-arrogant-ahole-gnomebutt day.

Garrett did the opposite, moving closer to the light until he was standing at the edge of it. "Shayla?" he asked in a tentative voice, reaching his hand up to touch the light.

The vision of a woman began to appear, misty at first, but quickly taking a more solid form. She was all white and then not, colors of her clothing and hair coming into focus. Ten seconds later, there she was, standing in front of us: a girl or a woman - I couldn't tell her age - not much taller than me, perhaps even the exact same size as me, with the same color hair, wearing brown leather pants and a linen tunic of a similar shade that was covered in plates of metal held together with leather straps. She had a dragon fang weapon strapped to her right leg and a sword at her left hip. The only thing that stopped her from looking like the sister I never had was the set of immense wings that were attached to her back, bright white and completely unblemished in any way. They stood out in stark contrast to her warrior garb, which looked like it had made it through more than a few battles, with some small dents in the metal parts and some spots on the pants that were so worn, the leather had gone shiny, mostly on her inner thighs and near where her weapons lay.

I smiled, unable to stop myself. "Damn, Shayla. You sure know how to make a badass entrance."

She looked at me and gave me a cocky grin. "Is there any other kind?"

She turned to Garrett and lost her smile. "Hello, incubus. Or should I say ... vampire?"

He nodded once. "Vampire would be the correct term for me these days. But not for long."

She lifted an eyebrow. "You've managed to earn another lifetime, eh? Who'd you have to sell out for that privilege?"

Garrett sighed heavily. "You know it doesn't work that way. Stop being bitter; it doesn't suit you."

Shayla rolled her eyes and turned away from Garrett to face me. "Dearest Jayne. You have brought me down from the Overworld. Now what, pray tell, are you going to do with me?"

My head started moving from side to side of its own accord. "I'm sorry. I'm having a hard time wrapping my brain around the fact that I'm standing under my mother's tree with a demon and an angel who probably shouldn't be here. I have a feeling I'm going to be in the biggest trouble of my entire *life*." I was getting indigestion from the thought of the council coming down on me in front of the whole fae community. And this time, it would be the Light and the Dark fae councils and the Light and the Dark fae groups all together. Hundreds of fae to stand witness to my stupidity and shame. Ben was not kidding when he called my screw-ups epic. This one was going to follow me around forever. Aidan and his dangling were-man parts in the council meeting had nothing on me.

I dropped my head into my hands, trying to get a grip on myself.

"Now look what you've done," said Garrett, coming over to stand next to me. "You've made her cry. Do you always have to be so cruel?" He patted me on the shoulder awkwardly. "There, there. It will be alright."

Shayla came over to my other side. "You must be joking. You are the *king* of cruel, as evidenced by the fact that you ended up where you did and I ended up where I did after the final battle."

"Pish posh. A mere accounting error."

"Ha! Accounting errors, my backside. Errors are never made, as you well know."

"Hey!" I yelled, lifting my face out of my hands. "I'm trying to work myself into a full-on breakdown here, and your bickering is making it impossible. Do you mind?" I frowned at both of them, trying to channel Dardennes' shame-inducing power into my expression.

Shayla studied my face for a moment before saying, "Well done, Jayne. I very nearly felt guilty over that one."

Garrett nodded. "Quite right, quite right. Well-played.

Please, continue with your breakdown. I shall wait until you are through before I finish berating the heartless silver elf over there."

"I'm no silver elf anymore," Shayla said proudly.

"What are you, exactly?" I asked, now too curious to focus on feeling sorry for myself.

She shrugged modestly. "I am of the Third Order, Silver House."

"Well, well," said Garrett before I could react, "well done, Shayla. Color me impressed."

She smiled, obviously proud of herself. "It has been fun."

"I'll say," responded Garrett, smiling at her and shaking his head in respect.

"What's that mean?" I asked. "Silver House. That's what Chase said when he was here." I swallowed the lump in my throat and beat down the feelings of jealousy that reached up to strangle me from the inside as I thought about Shayla being with him when I couldn't be.

"The Overworld is arranged in houses and in each house are levels of ... angels I guess you would call them."

"Fae like you ... with wings and all," I confirmed.

"Yes, although we are not fae with wings. We are guardians, but yes, you have the idea."

"Who are you guardian-ing?"

"Who did we used to be guardians to, you mean? Well, Fae, certain humans. Whoever is in the Here and Now needing it." Shayla turned to Garrett. "So you got here thanks to Maggie playing in her kitchen again. Lucky you."

He shrugged. "I have not yet decided whether it is a lucky thing or a very unlucky one. I guess we shall see." He stared at Shayla so hard, I knew there were layers of meaning there, but without their story I had no idea of knowing what those secrets were.

"So how do you two know each other?" I asked them both, ignoring for a moment that Shayla had suggested angels no longer acted as guardians.

Neither responded.

"Hello? Anyone want to confess, or do I have to beat it out of you?"

Shayla turned to me. "Don't make threats you cannot support." Her hand shifted to the butt of her dragon-fang weapon.

"Okay. Let me amend my threat, then. Confess or I'll put you into a coma." I folded my arms over my chest, quite confident in my ability to lose control of my power surges and send either of them into the Green for a while. I smiled, rejoicing in the fact that my earlier screw-ups were now sources of strength for me, and I didn't have to change a thing to make that happen.

"She looks a little too happy about the prospect of this coma for me to not be concerned," said Garrett, eyeing me carefully.

"I have heard of her near-comas in Silver House." She shifted her hands away from her weapons. "Very well. I am ready to shed some light on our past, Garrett. Are you?" She lifted her chin in challenge.

"Absolutely. Why not clear the air? We've only waited a thousand years or so to get to it, right?

She nodded, taking my hand in hers, drawing me over to the tree. "Sit down, Jayne. This is going to take a while." I watched as her wings faded and then disappeared from her back, making her able to sit on the ground next to me. I reached over to the space where they had been, waving my hand around, wondering if they were just invisible now. But they were gone. My hand greeted first nothing, and then just her back.

She smiled at me but offered no explanation for her disappearing appendages.

Garrett sat down across from us, leaning once again against the bark of the tree. He gestured gracefully at Shayla. "Ladies first."

"Ever the gentleman," she said, and then turned to me with a smile. "Once upon a time, long, long ago, Garrett and I were pledged to one another, me as a silver elf and he, as an incubus ..."

# Chapter Fourteen

SHE WASN'T THIRTY SECONDS INTO the story before I had to stop her.

"Wait? You mean silver elves and incubi can ... get it on? Like, officially?"

"Of course, if you mean by *get it on* that we can come together in an intimate way and procreate."

"For life? I mean, can you have babies and be married and all that?"

"Interracial pairings occur all the time. Don't tell me you're prejudiced," Shayla said, frowning at me.

"No, not at all. I just have never seen it in the compound. I have no idea how it all works, in the fae world."

"Great Spirit, they don't educate younger fae on the ways of procreation anymore? That just seems dangerous to me," said Garrett, shaking his head.

I smiled. "No, we know about all that stuff. It's just that I was human for most of my life, and fae birds-and-bees were never part of my training. So I just kind of ... I don't know ... never thought about it in detail."

"Let's just say that interracial relationships are common and can result in children of either race. Will that be enough of an explanation for me to go on?"

"Yeah, sure. Go for it. I get it now."

"Very well. As I was saying, Garrett and I were pledged to one another. But a great uprising occurred that interfered in our plans to actually go through with the binding ceremony. During the battle that followed the uprising - or during one of them, I should say, as there were many - we lost our lives in the Here and Now and went our separate ways. We have not seen each other since."

Shayla seemed very matter-of-fact about everything, but I could tell she wasn't unaffected by her story. She kept stealing glances at Garrett and then looking at the ground.

Garrett was still sitting with us, but his mind was far away, lost in the memories. "Of the many things I've been forced to bear as my punishment, *that* has been the most heavy burden of them all. Knowing that Shayla, the one I loved with all of my heart, was out there somewhere thinking ill of me while I was elsewhere and unable to see her or to explain."

Shayla leaned over and shoved his shoulder. "Don't get all maudlin on us, Garrett. It was an eon ago. And your selling us out does nothing to convince me you have any regret over losing what we might have had, or fooled ourselves into believing we had. You made your choice and had to suffer the consequences, like we all did. You should have moved on. I did."

My mind was going in about four different directions, wondering what it should clarify first.

"I am not being maudlin," he snapped back. "I have had a thousand-odd years to think about it and mull it over ... try to make sense of it. And, truly ... even after all this time, there is no sense to be made. You can believe what you want, but I sold no one out."

"Then tell us how you ended up in the Underworld, my friend. Tell us that," she said bitterly.

Garrett sighed. "I am too deeply ashamed of myself to confess my sins to you, but believe me when I say it had nothing to do with you and me. Let us talk about something else right now. I am certain Jayne would like to know about the uprising, as it is more applicable to her current concerns than the sorry state of our former love affair."

Shayla stared at Garrett for a few seconds before turning her attention to me, clenching her jaw a few times to get control of her emotions before speaking again. "He is probably right. The uprising was a big problem for us, and it appears as if you are about to suffer the same miseries that we did back then when we were young and foolish enough to believe we were invincible - and that love could conquer all."

"Shayla, please," begged Garrett.

She held up her hands in surrender. "Fine, fine. I'll stop. I'm sure your lifetime of guilt has done enough. At least I hope it has." She looked at me, putting her hands in her lap. "Prepare yourself, Jayne. What I am about to tell you will remove the veil of ignorance from your eyes. Are you absolutely certain you want that?"

"What, are you kidding? To know the secrets that everyone is keeping from me? Hell yes, I want to know. Lay it on me. Don't hold anything back, either. I can totally take it, no matter what it is."

"I know you can." She reached over and squeezed my hand once before pulling back again. "You are a strong girl, and I expected nothing less from my bloodline." She smiled proudly before continuing, drawing her sword from its scabbard and feeling along its edge carefully as she spoke.

"About a thousand years ago, when Garrett and I were members of your realm, we experienced an uprising from the Underworld. It began as you have seen recently, with orcs making sporadic appearances, several weaker fae channeling demons in both word and deed, and things being generally out of sorts. These demons caused many problems with our people and in our communities. There were some smaller battles and then one large one, fought in an area of the forest where several fae witches working with an elemental were able to trap hundreds of orcs within the trees there and close the portals through which they were entering this realm."

"That's not the worst of it. Tell her about the others ... the Time of Sadness," prompted Garrett.

Shayla bowed her head. "We lost many fae in our war with the Underworld. Some races were eradicated completely. The sorrow that rose up from the mourning covered our world with a cloak of darkness. The fallout was that those in the Overworld were overwhelmed. They could not keep up with the need for comfort and support coming from those in the Here and Now. The darkness and misery spilled over onto everything."

"Even good fae turned to darkness, finding no solace in the arms of light. Many of us lost our way," said Garrett in a quiet voice. "Others gave up everything, so that those remaining might find the light again." He looked up at Shayla, his pleading gaze making my heart spasm for him.

Shayla cleared her throat, and when she spoke again, her voice was hoarse. "The weapon you wear symbolizes the terrible sacrifices we were forced to make."

I looked down at the dragon fang on my leg. "You killed a

dragon to save the world?"

Shayla smiled bitterly. "That makes it sound very melodramatic. But it is close enough to the truth that I will let it stand."

"But what does killing a dragon do to change things? I mean, back then? Why did that made a difference?"

"The dragons guarded the portals between the realms. There were two. And while the beasts were there, while they stood sentinel, they made it possible for the doors between realms to be used. But once the dragons were exterminated, the portals were sealed forever, making it impossible for those in other realms to pass into this one."

"And yet, here you are," I said. "And there are orcs here, too. How is that possible?"

"An excellent question," said Shayla. "I wish I knew the answer, but I don't."

Garrett cleared his throat guiltily. "A-*hem*. I might be able to shed a little light on that issue, perhaps."

"By all means," said Shayla. "Light up the night with your truth, Garrett."

He smiled thinly. "We had two of the dragon souls in the Underworld, and believe me, they were not happy about ending up there, since all they'd ever done was their duty - according to them."

Shayla shrugged. "Someone has to be the bad guy."

"Exactly," agreed Garrett. "But they preferred to be the bad guys in the Here and Now, and not in the Underworld. They were never supposed to be there, you see. They were to remain immortal, in the Here and Now, carrying out their roles as regular as clockwork - as regular as the elements. I daresay they had begun to believe they were their own elements of sorts. Quite arrogant, if you ask me, really."

"So what happened?" I asked.

Shayla picked up the story. "The councils had decided during the Time of Sadness that the only way to get our realm back on track was to rely only on one another, and to stop leaning so heavily on the other realms and their inhabitants to right our wrongs and support us emotionally, or to do our dirty work. So they ordered the portals closed forever, which meant their dragon guardians had to go too."

"Talk about arrogant," I said. "Who gave them the power to do that?"

"Fae have always had the power to self-determine. The portals were a crutch. I don't necessarily think it was a bad decision then, and I still don't now. It was a terrible time for us. I cannot even now, with the wisdom of hind-sight, find a better solution."

"I agree with Shayla. The last thousand years of contemplation has not revealed anything more clearly to me either. We did what we had to do, and that was it. The problem was solved."

"Until now," I said.

"Yes. Until now," agreed Garrett. "Someone or a group of someones in the Underworld has discovered a way to come back here, and they want the portals opened up without their dragon guardians in place so they can come and go as they please. I believe *this* is what they are working towards, as we speak."

"But if they're already coming back here, why do they even need the portals opened?"

"Because what they are able to do now is only on a limited basis. They are restricted by time and in number. Should the portals be opened, however, they would not suffer these restrictions

## Clash of the Otherworlds: Book One

- and believe you me, even if the dragons were finally released back into the Here and Now, they would probably do nothing to stop them from coming through. I believe they would consider it the fae's and humans' just desserts for sending them to the Underworld unfairly."

"Where are these old portals?" I asked. "I mean, are they in a place, like on the map? Or is it more ... magical than that?"

"They are in places on the map," said Shayla. "Although those places move, as time continues on, but infinitesimally so. They are in the area you know as Europe. I don't believe they have changed spots on the map very much, if at all."

"Do you know the town names?"

"You would do better with showing us a map," said Garrett. "Towns move as people come in and out, families grow, or industries change. Showing you the coordinates based on the landscape would be more accurate."

"My friend Tony, he's a wrathe, he said he thinks the orcs and that demon came through in the Gray." I searched their faces for a reaction, but it had gotten too dark for me to see.

"I had assumed as much," said Garrett. "I gather it is not an easy task nor one that is accomplished without some magic; but I did hear that there had been some success."

"Where did you hear this?" asked Shayla, right before I was about to ask the same exact question.

"Oh, there were rumors going around."

"What's it like in the Underworld, anyway?" I asked. "Are you all just sitting around pits of fire or something? Waiting for your chance to come back here?"

"No, it is not nearly so dramatic," said Garrett, laughing bitterly. "It is very much like here, actually. Only the creatures living there have a different set of values than those here or in the Otherworld. And one special treat we enjoy as members of that realm is the constant, incessant reminders of the wrongs we brought upon ourselves and others in the Here and Now. We get to feel their pain and experience their emotions, over and over."

"Even after they're dead?" I asked.

"Oh, yes. Absolutely. Actually, I have found it to be a very effective deterrent. I am quite sure I never want to return there. When I get my second chance, I will take full advantage of my knowledge and painful lessons."

"How will you do that, being born with no memory of your torture?" asked Shayla. Her words were softer now, less angry-sounding.

"One cannot suffer as I have and not retain some of its echoes. I will remember enough, I am confident of that."

"Assuming Maggie and I haven't totally screwed you over, you mean," I said. I felt a little guilty now, thinking I might have sentenced him to more Underworld torture. It sounded awful. I could totally picture myself being punished, having to re-live all the times I did stupid stuff over and over, saying shit that hurt people's feelings. I vowed right at that moment to do whatever I could to avoid that destiny.

"I was brought here against my will. I will continue to function under the assumption that I will not be punished for it. And who knows? Maybe the demons will get their way and the portals will be reopened. Then everyone will be here and we can have a big party."

"That's not even funny, Garrett," said Shayla, standing. Her wings reappeared, lighting up the area with their blinding whiteness.

"Where are you going?" I asked. "Back to the Overworld?"

Shayla sighed. "Alas, I cannot. Like Garrett, now that I have been summoned, I am stuck here. Without the portals being opened, I am not free to travel back and forth."

"Did I do that?" I asked. "I mean, you were already kind of here in my head, right?"

"Yes, the veil between our realms is thin enough that with a strong enough desire, I was able to make a connection with you. But I could not cross over without you summoning me."

"Does that mean I can summon others?" I asked, my mind racing.

"Perhaps. And because of this, I must caution you. I believe your power to summon is equally strong in both other realms. Be careful of accepting pleas or invitations from creatures you do not know. You could bring someone to you who you do not ever want to see."

I swallowed hard, thinking about Torrie and how close I'd come to being his very unwilling lover. "Yeah, okay. Good advice."

Garrett stood and brushed off his pants. "Well, then, Shayla ... I hope it will not be too much of an imposition for me to spend the next few days with you, then, or however long we will be here. I have nowhere to go, and I suspect we would not be welcome in the fae compound."

"What are you guys going to do? Stay out here in the forest?"

"We are used to making shelter among the trees," said Shayla. "Do not concern yourself with our welfare."

"How am I going to find you? I mean, later. And shouldn't I tell the council you're here? I'm sure they'd want to talk to you."

"I ask that you keep our presence quiet for now. After Garrett and I have had some time to discuss our situation and compare what we've seen, we will know better our next course of action. Do you agree to this, Garrett?"

"Of course. I defer to your wisdom, oh guardian from Silver House."

"Stuff it in your saddlebags, Garrett."

"Of course, my lady," he said, a smile in his voice.

"When you are ready to see us again, just reach out for me in your mind. We are connected, you and I. When you are distressed, I can feel it," Shayla said to me, her hand moving to rest on her dragon-fang weapon.

"Oh, goody. Another empath."

"You know of another?" she asked.

"Yes. My best friend, Tony. The wrathe I told you about."

"I should like to meet him," she said.

"You will. And Tim, too. I can't keep secrets from either of them. How about tomorrow? After breakfast?"

"Very good."

"I will do what I can to find food," said Garrett, "but if I am not able to, Jayne, I would ask that you agree to provide for me once more."

Shayla hissed in a breath, spinning to face him. "You've fed from her?!"

"I had no choice," he said calmly. "What was I to do? Turn to dust in the witch's house? I think not. I have waited much too long to walk away from my next lifetime; and you know how it works ... ashes to ashes ..."

"...Dust to dust, yes, I know, Garrett. I don't need you to lecture to me as if I was a child."

"Sorry, guys, but I'm not following," I said, waiting for an explanation.

"I'll talk to you about it tomorrow," said Shayla, sounding tired. "Just do me a favor - no more blood letting until we talk, okay?"

"Sure, no problem. I didn't even like it, anyway."

"You didn't?" asked Garrett, sounding offended. "Well, of course you did. Don't be silly."

"No, actually I didn't. It stung and it hurt, if you really want to know. I feel very ripped off over the whole thing, to be honest. I was ready to be all drugged out over it, but instead I got zipped." I looked down at my arm and saw two swollen bite marks, oozing a little fluid but thankfully not bleeding.

Shayla started laughing and couldn't stop, resting her hand on my shoulder.

"Okaaay, so something I said was hysterically funny. Anyway, I'm tired and I have to go to bed. I'll catch you guys on the flip side."

I walked away hearing Garrett behind me asking Shayla, "Whatever does she mean by catching us on the flip side? Where is that?"

I wondered how long Shayla would keep laughing, since I heard the tinkling sound of it all the way back to the infinity door leading into the compound. I couldn't wait to get to my room and tell Tim all about what had happened. He was going to shit a brick over it.

# Chapter Fifteen

I BANGED THE DOOR TO my room closed, scanning the foyer and then inside the sitting room for my pixie friend. He was nowhere to be seen, but the instant my eyes fell on the pixie table, a little figure came buzzing up from amidst the flowers there.

"Oh, shit. I woke the baby," I said aloud.

"Woke the baby! Woke the baaaabyyyy!" said Willy, flying over to me in an even crazier, out-of-control flight path than normal. I snatched him out of mid air, worried he was going to splat himself into the door if he kept going.

"Hello, Lellamental!" he said, his little wings buzzing on and off as he sat in my palm with his legs straight out in front of him and his face split in a huge grin. "Wanna play?"

"No thanks, Willy. I'm too tired. I have to go to sleep now. That's what you should be doing, too." I looked around the room desperately. "Where are your parents, anyway?"

He yawned, flopping over backwards in my hand, splaying his arms out at his sides, bending his wings all up. "They're playing spider-nakies in the garden." He started swishing his arms and legs up and down like he was trying to make snow angels.

I reached down to try and lift him back up straight with my

finger, but all he did was giggle and push me away.

"Spider-nakies?" I asked. "What's spider-nakies?"

Willy sat up all of a sudden, his giggling forgotten. "Wanna play spider-nakies with me?!"

I closed my hand around him to keep him from falling out, laughing in spite of my fatigue and general uneasiness with being around a baby and no parents in sight. "I doubt it," I said, opening my hand a little in response to his now struggling form.

"Come on, let's do it. It's fun, Lellamental, you'll see."

"My name isn't Lellamental. It's Jayne."

"No it's not. It's Lellamental. Now take your clothes off like *this!*" He quickly stripped off his tiny pants and was wrestling with his shirt when I realized what the 'nakie' part of this game involved.

"Holy shit, Willy! You can't take your clothes off in here!" I looked around in a panic, worried someone was going to come in and see me with a naked baby sitting in my hand. I tried not to look, but he'd launched himself up into the air and was zooming all over the place now, coming in dangerous proximity to the ground and walls.

I ran after him, scrambling around the room with my hands out, trying to catch him long enough to throw him back into his bed. I figured I could put a pillow case over his sleeping area and at least keep him contained until his parents got back.

"Weeee!! Spiiiiiider nakiiieees!!" he squealed, finally succeeding in getting his shirt off and tossing it to the ground. It floated down slowly, like a piece of lint, while I tripped over a table leg, trying to keep the kid from hitting the wall.

He ended up on a tree growing out of the rock wall, gripping onto it with his hands and feet. He turned his head and looked at me, a mischievous grin on his face, out of breath from all the flying around like a maniac.

I couldn't help but laugh at the tiny pixie buns that were glaringly white compared to the bark of the tree.

"See, Lellamental? See me?"

"Yeah, I see you, Baby Bee. I'm not sure exactly what the hell you're doing, but I see ya."

I got closer and held my hands out below him in case he fell.

"I'm doin' spider nakies. See?"

I shook my head. "Well, you're naked. You got that part right at least."

He frowned. "I'm a spider. See? I sit on a wall! Just. Like. A. Spiiiider!" he yelled, launching himself up off the tree, into the air again. But his trajectory went narrow, and he didn't zoom around me like I think he'd planned. Instead, he came directly at my face, his eyes going wide and his little hands out in front of him to grab for the nearest thing they could find.

I stumbled backwards, trying to avoid the inevitable, but my foot got hung up in the rug and I fell - but only after Willy had flown straight into my face, gripping onto my nose with his arms and legs for all he was worth.

I shouted as I went down, spitting raspberries upwards in an effort to get him off me, my arms flying out to the sides trying to break my fall.

The small table with the lamp on it didn't have a chance. It crashed to the cold, hard floor right along with me, glass shattering into a million pieces. My head snapped back with the downward force and slammed into the stone, making my vision fade blissfully to black. The last thing I remembered thinking before my brain completely shut down was how difficult it was to breath through my nose when there was a naked pixie baby attached to it.

# Chapter Sixteen

I WOKE IN MY BED to the sound of Tim giggling like a patient in an insane asylum.

"Shhh, Tim. She doesn't want to wake up to the sounds of your hysteria," scolded Abby.

"But she ... but she ... but shhh ..." Tim couldn't finish his sentence, he was laughing so hard.

"Come on, Baby Bee. Let's go back to bed," said Abby.

I cracked an eye open in time to see her leading him away while he whined behind her, his naked ass blowing in the breeze. "But she *likes* playing spider nakies! I don't wanna go! I'm not *tired!*"

Tim caught me awake and zoomed over to float in front of my face. He tried to school his features to look serious, but he just couldn't do it. He bent in half, holding his stomach, laughing so hard he farted three times in rapid succession.

"Jesus, Tim, get a grip, would ya? I have a friggin headache already. And I'm pretty sure I'm scarred for life now, getting a baby pixie wiener to the nose. Do you mind not polluting my breathing space with your butt stink?"

Tim flipped over onto his back and fell to my chest, his

hysteria now having moved into the silent scream zone, where all he could do was turn purple and gasp for air.

"Yes, it was awesome. Playing spider nakies with your little friggin hippy child. Get some clothes on that kid, would ya?" I turned my head to the side, hiding my own smile. It *had* been pretty funny, seeing him clinging to that tree with his little butt hanging out. I could only imagine what it must have looked like attached to my face.

I lifted Tim's limp body up off my chest. "Hey! Quit laughing," I ordered, dangling him over my face. "I have massively major secrets to tell you, and I'm tired and I have a headache, so if you don't shut up you'll have to wait until tomorrow to hear them." I frowned, looking around me, thinking about secrets and other people hearing them. "How did I get up on this bed, anyway?" I leaned over and looked at the floor nearby. There was no evidence of a mess in here, so I probably hadn't crawled in myself. The accident had happened in the other room, and I could hear noises out there.

Ben stuck his head out my bedroom door, just as I was thinking about getting up to investigate. "How are you feeling? Better?"

"Yeah, she's better," coughed out Tim. "Now that she doesn't have wee Willy's winkie in her face!" And then he seized up into fits of laughter again.

I shook my head, throwing him over onto the other side of the bed where he landed in a *poof* of down comforter.

"I'm fine. Thanks for putting me in here. I assume you're the one who came to my rescue?"

"Yeah. I heard a big crash and came over to see if you were okay. I found you on the floor with ... uhhhh ... a baby pixie stuck to your face."

I smiled. "Little fucker jumped me."

Ben moved his mouth around, looking like he was trying not to laugh. "Yeah, so, anyway, I put you in bed, but I didn't get a witch or medical expert in here. Do you want me to find a doctor?"

"No, I'm fine. I just have a little headache. I'm going to sleep. You can see yourself out, if you don't mind."

"No, not at all. I'll see you in the morning?" He made as if to step into the room, but I quickly rolled over.

"Yeah. Tomorrow. At breakfast," I said, staring at the wall, stopping myself from announcing my intention to eat with my friends. He'd been nice enough to save me not only from a cold night on the floor, but the embarrassment of a talking about the pixie penis-plant to the face, so I let it go. There would be plenty of time to duke it out with him tomorrow. I yawned loudly. "G'night, Ben."

"Goodnight, Jayne," he said softly, closing the door behind him.

I laid there watching Tim struggle to sit up and then crawl on his hands and knees over to me, before falling onto his back again near my face.

"That was *the* most awesome thing I have *ever* seen in my entire life," said Tim, sighing loudly, still suffering an occasional spasm brought on by a snort or giggle. "I wish I had a camera. Or a freeze-frame spell. Holy flaming pixie butts, that was classic." He rolled over to look at me again. "How much could I pay you to do that all over again?"

"You could never come up with enough money or power or promises to convince me to play spider nakies with your kid again. Ever. *Never* ever." I reached back to touch the lump on the back of my head. "What kind of a fucked up game is that, anyway?" I sighed, rolling over to look up at the ceiling covered in tree branches and leaves, wincing at the pain from my head injury.

"It's something he made up himself," said Tim. "Apparently he's not fond of wearing clothes, so any excuse he can find to take them off, he jumps on it."

"Great. A nudist rebel pixie baby. In my bedroom."

"You don't want us to move, do you?" Tim had stopped laughing and sounded concerned.

I sighed. "Yes and no. But ultimately, no. Just stay. I'll wear a hockey mask or something to keep the pixie wieners at bay."

Tim giggled again. "Good plan. It'll look good on you."

I yawned again, loudly. "Tim, I'd love to shoot the shit with you all night, but I'm beat. I have to go to sleep now. I'll tell you about the end of the world as we know it tomorrow, 'kay?"

"Yeah sure, Spider Girl. Talk to you tomorrow," he said, flying up above me and then disappearing out the door Ben had left cracked open.

I fell asleep, rubbing at my nose, wondering if it were just my imagination, or if I were actually smelling pixie-privates talcum powder left over from my collision with Baby Bee.

# Chapter Seventeen

IT WAS DARK, AND I could hear the sound of my own breathing, loud to my ears. Something was wrong, but I didn't know what. I thought the space around me was black because my eyes were closed, so I blinked them a couple times. Still ... there was nothing but blackness. I'd never been in a place like this before, and it gave me a very bad feeling. Goosebumps stood out on my skin.

"Tim?" I called out into the cool, damp air around me. "Are you there?" I waited but no response came. "Baby Bee?" I was pretty sure this was a place his parents wouldn't want him to go, but thinking if he were already here, he'd be better off with me than flying around and banging into things in the dark. But no buzzing greeted my ears and no annoying little voice yelled out with plans to dig into my nose or fly around naked. I couldn't believe it, but I was missing that baby pixie. If I were going to die in some deep dark hole, it would have been nice to have a familiar face around when it happened.

I concentrated hard on finding a way out of this place, squeezing my eyes shut so the blackness would we a little less frightening. *Somebody help me. Somebody come and get me.*

I heard a shuffling sound off to my right, so I turned quickly, opening my eyes and facing whatever was coming. "Who's there?" I said, my voice echoing just a little. It sounded like I was in a room, not much bigger than the bedroom I last remembered falling asleep in.

"Well, well," said a vaguely familiar voice. "Look who dropped in for a little visit." Whoever it was laughed, and it was then that I knew who the voice belonged to.

*Oh, fuck and double fuck. If he gets any closer I'm going to have to bust out every single karate move I ever dreamed of having, because I will not be sleeping with a demon tonight. Over my dead body.*

"What's the matter? Buggane got your tongue?" he asked.

"Go to hell, Torrie. Or should I call you Rick the Dick?" I had no idea if my former, murdering step-father was still riding shotgun in Torrie's leathery hide, but I really wanted to know who I was dealing with. If it were Rick, I would surely have extra kickass powers, because my hate for him gave me serious wings.

I tried to pull the Green up into me, but where it usually waited for me to connect, right now there was nothing, just an empty void. It reminded me of how I felt as a human teenager - powerless and abandoned. It pissed me off that I was going to have to face this beast as weak as I was right now.

"Where the hell am I? And where are you?" I asked, putting my fists up in front of my chest, ready to do a couple quick jabs.

"I'm standing right in front of you," he said, and I knew from the volume of his voice that he was telling the truth and only a few feet away.

*Damn my vision. Why can't I see him?*

"You summoned me here, so forgive me if I find it hard to believe you don't know where we are." He chuckled at that, and I hated him even more for knowing things I didn't.

"So, what's the plan?" I asked. "Are you here to kill me? Maim me? Rape me? Because I'm not on board with any of that. I won't go down easy, either." I reached down and felt along my thigh, wishing I had Blackie with me, but I'd taken it off and put it next to my bed when I'd gone to sleep. My shoulders slumped as I realized I was facing a demon with nothing but my feminine wiles to save me. I was definitely doomed.

"I wish," he said, sounding regretful. "Unfortunately, you've made that quite impossible. And since I cannot accomplish any of those rather intriguing activities you've mentioned, I would appreciate you sending me back."

I frowned. "Send you back? Back where? To Florida?" It was the last place I'd seen him before Ben and I had banished his soul from the Here and Now, and it was also one of the last places I'd send him to if I could. I still had some friends there.

"It is really quite insulting how ignorant you are, dragging me from my realm only to end up playing twenty questions. A girl like you should not be permitted to have this kind of power. The universe has made another error - this one, however, not in my favor."

"I have power? I did this?" I asked, recognition dawning.

"Why don't you turn on a light so we can enjoy the moment together, eh?"

"Where's the switch in this room?" I asked, putting my hands out the sides, hoping to find a wall there. All they met was air.

"Don't be ridiculous. Why would there be a switch when this is no *room*?"

"Where *are* we then? Jesus, I've asked you like ten times now!" I stomped my foot in frustration, not sure who I was more pissed at - him or me.

He growled something unintelligible before answering me and nearly giving me a heart attack in the process.

"We are in your mind. Just let in the light, and we'll get down to business."

I swallowed hard, trying to understand, first, how I'd invited a demon into my brain while I slept, and second, how a person could turn on a light in her mind. My inner flashlight seemed to be broken, so I fell back on something as basic as I could imagine - picturing myself flicking on a light switch. The space went from black to brightly lit as soon as my imagined finger finished its motion. I snorted. *Screw you, demon. This is too a room with a light switch.* And then I nearly gagged at the vision before me.

"What's the matter? Not what you expected?" he asked. He spoke with Torrie's voice, but he didn't look at all like the demon I had met at my mom's house.

"What are you doing here with Torrie's voice coming out of your mouth?" I asked, searching his face, my brain not able to make the connection. *Why is Ben here, acting like a demon? Why did his voice change? Why was he acting so stupid and mysterious?*

I tried to back up away from him, but an invisible wall behind me stopped me in my tracks.

The Ben Monster smiled, stepping closer, apparently not suffering the same effects as I was.

"Don't go," he said silkily, "we've only just arrived. Tell me ... who do you see standing in front of you right now?" When no answer was forthcoming, he looked down at his hands. "A young fae, or one who looks to have the hands of a boy not that much older than you in appearance." He held out his right arm, flexing it, watching it the whole time with unabashed curiosity. "Strong ... tall ... Who could this be, I wonder, who strikes so much fear and loathing into your heart that you would draw me into your dreams and yet see him in front of you?" He dropped his arm back to his side.

"I'm *dreaming* this?" I asked, even more mystified than I was before.

"What do you think?" he asked, coming one step closer, now just a foot away from me.

I had to look up to see his face, and even this near to him, I could see nothing but Ben in his eyes. "That is just sicker than sick," I said, disgusted with myself and now not as afraid as I had been. "I fall asleep after being molested by a naked pixie baby, and now I'm dreaming up demons and ... other fae ... just to freak myself out." I reached up to push him out of my way. "Go away. I'm tired. I have to get up in the morning and talk to the council."

He grabbed my hands as soon as they touched his chest and clamped onto them, squeezing them hard enough to make me scared again. This clearly was not the Ben I knew and at least liked now and then. And pain was still possible here, I quickly realized, making me lose whatever confidence I'd had a second ago.

"Who do you see in front of you? Who am I, here in your mind?" he demanded angrily.

"Don't you know?" I asked. *How can he not know he's Ben?*

"I would have thought your greatest fear was me as you've seen me before. Not this fae ... this mystery boy. Who is it that you fear so deeply? Tell me!" He yanked my arms towards him painfully.

I opened my mouth to answer him, but then thought better of it, clamping my jaw shut. My brain was moving as fast as it could in this weird place with almost no clues to help me figure things out. The only thing I could come up with was that I should never

*ever* give a demon what he wanted, and since he wanted to know Ben's name, that would be the last thing I told him.

"I don't know who it is. I've never seen him before in my life," I lied. I was trying not to freak out any more than necessary, but this demon even smelled like Ben which was wrong, wrong, wrong.

"Don't lie to me," he growled, squeezing my hands harder.

*Ben, you stupid jerk, why are you coming to me like this?!* I didn't know what else to do but yell out in my own head, which was surely a sign I was losing it. But I was panicking, picturing myself stuck here in this dark place with only the Ben Monster to keep me company for all eternity. I closed my eyes and focused hard. *Come to me, Ben. Come to me. Save me!*

"What are you doing?" he asked, breathing down on me with Ben's breath.

"I'm trying to wake myself up."

He dropped my arms. "Do you mean to suggest that you cannot reverse this spell?"

My eyes popped open. "This is a spell?"

"Curse the dragons!" yelled the Ben Monster, spinning away from me, taking a few angry steps before facing me again. "You are the most inept elemental I have ever had the misfortune of dealing with, do you know that?"

"*Pfft.* Not so inept that I wasn't able to send your sorry ass back to the Underworld." I was feeling cocky again.

"Not without the help of your lover, the other elemental. What's his name again ...? Ben was it?"

My eyes widened. *Oh, shit. He knows about Ben.*

The Ben Monster moved back over to stand in front of me, watching me closely. I tried to school my features to look unconcerned or bland, but he wasn't falling for it. I could tell the way the smile started to creep across this face. And it was more than a little disturbing to see Ben looking so happy. He was usually so brooding, but now I could truly appreciate how gorgeous of a specimen he really was with his demon doppelganger smiling like that.

"Why do I think now that the fae you see standing before you is this elemental ... Ben?"

I shrugged. "I have no idea. I'm bound to him, so he'd be the last one to show up as my worst nightmare."

We both turned at the same time we heard the sound.

"Who's there?" I said, my throat constricting on my words, making them squeak out. *It's probably Gorm, the buggane. He's next on my list of the last creature I'd like to see in my head at night.*

But it wasn't. As soon as he entered the light, I breathed a sigh of relief. "Ben," I said, walking quickly over to him and taking his hand in mine. "Thank the Overworld you came. I'm stuck in here with this turd, and I don't know how to get out." I gave him the biggest smile possible, just realizing now that he was about to figure out exactly how I felt about him, seeing Torrie inhabiting his body.

The new Ben looked from me to Torrie and back again. "What's the meaning of this?" he said haughtily, not sounding at all like Ben.

I dropped his hand like a hot potato and took three quick steps back. *"Leck?!* What in the hell are you doing here?"

"What's Ben doing here?" he asked.

"Ah *ha!"* yelled Torrie. "I *knew* it. This is Ben!"

"That's not Ben's voice," said Leck, narrowing his eyes. "An imposter." He turned to me. "I ask you again. Why have I been compelled in here, and what is this imposter doing with Ben's corpus?"

"Probably the same thing you are doing with it," said Torrie, cockily. "Apparently this young elemental fears him and us. Quite charming when you get past the fact that we have been brought here by a fool who does not know how to release us or herself."

"You cannot be serious," said Leck, at first appearing as if he thought Torrie were joking, but then getting an angry look on his face. "Oh, for the love of ..."

"Hey! I'm standing right here! No need to be rude about it."

"What do you expect for us to do?" asked Leck in his most obnoxiously stuck-up voice. "Act as good buddies like you and your little water sprite and green elf friends, and sit in a circle playing pat-a-cake?"

"Wow, Leck. Being Maléna's right hand wrathe has really done wonders for your personality." I wasn't sure who was worse between the two of them. She was a pain in my ass, but Leck had actually tortured me a couple times when Ben had held me captive. I wasn't one bit sorry I'd interrupted Leck's sleep to drag him in here. Anything I could do to pay him back was fine by me.

"You are acquainted with Maléna? The silver elf?" asked Torrie, some of the menace missing from his tone.

Leck lifted his chin, which looked ridiculous on Ben's face since it seemed to be a sign of self-bolstered confidence. Ben didn't need things like that.

"We are more than acquaintances."

Torrie's lip curled in disgust. "I can only see you as this Ben fae now, but even so ... I am not impressed."

Leck was getting ready to let Torrie have it, so I stepped between the two Ben imposters and held up my hands. "Okay, boys, let's drop the super stupid jealousy act and move on, shall we? I mean, seriously ... she didn't like you when you were alive, Torrie, so trust me - she's going to hate you now. Not only are you ugly as sin, but you smell bad, too. And Leck, you are her do-boy, plain and simple. I hope you haven't fooled yourself into thinking otherwise. She could probably have anyone she wants; she's not going to settle for a simpering wrathe who can't control his temper."

"Did you just call me ugly?"

"Did you just accuse *me* of *simpering?*"

Both Bens stood staring at me with mouths agape.

Before I could answer, another voice came out of the darkness. "Who's there?"

A fae who looked like the real Ben walked into the light, joining us. I breathed a sigh of relief when the voice and face matched.

"Is it really you, Ben?" I asked, moving closer to put my hand on his arm. I squeezed it, finding it warm and solid. I searched his eyes for answers, but they looked exactly like the other Bens' eyes.

"Where are we?" he asked me. He looked at the other two. "And why are there three of me here?"

"Wellll ...," I started, nervously, "see, I was having this dream, I guess, and I somehow managed to pull the demon Torrie and the wrathe Leck in here. And I'm not sure how to send them out or how wake up at this point."

"And you called me to help you," he asked, his expression neutral.

"That's the gist of it, yeah."

"Which one of you is Torrie?" Ben asked, looking from one to the other.

Neither answered, so I pointed to him. "That one."

"Did you answer a call or were you compelled?"

"Compelled," he admitted.

"And what about you?" he asked Leck.

"Compelled," he said, sighing.

"So I am the only one summoned?"

The other two Bens nodded.

"What's the difference? What does it mean?" I asked. It seemed significant, the way he acted, but for the life of me I couldn't figure out why. All of the biggest jerks I knew were here, and I wanted *none* of them here. How they got here didn't matter to me. I just wanted them all gone.

The real Ben turned to me, his face a mask of coldness. "End this now, Jayne. I have to get my sleep. We face a challenge from Maléna tomorrow, and I cannot enter it tired."

"A challenge?" asked Torrie. "How interesting. What are the stakes?"

"None of your business," Ben said over his shoulder.

"Perhaps I could be of assistance," said Torrie, a hint of slyness entering his voice.

Normally I would run from it, but in this case, I thought better of it. "Like what kind of assistance?" I asked, curious about what a spurned lover of Maléna might be willing to offer.

"Shut your mouth, demon!" yelled Leck. "You have no place in Here and Now business!"

"Much as you might like to believe that, I must assure you, it is not correct," said Torrie, turning back to me before continuing. "Send the wrathe away, and we shall talk. I'm sure we can reach an agreement."

"Send them both away, Jayne. We need to leave here. Dwelling in your mind for too long is never a good idea," said the real Ben.

I bugged my eyes out at him and put my hands on my hips. "Don't you think I would have already done that if I knew how? *Shit*, that's why I called you! Help me send everyone away. *Including* you."

Ben's lips pressed into a thin line for a few seconds before he answered quietly, so only I would hear. "You will answer for this later. But for now, you may send all of us back by just making it so."

My mouth dropped open and stayed that way until I had the presence of mind to start talking again. I whisper-yelled back at him, "Are you fucking kidding me? That's not an *answer*. That's not a method for undoing this mess! Give me something real I can use, you idiot!"

Ben's nostrils flared. "Use the power of your mind. That's what got them here in the first place. Apparently, you hate me so much, you've drawn in your worst fears and put my face on them." He shook his head in disgust. "I don't know why I've bothered. Just send us away. Picture it in your mind."

I was pissed. "You act as if you're the only one trying to make this work. But when you do try, you do it for a little while and then you just act like an ass again. Like right now, for example."

"Better than acting like a spoiled bitch."

"*Ass!*" I yelled, pushing him hard in the chest.

He flew backwards, into the darkness, as if I had some kind of super-strength that lifted him right off his feet. And then I heard nothing more.

"Ben?" I called out tentatively. "Are you there?"

"I think you may consider him de-summoned," said Leck, snickering.

"Oh yeah? Well, guess what, Leck? You can consider yourself

de-summoned *too!*" I strode up to him and gave him a two-fisted punch to the chest. "*Ass!*"

He went flying off into the blackness too, leaving me alone with Torrie.

"Technically, he would be de-compelled," said Torrie, barely controlling his laughter.

I walked over and raised my fist into his face. "Shut up, or I'll de-compell you too before you have a chance to make me a deal I know I shouldn't take."

He lifted an eyebrow. "And you do the de-compelling so well. I like your style, elemental."

I nodded, actually kind of proud of myself. "Yeah, me too. Who'd-a-thought the magic word would be *ass*? I like it."

"I'm quite sure you could use any word you wished, or even no word at all."

"No thanks. I'll keep using *ass*. It seems to fit the situation perfectly."

Torrie wisely said nothing, briefly giving me the illusion that I was in control here.

I mentally slapped myself to bring my brain back to reality. Nothing good could ever come of me forgetting who he was and what he'd done. Even wrapped up in a pretty face and body, he was still evil to the bone. I'd seen his real soul, and it was as ugly as sin.

"So what's your proposal?" I asked. "I need to know Maléna's weak spots. I want to either get a full-on kill-shot on that bitch or figure out some way to incapacitate her so I can at least win this challenge."

"What, may I ask, are the stakes?"

"Head of the council, I think." I decided the less Torrie knew the better, but if the gleam in his eye was any indication, it was motivating for him to think he was going to help me take her down a few notches, so I added, "Essentially the question is whether Maléna answers to elementals, or elementals answer to Maléna."

Torrie nodded. "I can help you. The question is, what will I get in return?"

I laughed. "Before you even go there, I have to tell you that you can keep your demon wiener to yourself. I'm not interested in giving birth to the spawn of the devil, and there is nothing you could give me that would make that happen. I'd kill myself first."

"I'm sorry you find laying with me so distasteful. Your mother didn't seem to share your abhorrence."

I reached my hand out and slapped him hard across the face, sending his head sharply to the side.

"Don't you *ever* talk about my mother again, do you hear me?! One more word of disrespect towards her and I will *rip* your friggin *head* off!" I was shaking with the sudden flare of anger and disgust that took over me. The light in my mind turned a sickly green. Flashbacks of my mother's beaten and bloody body assailed my inner eye. I felt sick to my stomach and wanted to cry with the memory. This beast had done that to her. He was the one who'd ruined that part of my life. Never again would I have a human home to go back to.

Torrie stood back straight, wiping a drop of blood from his lip, nothing but a blank expression on his face. "As you wish, elemental," he said in a controlled voice.

"Let's get one thing straight, demon. We are not friends, got it? You might help me today, but that means nothing to me. Nothing at all. I'm just as happy sending you back like I did with Leck and Ben."

"Then why should I help you at all?"

"I don't know. Maybe to get back at your old girlfriend. I hear she dissed you pretty hard."

Torrie took a deep breath, flaring his nostrils, but saying nothing.

"You've got five seconds before I de-compell your sorry ass out of my head."

"You can incapacitate Maléna, or any silver elf for that matter, by pulling her Wind away from her."

My anger abated just a little at his offer of help. "How can I do that? I don't command Wind."

"All of the elements are connected. You might not command it, but you can influence it. It takes practice, but I'm confident you could do it. With the right training."

"Who could train me with that?"

Torrie raised an eyebrow. "Are you sure you don't already know the answer to that question?"

I sighed. "It's Ben, isn't it?"

He nodded once.

"Fine. Thank you. You can go now."

I lifted up my hands to shove him away from me, but he stepped back out of my reach.

I frowned. "Get back here. It's time for you to go."

"But I haven't had my chance to ask you for what I want. We had a deal."

"I already told you to keep your demon parts away from me," I said, stepping towards him again.

"Just promise me ... that if you ever have the chance in the future, that you will speak the words to send me back to my home."

"What? That makes no sense at all."

"It doesn't now but perhaps someday in the future it will. Promise me."

I thought about what he was asking. His home was in the Underworld, and I had no problem sending him back there at all. It seemed like a no-risk proposition to me. "Fine. If I ever have the chance, I'll be happy to send you back home where you belong."

He smiled, a little too happily for my comfort, but what was done was done; there was no going back now.

"Speaking of going back home," I said, smiling maliciously, "see you later ... *ass!*" I shoved him hard in the chest, sending him back into the darkness. His form disappeared in the blink of an eye.

I listened for a moment, hearing no voices or breathing other than my own, turning around in a circle to make sure I was truly alone. My feet made scraping sounds on the ground that echoed out into the empty space.

"What now?" I said loudly. "Do I call myself an ass?" I laughed, deciding that even if it wasn't necessary, it might still be fun to do it that way. I spread my arms out wide, dropped my head back, and yelled, "Send me back to my bed, *ass!*"

# Chapter Eighteen

I WOKE UP WITH A headache and butterflies in my stomach. *Will Ben remember he was my worst nightmare?* I wasn't ready to know the answer to that question. I just wanted to figure out the more basic things in life first. Like where I was going to get some breakfast.

I slowly got out of bed, and within seconds of my feet hitting the floor I had to duck, barely surviving a midair collision with a baby pixie who appeared out of nowhere and almost splatted into my face.

"Holy shit, Baby Bee! Watch out!" I yelled, following his progress across the room and then looking anxiously towards the door for his parents.

Abby came flying in after him. "Sorry, Jayne. He's on a tear right now. I caught him in the honey." She had a frantic look on her face as she flew by me, heading to the spot on the wall where he'd disappeared into some branches coming out of the stone.

I smiled, silently cheering him on. Little fucker was hiding from his mother. I wondered if honey was like pixie crack or something. It probably was. And with all that sweetness in his tiny body, there was no telling the mischief Willy could get into.

I hurriedly opened my dresser, pulling out clothes and a towel so I could hightail it to the shower before he made another appearance. I couldn't handle another game of spider nakies right now. I looked up, searching the walls of the room, realizing I had no idea where my shower even was. *Do I not have a bathroom in this place?* That made me really have to pee, knowing I couldn't right now. My eyes were nearly crossing with the instant, overpowering need.

"Tim!" I yelled out towards the adjoining room.

"Yes, my liege?!" he yelled in his best movie announcer voice, flying into the room. "Back to the land of the living, I see. Nice of you to join us. Breakfast is already over, you know." He paused and looked at me suspiciously. "What's wrong with you?" He was back to using his normal voice. "You look like you're about to pass out." He lifted up his arms and sniffed his pits. "Do I smell?"

"No, stupid, I have to pee! Where's the damn bathroom?"

He grinned, pointing to the corner of my room. "Oh, it's right over there. Phew, for a second there I thought I'd lost some of my charm. You know ... the stuff that oozes out of my every pore?"

I turned and tiptoed in the general direction he'd pointed to, my bladder spasming, wondering how long I had before I lost it all on the floor. "Where's the door? I can't see anything but tree bark!"

"Follow me. We can chat in the potty like old times." He flew past me and stopped by a break in the trees that I only noticed once I was close. "Just put your hand in there and grab the door handle."

I did as he instructed, finding a metal thing behind some leaves. I pulled and a whole section of the treed wall separated itself from the rest of the greenery and swung open. I stepped into a cozy bathroom, complete with a toilet, a claw-foot tub, a white pedestal sink, and a large, tiled shower.

I didn't waste any time, dropping my clothes and towel on the floor to run over to the toilet that was separated from the main part of the room by a short half-wall. Tim flew over to the tub and sat on the faucets, facing me. I could just barely see him as I peered over the edge of the divider, relieved I'd made it before wetting my pants.

"Wow. Talk about Niagara Falls," said Tim, snorting.

"Shut up. I've been holding it for like twenty-four hours or something." I wiped the sweat off my upper lip. "Phew, that was a close one."

"Well, you missed all the fun. I was tempted to invite Spike into your room to give you one of those sleeping beauty kisses, but Willy kept assuring me you were breathing, so I didn't bother."

"You let Willy hang out near my nose?"

"What can I say? The kid is obsessed with your nostrils." Tim shrugged. "It keeps him out of trouble, anyway."

I shook my head, getting ready to stand up and strip for the shower. "How him hanging out in my nostrils is considered staying out of trouble, I'll never know." I wiggled my nose around a little, trying to figure out if anything was amiss. I wouldn't put it past him to stick things up in there, but everything felt normal. "Are you staying in here? I have to take a shower. I reek almost as bad as you do." I stood and stripped my clothes off, walking carefully on the shiny, slippery floor over to the glass shower door so I could turn the water on.

Tim was back to sniffing himself again. "Seriously? I can't smell anything. Stupid pollen has my nose all messed up."

I laughed, stepping under the deliciously refreshing warm water. "You're allergic to pollen? And you're a pixie? Now, that's funny."

"No, I'm not allergic, *Lellamental*. I just get too much in there sometimes, and then all I can smell is pollen. Everything else just kind of fades out when that happens."

"Sounds like an allergy to me," I said, putting shampoo in my hair and scrubbing it around.

"It's not an ..." Tim shook his head. "Why am I arguing with you? You have no idea what you're talking about, amateur elemental that you are. Besides, we have gossip to get to, so let's drop the pollen talk and get down to the juicy stuff."

"What kind of gossip?"

"Oh, I don't know ... like the gossip about Maléna getting ready to fry your butt. And the gossip about Tony. Or maybe the gossip about Chase possibly coming around..."

"What?!" I flicked my head so fast in Tim's direction I threw soap in my eyes. "Dammit! Ouch, that hurts." I rinsed my face while I continued, making me sound like a talking fish. "Chase is coming?"

Tim laughed. "Out of all that, the most important piece of information was about Chase? Man, you need to get your priorities straight."

"But it's *Chase!*" - my guardian angel who'd masqueraded as my daemon long enough for me to totally fall for him. "What could possibly be more important than him coming back?"

"I guess you didn't hear the part about Maléna getting ready to end your life."

"I heard that. I'm not so worried about her."

Tim flew over to the glass, making sure to stay out of the range of my splashing as I rinsed my hair. "Did Baby Bee stick something up your nose? A stupid spell or something? Because if you aren't deathly afraid of her, you're either fooling yourself or under the influence of some bad juju."

"I got some inside info on her ass. I'm gonna blow her away. Like, literally." I smiled, just thinking about it.

"Where'd you get that?" asked Tim, now pushing his nose and hands up against the glass.

I took a soapy finger and pressed it up to his face, wishing I could actually reach his schnoz through the barrier. "It's a secret."

"How many times do I have to tell you that the roommate code forbids secrets?" He flew around so the glass wasn't separating us anymore, risking getting hit with heavy drops of water in favor of being able to give me his sternest look possible. "Tell me everything and leave nothing out."

I shut off the shower, finished with conditioning my hair and soaping myself down. My hairy legs would have to wait until later. I was too hungry to take the time to shave right now. "I fell asleep last night, and some weird shit happened. I ended up talking to Leck and Ben and Torrie." I said the last name when my face was in the towel, muffling it on purpose.

"Say what? Say *who*? Did I just hear you say ...? *No.* No, I did not. I'm *sure* I didn't. Repeat that last one, would you? The pollen has apparently reached my gray matter. I think I could possibly need brain surgery later."

I pulled the towel away from my face and walked into the bedroom, carrying my clothes with me and patting and squeezing my hair as I went. "I said, that I talked to them and they told me some stuff."

"Them *who?!* Stop playing games, Jayne, or I'll get Willy in here to do a nostrilectomy on you."

I laughed. "Is that even a real procedure? Is he qualified for that?"

Tim came flying over and hovered right in front of my face.

"Five seconds. That's all you get. Five ... four ... three ... two ... "

"Alright, already! I'll tell you." I pulled my underwear and jeans on. "I talked to Torrie the demon, okay? He told me how to take advantage of Maléna's weaknesses, so we're all good."

Tim started gasping like a fish out of water. Then he zig-zagged around the room a few times before freezing above my bed and letting himself plummet down to land on his back. He laid there, his arms and legs spread out around him, gagging.

I put my bra on and threw my tunic over my head as I waited for Tim to finish his histrionics. He was giving it his all, that was for sure. I watched him feign some seizures before deciding to explain some more.

"It wasn't my fault; it was a total accident. I compelled him into my dream and he showed up. And that's not the worst part, Tim."

Tim's seizures stopped and he turned his head towards me weakly. "Please tell me you're joking."

"No, unfortunately, I'm not. The worst part of all of it was that he came into my dream in Ben's body. And so did Leck."

Tim threw his arm over his eyes. "Woe is me! I'm roommates with the dumbest elemental to ever walk the Here and Now. *Oh, the humiliation! Oh, the pain!*"

I threw my towel over him.

"And the last part of my story is that Ben came when I called him and saw those two assbags wearing his skin. I'm pretty sure he wants a divorce now."

The towel moved around as Tim desperately tried to free himself from beneath it. I couldn't hear what he was saying, but he sounded cranky.

"I can't hear you, dope. But anyway, after I sent Leck and Ben out, Torrie and I made a deal; and he gave me the kill-shot on Maléna ... or the put her out of my way shot ... so all's well that ends well." I sat on the bed fully dressed, ready to brush my hair out, pulling the towel off Tim so he could scold me properly.

He stood there, sunk down into the covers of my bed, his hair sticking out all over and his clothing askew. His mouth was opening and closing, but no words were coming out.

"What's the matter? Buggane got your tongue?" I smiled for a second until I realized that I had just used the demon's own words. My grin disappeared to be replaced with a grimace of misgiving. *Holy shit, I hope none of his evil rubbed off on me in there.*

"Okay, okay," said Tim, holding his hands out in a calming gesture, "let's just try to get a handle on what happened in here last night ... at the scene of the crime." He clasped his hands together and put them up to his chin. "So you were sleeping and somehow managed to pull other fae and a demon into your dream is that right?"

I nodded my head, drawing the brush through my hair and squeezing the extra water out onto the towel. "Yep."

"And Ben realized that you consider him your worst nightmare? Like, worse than Torrie?" Tim started tapping his clasped hands on his mouth.

"I'm not sure if I consider him worse than Torrie, necessarily, but that's the basic idea, yeah."

His hands froze out in front of him. "And you made a deal with the demon? You actually *did* that?"

"Well, kind of." I was feeling nervous all over again. "He offered me help in exchange for a promise."

Tim dropped to his knees, his hands held out in prayer now, looking up at the ceiling. "I tried, Great Spirit. I tried. But she keeps putting her head in her butt, and there's nothing I can do to stop her, apparently. I don't know what to do! Please give me your guidance!"

I leaned over and pushed him onto his side.

He fell stiffly, not moving his hands or changing his pleading expression.

"Shut up. It's not that bad."

He laid there, his hands still clasped together, but now he was looking at me. "What did you promise? Please tell me it wasn't your first-born."

I frowned, trying to remember exactly what I'd said.

"What? Tell me!" he demanded, his hands coming unclasped and dropping to the bed next to him as he stared at me, the anticipation of hearing really bad news written all over his face.

"I will. I just want to remember it right. I think I said that I'd send him back to where he belongs one day when he asks me to."

"Where he belongs? Did you specifically say *belongs* and not the *Underworld*?"

"Maybe," I said meekly, now realizing I probably should have used a better, more specific word.

Tim stood and straightened his hair and clothes out, tugging the bottom of his tunic down to pull out the wrinkles. "All I have to say is, you've got a lot of nerve calling Baby Bee a spaz after that stunt."

"I never called him a spaz."

"Well, you thought it."

"That's probably true," I admitted. "But what the hell else was I supposed to do? I'm fighting Maléna someday, and I need to know what to do to take her down."

"First, you are fighting Maléna *tomorrow*, in fact; that's one of the bits of good news I had planned to share with you before you blew me out of the water with your doomsday prophecy. And second, I hope the information he gave you is, like, sea-scroll-worthy, because you traded it for something I have a very sick feeling you're going to regret."

"He told me that to take her out I had to take her Wind from her. Without it, I guess she's nothing."

"Did he perchance tell you how to do this?"

"No. He said Ben would teach me."

Tim started laughing hysterically, maniacally even, bending over and holding his stomach as he stumbled around the top of bed.

"Shut up," I said, frowning at him. I felt monumentally stupid, and he was making it worse with every second.

"I can't ... I can't ..." He was holding one arm out to the side, in a stop-gesture.

"Laugh all you want, twerp. I'm going to talk to Ben about it."

"Wait! No!" he yelled, trying to fly after me. But his laughter made it impossible for him to go straight. He ran into one of the trees coming out of the ceiling and had to grab onto a leaf to keep from falling. He dangled in front of me, up above my head a little. "Don't leave. I have too much to tell you. And the Ben thing ... we need to talk before you go."

I crossed my arms over my chest. "So talk. You have five seconds. Five ... four ... three ..."

He let go of the leaf and hovered in front of my face, shaking a finger at me. "No fair using the parental counting technique on me, Jayne. You're not the parent."

"Neither are you, but you used it."

"Some might argue with you on that, but let's move on. Fact

is, right now you might want to avoid Ben. Seems he came out of his little trip into your dream in a bit of a mood. Now I know why. And second, we need to talk about the Maléna thing and your training. And last, we need to talk about what Tony has found. And his little, er, issue."

I dropped my arms to my sides. "Wow. That's a lot of shit to discuss when I'm this hungry."

"Just wait a second, and I'll be right back." He had flown towards the door, but came back to my face again. "Promise you won't leave or make a deal with a demon or go to sleep or put anyone in a coma until I return."

I smiled. "You've got five minutes."

"Wench!" he yelled, flying out of the room.

"Make that *two* minutes!" I shouted out after him.

I walked over and stood in front of the mirror to finish with my hair. I was using the damp towel to fluff it out a little, hoping I could get it somewhat dry before putting it in a ponytail when I heard a giggling from the wall near the bathroom door.

I sighed. "Come on out, Willy. Your dad's gone."

The little bug flew over to join me at the mirror, bumping into it before falling down to the dresser where he landed on his butt. "Where'd Papa go?" he said, smiling brightly up at me.

"He went to get me some food, I think."

"Your nose is pretty inside."

"Thanks. I think. But you really shouldn't go in there."

"Why?"

"Because it's my *nose*. And it's ... dirty."

"Why?"

"Because all noses are dirty."

"Why?

"Because we breathe shit in all day with them, I don't know."

"Why?"

I leaned down until I was just an inch or two away from him. "Because if we don't, we will die and turn all stiff and then our bodies will explode and our guts will come out everywhere and stink like dead, rotten animals."

He looked up at me sweetly and said, "But why?"

"Jayne!" gasped Abby from behind me. "What are you saying to my child?!" She buzzed around my face and swept Willy up into her arms. "Come on, Lovebug, Momma needs to get you to the garden." She frowned at me harshly as she zoomed past with Willy struggling in her arms.

"Don't wanna go! Wanna stay here and talk about the guts! Wanna talk about the *guts!* Bad, mommy! *Bad!*"

It was the last I heard as they left the room. Tim passed her in the doorway, not stopping for an explanation, but continuing his journey over to me flying backwards.

"What was that all about?"

"Uhhh ... nothin'."

Tim faced me. "Corrupting the child again, are we?"

"I guess."

"Nicely done," said Tim, grinning. "Abby's too uptight. Poor kid needs a little distraction now and again."

I grinned back, glad I wasn't in trouble with him too. "I'm not sure your wife agrees with you."

"Meh. She'll come around. And if she doesn't, well, I'll send her to a pixie colony."

"Tim!" I yelled, barking out a laugh. "How can you say that? I hope you're not serious."

"Of course I'm not serious, gimme a break. I could sure *try* to do that, but believe me ... Abby's stubborn. She'd refuse to go."

"Well, I hope so. This isn't the sixteenth century, you know."

"Oh, that it were ..." he said, getting a faraway look in his eyes.

I poked him to bring him back to the present. "Did you get me some breakfast? I'm dying here."

"Yeah. Netter will be here soon. In the meantime, I've got to fill you in on the latest and greatest. Which do you want first? Chase? Tony? Ben? Pick your bad news."

"All of it's bad?" I asked, feeling sorry for myself again, wondering when it was going to be a list of good news to choose from.

"Yep. Pretty much."

"Tony, then. If he's in trouble, I need to help him first."

"Okay. Well. Tony is a Gray-walker, right? So he's walking in the Gray while you were playing sleeping baby-pixie-in-the-nostril girl, and he stumbles across this group of Underworld creatures wandering around in there. And you know Tony, not being the most muscular of fae, he just ... you know ... did the best he could with what he had."

I slammed the brush down on the dresser. "What?! What happened?!" I was ready to grab Tim and squeeze the juice out of him.

He must have seen the pixie-squeezing gleam in my eye because he flew out of my reach. "He's okay, he's not dead. But he's in recovery, and he wants to talk to you."

I ran over to my side table and grabbed Blackie, strapping it onto my thigh as I walked to the door, stopping only long enough to tie the bottom strings around my leg.

"Wait! I'm not done!" yelled Tim.

"Just talk while we run."

"But you haven't eaten!" he shouted, following me out into the sitting area.

Netter came into the room through the main door, wheeling a cart with some dishes on it.

"Hey, Netter. What's up?" I said, running over to the cart and grabbing food off the plates, shoving it into my mouth.

The brownie stared at me in open-mouthed fascination.

"Forry. I gotta go mow. My fweind's fick." I took two rolls and pushed them into my pant pockets and rolled up two slices of meat to eat on the way. I swallowed so I could say goodbye. "I'll get you some tokens later, okay? Tony's in the hospital."

"Is there anything else I can do?" he asked, waving his hand over the mess I'd just made. I knew that meant soon it would be all cleaned up with his brownie magic.

"Maybe later. Sorry ... gotta go!" I grabbed the door and yanked it open. Becky was standing out in the hall with her hand up like she was about to knock. Finn was standing behind her.

I grabbed her tunic and pulled her along. "Come on. I'm going to see Tony."

"That's what I came to tell you. He's been moved. To his room."

I stopped. "Oh, shit. I have no idea where his room is."

"Follow us," she said brightly, going in the opposite direction as I'd been headed.

I took her good mood as a positive sign, even though she would probably be smiling the same way if Tony'd been turned into a frog.

# Chapter Nineteen

"IS TONY BETTER?" I ASKED as we strode down the hall.

"Yes. Much," she said, a little too brightly for my comfort.

"What the hell happened?"

"Didn't Tim tell you?" Finn asked. "I'd-a-thought that'd be the first thing you heard when you finally woke up."

"He did. He tried, actually, but I had news too, so it all got kind of messed up."

"What's your news?" asked Becky.

"I'll tell you later." I wasn't anxious about sharing another story of monumental screw-up, and if Tim's reaction was any judge, that's what it was. I needed to find out about Tony first, anyway. Everything else could wait.

We stopped at a door that appeared on the wall, and Becky pushed it open, tapping on the wood as she went. I pushed past her to get to Tony's bed.

He was covered with a quilt, only his pale face showing. His eyes were closed, and for a moment, I thought he was dead.

"Tony!" I screamed, running over to his bedside, dropping on my knees to the stone floor, my chest instantly starting to ache.

His eyes opened slowly and looked at me. "Hey, Jayne," he

said in slightly slurred speech. "Where'd you come from?"

"What the hell happened to you?" I asked in a more normal tone of voice, a little less concerned now that he was going to die in the next two minutes. But he didn't look good at all.

"I got jumped in the Gray, I guess. I don't remember all of it."

I looked around at my friends. "Who in the hell is responsible for this? Who was supposed to have his back?" I looked at Tony again. "Was it Gregale? Was he supposed to be there?"

Tony shook his head slightly. "No. I was alone. No one was supposed to be there."

"My ass," I said, standing. "Someone go get Gregale for me, please. I have a few things to say to him."

"Are you sure you want to do that, Jayne?" asked Becky, giving me a nervous smile.

"Yes, Becky. I am. Now either you pop over there and get him, or I'll do it my way. You choose."

She shook her head quickly. "No, I'll go. We don't need you sending the werewolves into a frenzy again." She gave me a scolding look before disappearing into thin air.

"Man, I wish I could do that," said Finn, staring at the space where she'd been standing.

"You can use telepathy with the other green elves. She can't do that." I reminded him.

"Yeah, but still ... nothin's cooler than zippin' 'n zappin' all over the place like them water sprites can do. Plus they get to breathe underwater."

"Awesome. Breathing in fish crap. Sounds nice. You're right," said Tim. "We should all be jealous."

I turned my attention back to Tony, while translating Tim's reaction to the envious green elf. "Tim says they breathe in fish crap, so he's totally jealous too."

Tim blessed me with a pixie fart, impressing me again with his ability to produce them at will.

"Nice," I said, shaking my head.

"Do they do that? For serious?" asked Finn, now looking less excited about the idea of being a water sprite.

"Would you focus, Finn? You're too brave and too much of a good shot to be a wienie water sprite anyway."

He pursed his lips and nodded. "You got that right. Okay. Let's get down to what's happenin' here. Looks like ol' Tony got his butt whooped in the Gray. Is that right, Mister Wrathe?"

Tony nodded his head. "Pretty much."

"Who did it?" I asked, ready to make a plan for their imminent demise.

"I don't know who they were. Just some guys. I guess they were demons, but they looked like regular fae." He closed his eyes, and for a second, and I thought he'd fallen asleep.

"Tony?" I pulled the covers back and pulled one of his arms out so I could hold his hand. It was like ice. "Holy shit, why are you friggin cold?"

"Aftereffects of the Gray. I stayed in too long," he whispered.

I pulled the covers back the rest of the way so I could get in next to him. "Come on, Finn. You get in on the other side. We need to warm him up."

He looked at us with extreme distaste. "Oh, *hell* no, I ain't doin' no cuddlin' with that boy. Huh-uh, no, sir. I ain't gay."

"Fuck, *Finn*, would you shut up about the gay stuff and get in here, already? No one's gonna think you're a homo for helping a friend get warm."

"I will," said Tim, giggling up near the ceiling.

I ignored him, knowing Finn couldn't hear him.

"Says who?" asked Finn, not moving.

"Says me! I'm the boss of the whole compound, in case you haven't heard, so get in here. You're letting all the cold air in."

Finn grumbled, but he complied. I snuggled in close to Tony, turning so I could face him. I tucked his arm in tight to his side and rested my head on his chest. Finn laid down on the other side, facing out. Once we were both in place, I pulled the covers up to our necks, and then reached into The Green to bring its healing energy to my friend. As the green glow crept over us, it began to warm up under the blanket. But Tony's skin remained frigid.

"What the hell, Tones? Why is your skin like this?"

"Gray," was all he said before he closed his eyes again.

The door opened and Tim buzzed to the other side of the room, as far from the door as he could get. I craned my neck sideways to see who it was.

"Well, doesn't that look cozy," said Spike's voice from the doorway. It was soon joined by two female ones.

"I want in!" said Felicia.

"Why didn't we get an invite to the orgy?" said Theresa.

I rolled my eyes, turning my head back to Tony. "It's not an orgy. We're trying to warm Tony up. He's got some Gray in him or something."

My incubus and succubi friends moved to the foot of the bed where I could see them better. Spike still looked goofy-happy, but the girls not so much.

"What?" I asked them. "I don't like the looks on your faces."

"Getting Grayed is not good, Jayne," said Felicia.

"Bad news, sister," said Theresa. Their heads moved in perfect unison, both of them shaking slowly from side-to-side.

"Why? What does it mean? How can we get it out?"

Before they could answer, Spike spoke up. "Is that Finn in there? Hey, dude ... what are you doing under the covers with Tony?" He laughed, knowing exactly what he was doing.

"Shut the hell up, okay! I was ordered to git in here, and I ain't happy about it, alright?"

"Okay, okay, ease up. I just didn't know you swung it like that, is all." Spike winked at me.

"That's it," growled Finn. "I ain't doin' this no more. Come on, girls. Have at it. I'm done with this body-warmin' shee-it."

Theresa and Felicia scampered over, shoving each other out of the way to be the first at Tony's side.

"Move, Felicia!"

"No *you* move, Theresa! I'm going in, not you!"

"Hey!" I yelled, sitting up, bracing myself with my hand behind me on the bed. "Neither of you are coming in here unless you can *help* the situation! I don't want anyone sucking whatever life he has left out of him, do you hear me?"

They both stopped at the edge of the bed opposite me, looking at one another first and then at Tony. "We could help," said Theresa, "but you might not like how we'd do it."

"I have no problem with you cuddling with him to warm him up," I said.

"It wouldn't be just cuddling," said Felicia, the nicer of the two, usually.

I clamped my mouth shut, not sure I wanted to know what she meant.

"You should strongly consider it, Jayne. He's in bad shape," she said, looking sad.

"How do you know he's in bad shape?" I asked weakly, staring at his really pale face. *But the medical fae sent him back to his room, so how bad can he be?*

"We can sense these things. He's got dead spots," said Theresa.

My heart leaped into my throat. "Dead spots?" It sounded worse than awful. I sat up more fully, looking at Spike for confirmation. He wasn't as experienced as his succubi girlfriends, but he had to know something. Spike bit his lip and rolled his eyes to the ceiling. When he started whistling I knew something was up.

"Spike, come on. Stop fucking around."

His eyes left the ceiling and met mine. "Yeah, he's got some dead spots. They're not lying." It sounded like he was ringing Tony's death bell.

"So what's the cure?" I asked, looking from one girl to the other. "A witch's spell? Hot tea with lemon and honey? What?"

Theresa shrugged. "You can cut the dead spots out. Leave them. Or try to heal them over. It's a crap shoot any way you do it."

"A crap shoot? What the hell does *that* mean?"

Felicia explained. "What she means is, that if you leave them, Tony will not be like the Tony you knew anymore. Dead spots on your soul are never good for the personality. And cutting them out ... well, that's painful and dicey at best. It's not a precise magical science and so is prone to errors. Bad errors can be, like, really bad. Like, cutting out good parts instead of bad parts. So your best bet is to try and heal them; but to do that, you need us to get busy."

"Get busy as in ... "

"She means like *get busy*, get busy," said Spike. "Like serious sexy time. Energy sucking and other things, if you catch my drift."

I laughed in a sick way, feeling totally bereft at the idea of either losing my best friend or seeing him changed in irreparable ways. "So what you're saying is, he needs some sexual healing."

"Yep. Pretty much," said Theresa.

"But we'd be gentle with him," said Felicia. "As gentle as we can be, anyway. We know he's special to you."

"Oh, to be a fae with a dead spot on my soul," said Tim, staring at the twin succubi wistfully.

I really wished I had something to throw at him, but since I didn't, I did the next best thing. "The succubi don't do micro-wieners, Tim, so you're not allowed in the line for sexual healing. Better go see Maggie for what ails you."

He came flying down to buzz my face. "I'll have you know I am *more* than fully endowed in that area, thank you very much! And I'll thank you to not be *talking* about my *junk* in front of all these *children!*"

I laughed, ducking his slappy little hands. "Man, you are so not fun now that you've become a father."

He screeched something unintelligible as he flew out the door.

"What'd he say?" asked Finn, watching him go with an expression of awe on his face.

"He denied having a tiny pixie dong."

"Oh, shee-it, why'd I even ask?" he said, hanging his head and shaking it slowly.

"Anyway, back to business," said Felicia. "Do you want our help or not?"

I looked down at Tony who appeared to be sleeping. "I think I'd better ask him first." I knew my best friend was still pretty innocent where girls were concerned, and this felt a little too close to virgin sacrifice for me to make that decision so easily. I looked back up at my friends. "Could you guys give me a minute alone with him?"

"Sure, no problem," said Felicia, pushing her twin towards the door. Theresa just stared at Tony, a hungry look in her eye.

I sat cross-legged and pulled his hands into mine while they filed out of the room. When they were gone and the door was closed, I jerked on his hands a couple times to wake him up. I let The Green go back into the Earth so it would be just the two of us.

His eyes opened.

"Hey," I said, "listen ... I have to ask you a question, and it's totally important. It's not a sick joke, but it's going to sound like one, okay?"

"Sure. Go ahead." His lids slid shut again.

I jerked on his hand. "No, open your eyes. You have to look at me when I ask you."

He smiled and opened his eyes again slowly. "You look like you're about to propose." He tried to laugh, but he didn't have the energy. His smile slipped away when I didn't laugh with him.

"I just found out that your soul has spots on it or something from whatever happened in the Gray. The twins say they can help you out ... but I think it's going to mean losing your virginity. And I really hope I can convince you to say yes ... that you'll let them do it, because I love you so much, and I can't stand the idea of you not being your perfect Tony self." I tried to keep my tone even, but I was ready to cry and my voice was getting more and more strained with every word.

He winced, and I quickly realized it was because I was squeezing the crap out of his hands.

"Oh, shit, sorry." I smiled weakly, loosening my grip. "I'm freaking out. I'm so sorry I have to ask you to do this."

Tony pulled one of his hands away and patted me on the knee, leaving it to rest there when he was done trying to make me feel better. Then he smiled. "So let me get this straight ... you're telling me that I have to lose my virginity to the two most beautiful, sexy girls in this entire compound, in order to save my soul ... and you think I'm going to be upset about that?"

It took me a second to compute what he was saying. "Uhhh, yeah, I guess I was. I thought maybe you were saving yourself for someone special or something."

He closed he eyes again, but the smile never left his face. "Bring on the healing."

I shoved his hands away from me, smiling so hard it almost cramped my face. "You dog. You guys are all the same, you know that?"

He laughed. "What can I say? I may be a little inexperienced, but I'm not blind, you know."

I stood. "Fine. I'll go get your honeys. But just don't come crying to me if they, you know, do something wrong or whatever."

He turned his head to look at me. "I'm pretty sure they're experts at what they do. I don't think I'm going to be complaining."

I walked over and grabbed the door handle. My emotions were so tied up right now, I didn't know what to say, so I said nothing for a moment. But then I changed my mind and ran back to his bed, leaning down to give him a quick kiss on the cheek. "Just remember, no matter how much they love you, they'll never love you as much as I do." I had to catch the tears before they could fall, refusing to make him feel bad about the choice he had to make but also wanted to make.

"I know. And same for you. No matter how many angels you fall for or how many deals you make with the devil, I'll always be the one who loves you most."

I was getting ready to stand again, but I froze. "How did you know about that?"

"I was watching you from the Gray. That's how I got jumped. Torrie was keeping you busy and luring you in, and I tried to stop you but I couldn't reach you in time. I got distracted."

I shook my head. "Fuck me," was all I could think to say. I'd let my guard down with that evil creature and had nearly destroyed my friend's soul.

Tony grabbed my hand before I could leave. "Don't."

"Don't what?!" I nearly shrieked, my tears choking me.

"Don't get upset with yourself like that. It's not your fault."

*"Everything's* my fault. I had no idea..."

"Of course you didn't, silly. That's why you can't get upset about it. There's good news, though. I'm happy it turned out this way. I learned some good things, which I'll tell you later. I'd tell you now, but I have other things on my mind, and I'm getting weaker."

I panicked. Too much shit was going down right now, and I didn't know what needed to happen first - confessions, healings, fights to the death. *Argh!* "Okay, fine. Sexual healing, and then you and I are going to have a looong talk, which may or may not include details about you losing your virginity."

Tony smiled. "Deal. Now, go."

I strode from the room, throwing the door open, at least now feeling resolved about what needed to happen first. "Girls! Batter up! Time to get some healing done!"

They both squealed with delight, clapping their hands as they shoved past me into the room.

I shook my head as I shut the door behind me. "Friggin virginity-stealing cheerleaders."

"Lucky bastard," said Finn, staring at the door.

I punched him in the shoulder. "Yeah. Got his soul shit on by some evil spirits. He's lucky alright."

"I don't know," said Finn, a teasing note in his voice, "I'd consider some tay-ta-tay with some evil spirits if it meant I could ..."

Becky appeared at his side. "If it meant you could what?" she asked innocently.

Finn nearly choked, throwing his hand up to his chest. "Damn, girl!" he burst out. "You nearly gave me a dang heart attack!"

"If it meant you could *what?*" she asked again, looking pointedly at the door.

"If it meant ... uh ... some cute water sprite could come in and do a healin' on me," he said sheepishly.

"Yeah. That's what I thought," she said sassily before turning to me. "Gregale is almost here. I offered to transport him with me, but he declined."

"You can do that?" asked Finn, interrupting her in his enthusiasm. "Oh, man ... " He held out his arms. "Do me. Transport me. Come on, I'm ready."

She smiled evilly. "You won't like it."

"Oh, no. I'm gonna love it, trust me." He was grinning like a fool.

"You sure?" she asked slyly.

"Damn sure. Let's go. Lay it on me, water sprite. I've been wantin' to do this forever."

She shrugged. "Okay. Can't say as I didn't warn you."

I started to interrupt, knowing full-well there was something going on in her tone that Finn was ignoring. But before I could get the words out, she grabbed his hand and they both disappeared.

"What the hell?" said Spike, turning to look all around the hallway.

"Since when has she been able to do that?" I asked.

"I have no idea," he said, coming up behind me to rub my shoulders.

I felt like melting under his firm touch, the muscles in my neck and back losing some of their stress almost instantly.

He leaned in by my ear and breathed in deeply, giving me goosebumps. "Mmmm, I think someone else could use a little incubus healing today."

I shrugged him off and turned around. "Keep your incubus parts to yourself, Spike. I have enough shit to deal with without adding cheating on my partner to the pile."

"It's not cheating, Jayne. You should know that. Especially when you're partnership isn't exactly a love match."

"Listen, Spike ... no one is allowed to be bitter about this situation except me. And maybe Ben. We did it because we had to, not because we wanted to. But that doesn't mean I'm free to just mess around with anyone, you know? And it wouldn't be with you anyway." Images of an angel and another fae flashed into my head, shocking me enough that I immediately brushed them out of my mind and continued with my scolding. "I have to focus on other things and not my love life, okay?"

He put his hands up in surrender. "Okay, okay, geez. Shoot a guy down, why don't you. Shit."

I punched him. "Stop. Seriously. I need your friendship now so you need to quit getting weird on me."

He sighed, putting his arm over my shoulders. "Come on, Jayne. You know me. Friends for life, man." He put up his fist for a bump from mine, which I gave him. "There. Now tell your buddy Spike all your problems." He glanced at the door. "They're gonna be in there for a while, so you might as well."

I looked from the door to him, trying to gauge his reaction to their offer. "You don't seem jealous or anything."

"Why would I be?"

"Well, because I guess I thought they were your girlfriends."

"Nah. Incubi and succubi don't do the girlfriend-boyfriend thing. We just hang out and have fun together."

"Well, how come you're always trying to convince me to be with you, then?"

He smiled. "I'd make an exception for you."

"Shut up, I'm serious."

"So am I." He lost his smile.

I dropped my face into my hands and spoke through my fingers. "Stop now or leave. I'm serious. I cannot take the stress of your flirting."

I looked up two seconds later to berate him some more, but he was gone. All I'd felt just before my hands came off my face was a little fluff of wind on my arms. *Friggin incubus.* I hated that they could run that fast. I was like a turtle in comparison.

I'd thought Spike was over my numerous previous rejections, but seeing his reaction just now made me question that. *Great. All I need to add to my shit pile is a mooning incubus.* I decided I was going to put Spike into a coma the next time I saw him, just because I could. I smiled, imagining him floating around in The Green. Maybe that would finally put him off flirting with me.

I heard footsteps in the hallway and turned to see Gregale making his way towards me, his tunic easily marking him as a member of the gray elf race - the group responsible for strategic planning and analysis of all manner of things. Tony was unofficially a part of their group, even though he was a wrathe.

"Hello, Gregale. Long time no see."

"Yes, Jayne," he said, stopping in front of me and giving me a half-bow. "It has, indeed. So very nice to see you again."

"Thanks for coming. I have some questions I wanted to ask you about Tony."

"I suspected that was why you sent for me."

I tilted my head to the side. "How come you didn't let Becky transport you here with her?"

His hand flew to his heart. "Surely you did not expect that of me! How urgent is this matter?" He looked stricken.

I laughed, confused. "It's important, but I wouldn't say urgent. What's the big deal of teleporting with the water sprite?"

Gregale's hand slowly left his chest. "I forget sometimes that you are so lacking in knowledge of our kind."

"I don't see how that's possible when I am constantly giving you reminders," I said dryly.

"Quite right, Jayne, quite right."

I raised my eyebrows at him, gesturing for him to get to the point.

"Ah, yes, well ... to answer your question, water sprites use their affinity to Water to travel through the humidity in the air. The rest of us fae do not have such a connection. We are essentially dragged through that element by the sprites when they do this accompanied teleportation, and believe me, it is not a pleasant experience. And that's putting it lightly."

"Oh, shit. What happens to the fae who isn't a sprite?" I was wondering what Finn looked like right now.

"Well, I have heard that it is a bit like being drowned. But since I have never experienced it myself, I cannot say for certain."

I laughed.

"What is so funny about being drowned? I do not understand."

When I recovered a few seconds later, I said, "Nothing. Just ... my friends goofing around. Anyway, I wanted to talk to you about Tony. You heard about his accident, I assume?"

"Yes, of course." Gregale folded his hands in front of him.

"I wanted to know why someone wasn't watching his back when he was in the Gray. He got jumped in there, and I feel like he shouldn't have been left so vulnerable."

"You are quite right," said Gregale, his expression revealing nothing.

I sighed in frustration. "Okay, so if I'm right, why did this happen?" I wasn't entirely comfortable with acting like I deserved explanations. I didn't like swinging my weight around as the Mother of the Fae or whatever it was they were calling me these days. But this was my best friend and brother from another mother. Someone had to answer for this, and if no one else was calling that someone out, I was going to.

Gregale cleared his throat. "It is our understanding that another fae was with Tony at the time, but for one reason or another, was not able to assist him in his activities."

My mouth thinned into a line as I ran through the list of possible fae who might have been qualified and able to assist him in the Gray like that.

"Was it a gray elf?"

"No. We cannot be fully present in the Gray like Tony can. Like *any* wrathe can." Gregale didn't have to say anything else. The look on his face said it all.

"The only other wrathe I know in this compound is Leck."

"Precisely."

"And so Leck was supposed to be with him, helping him, is that it?"

"Yes, I do believe that was the case."

I bit my lip. *Is this my fault?*

"What is wrong? You look confused. Perhaps I can enlighten you regarding what concerns you."

I took a big breath in and out, trying to make sense of everything. But it was all too jumbled up with things I just didn't understand or even know the first thing about.

"I think what happened to Tony might be partially my fault," I admitted, feeling the heat of shame crawl up my face.

"What do you mean?" asked Gregale, no judgment or censure in his voice. It made me feel even worse that he didn't instantly agree with me.

"Last night I compelled two people ... or creatures ... into my dream, and then I summoned another one who answered me and came on his own."

Gregale's mouth dropped open, and he stared at me for a few seconds. Then he shook his head briefly and said, "Fascinating. Truly ... I would love to hear about your experience." He nodded his head quickly, encouraging me.

"Well, first I brought in a demon. You know, the one that was at my mom's house."

"Yes, I have heard the story."

"And then I brought Leck in."

"Go on."

"And then I couldn't figure out what to do, so I summoned Ben to join me."

"And did he?"

"Yes."

"And what occurred in this dream of yours? Give me every last detail; it could be important." Gregale pressed his hands together and put his fingers to his lips as he concentrated on my face and words.

I thought back to last night, trying to get all of my facts straight in my head. "Well, I was sleeping, of course. And then all of a sudden Torrie was there. But he was in Ben's body. The only thing that was different was his voice - he still had Torrie's voice."

"What about his eyes? Did you see his eyes?"

"They were Ben's for sure. I remember being surprised about that."

"Okay, continue ..."

I related the entire conversation to Gregale and everything about the event I could remember. It was difficult because I could feel that some of the details had already left my mind. The memory was fuzzier than it had been just an hour ago.

Gregale nodded his head throughout my tale, asking a couple questions and never giving any clue as to how he felt about any of it until I was finally done.

"Well, this is beyond interesting for me. I hope you do not mind that I intend to share all of the details with the other gray elves and perhaps the council as well. We need to analyze this for all of its possible import."

"Do you have to? I mean, share with everyone? I appreciate you wanting to get to the bottom of it, but it's kind of humiliating that everyone was wearing a Ben-suit in there." I looked down at the floor, not wanting to see the frown of disappointment I was sure would be on his face.

Gregale lifted my chin with his finger. His expression held

only pity. "You are so young, elemental. No one expects you to be perfect. And even I, the most rational fae in this compound, do not expect you to fall in love with a boy just because it would be good for the world if you did."

"You don't?"

He shrugged. "Certainly it would be convenient. But that is one thing that none of the gray elves, nor anyone we know for that matter, has never been able to figure out."

"What's that?"

"The whims of love. Only the Great Spirit knows the wherefores of that great mystery. And we have come to the conclusion that if we solved *that* particular puzzle, there would no longer be a need for us to be here. And so, we do not try too hard." He smiled at me.

"So, what you're saying is, if I don't fall in love with Ben and have his children, no one's going to hate me?"

He shrugged. "I cannot speak for the other fae, but as for the gray elves, I would say no. But we do hope that you will continue to act as his life partner and do what you can to heal the rift between our people and move towards peace for all our sakes."

My tentative smile disappeared. "No pressure, eh?"

He patted my shoulder. "Only that which you accept and put on yourself."

"So what's the deal then, Gregale? What's up with this dream of mine and the compelling and summoning crap? I didn't do it on purpose, and I don't particularly want to do it again."

"Well, I will have to discuss this with the others, but I can tell you now that this power you have to compel these creatures is quite unknown in our circles. I will have to consult the records to see if there is a mention of it in the past. The fact that they all appeared as Ben, right down to the eyes is disturbing. You have heard they are the windows to the soul, I assume. But we shall do our best to determine the cause or effect, as it were."

"Do you think it matters that Tony was walking the Gray at the same time?"

Gregale nodded slowly, staring off into space. "Perhaps. It is an interesting hypothesis. You are both very strongly connected. His empath skills are definitely enhanced where you are concerned. I will put that question to the group and see what the others think."

"Okay, and what about the Leck thing? Do you think he sabotaged Tony or that maybe I screwed things up by bringing Leck in?"

"Another astute question," said Gregale, smiling proudly at me. "I should like to have you as a guest speaker at one of our meetings someday." His eyes took on a faraway look, a grin spreading across his face and lighting it up. "Oh, the lively debates *that* would engender!" He looked at me, now back in the present. "Perhaps when all of the current confusion is cleared up, we could look forward to this?"

"Perhaps," I said, not sure I wanted to be standing in front of a roomful of superbrains who would probably make me feel like a complete imbecile inside of five minutes.

"I will share the wonderful news. And now, I bid you goodbye. I must return to the meeting I left when I was summoned here by your water sprite friend." He bowed once more and turned to leave.

"Wait! But what about Tony?"

"Where is he now?" asked Gregale, hesitating, looking back at me.

"In his room. With the succubi girls."

Gregale grinned. "There is nothing for me to do. He is in good hands. Goodbye, Jayne!" He strode down the hall, quickly moving out of sight.

"Dammit," I said, out into the hall. "What am I supposed to do now?"

"Wanna play spiker nakies?" came a little voice from over my shoulder.

I jumped about a foot in the air, grabbing my chest when I landed. "Shit on a friggin *stick*, Willy! You almost gave me another heart attack!" I turned to face him. He was bouncing around in the air near my face. "You really need to stop sneaking up on me."

"But I like to 'neak up," he said, pouting, looking like he was going to cry.

I held out my hand for him to sit in. "Feel like going for a walk with me?" I asked, trying to cheer him up. I seriously did not like making babies pout.

"Yes!" he said, flying down to my hand and jumping up and down on it. "Take a walk! Take a walk and shit on a *stick!*"

I laughed. "Do not tell your mom that word."

"Stick, stick, stick!" he said, grinning up at me.

I put my finger to my lips. "Shhhhh. Stick is a baaaaad word."

Willy jumped up off my hand and flew out in front of me as I walked down the hallway. "Stick, stick, sticky, stick. I love stick, sticky, stick!"

I felt proud of myself. *I may be a totally inept elemental, but I'm great with kids.*

"Shit on a stick. Sticky stick. Shitty sticky sticky shit!" came the little voice in front of me.

*Or not.*

I sighed, imagining the Infinity Meadow in my mind so the

## Clash of the Otherworlds: Book One

door to it would appear for me.  *Time to go talk to some more creatures from the Otherworlds.*

# Chapter Twenty

I REACHED THE MEADOW AND sat under my mother's tree, even though it was much colder there, being out of the sun in the deep shade. I pulled my knees to my chest and rested my chin on them, wrapping my arms around my legs. Willy buzzed around my head for a while and then disappeared into the last of the flowers that were still hanging in there. I quickly lost sight of him.

I had just started to mull over the recent events in my mind when Shayla appeared in front of me, still far enough away that she was out of the shade of the tree and in the full sun. I picked my head up and admired her wings as she walked over. They were big, almost as huge as Chase's had been. Hers were not quite as bright though, if I remembered correctly. It made me sad to think of him, because this was one of those times that I really could have used his strong, steady presence.

"Hello, once again," she said as she approached.

I let my legs go and crossed them, dropping my hands into my lap. "Hi. What's up?" I snapped a nearby piece of grass off and wrapped it distractedly around my finger.

Shayla lifted an eyebrow, sitting down across from me as her wings slowly disappeared. "The sky. The stars. The clouds.

Numerous things."

"Ha, ha. Where's Garrett?"

She shrugged. "Who's to know? I am not his keeper."

"I am here," came a voice from behind the tree. A split-second later he was standing next to Shayla, and she had her dragon fang out and in her fist, pointed at his groin.

He quickly moved his hands to cover his tender parts. "Be careful with that thing! I am not immune to its charms here!"

"Exactly. Keep that in mind before you decide to use your vampire speed near me again."

Garrett sighed. "Shayla, you know I would never hurt you."

She snorted. "No, I do *not* know that. So I will repeat myself once more: guard your speed in my presence, lest you feel the sting of dragon fire against your manly parts."

Garrett looked at me. "She always was one to go for the ... throat."

I smiled, proud of my ancestor's fierceness. "You're not going to get any pity from me, Garrett. I'd sting you too if you snuck up on me like that."

"What brings you to the meadow?" asked Shayla, ignoring Garrett and putting her weapon back into the sheath on her leg. "You seem distressed."

"I am. All kinds of shit has gone down since I saw you last. I'm not even sure where to start."

"What is most distressing?" asked Garrett. "That, for me, is the best way to prioritize, worst to least."

"Well, I guess the worst part used to be that my best friend had dead parts on his soul from being jumped in the Gray; but now since he's being healed by a couple of cheerleader succubi, my biggest and most distressing problem is the fact that I had a dream last night that I pulled a bunch of fae into, and I don't know how I did it."

"A Dream Walker," said Shayla in a reverent voice.

"Don't be too hasty," said Garrett. "It is not the only explanation."

"She wasn't in the Gray, you know that," she said angrily at him.

Garrett paused for a moment and then admitted, "Yes, that is true. I would have sensed her there the second she arrived."

"Is that where you guys hang out?" I asked.

"It seems to be a place we can get into and out of from here quite easily," answered Garrett. "We just can't continue on to the other sides of it. That way appears to be closed to us right now."

Shayla nodded but said nothing.

I felt a little guilty that I had a hand in them being trapped on this side of the Gray, but before I could apologize, Garrett continued.

"Who was in this dream with you? And do you know how they got there?"

"Well, first it was a demon named Torrie. He said I compelled him in. And while I was doing that, my friend Tony was in the Gray, and he got jumped in there by some demons or something. He said they looked like regular fae but were from the Underworld. That's what he thought, anyway."

"Anyone else?" asked Shayla, her hand resting on the butt of her weapon.

"A wrathe named Leck was compelled in too; and he was with Tony in the Gray, supposedly watching his back. I'm not sure if Tony got jumped before or after Leck got compelled into the dream."

"What difference does it make?" asked Garrett.

"Well, if he was doing his job for Tony, and I screwed it up, then I won't kill him. But if he sold Tony out to those demons, well, I will do what I have to do."

"You will punish him for his infidelities towards your friend." This came from Shayla but was clearly meant for Garrett. She was shooting daggers at him.

"Oh, *do* give it a *rest!*" said Garrett, clearly frustrated. "How many times do we have to rehash this? I did *not* do anything disloyal to you *or* your friends!"

"Denial? That's your best defense?" Shayla snorted. "I should have guessed. Pitiful." She shook her head.

"Hey, lovebirds!" I said, getting frustrated. "I appreciate that you have a history, but right now, I'm not all that interested. Some bad shit is happening, and I really need your help with answers. No one seems to know what exactly is going on with these demons walking around in the Gray."

"Right," said Garrett, smoothing down the front of his tunic, visibly collecting himself. "So, disregarding for the moment this issue of whether this Leck has been disloyal or not, let us discuss the other problems that concern you. I assume it would also include the question of how you managed to do this feat, pulling demons into your dream?"

"Yes. Definitely."

"And what the demons did to your friend?" added Shayla.

"Yes. Or what the heck they're even doing at all. I know it's something really bad."

"On that, I believe we all can agree," said Garrett, looking over and receiving a nod of assent from Shayla.

"How come you think it's bad too, when you yourself come

from the Underworld?" I asked Garrett. It was as if he were talking bad about his own people, which seemed weird. I didn't get the vibe that he was faking it either.

"I may be an inhabitant of that realm, but that doesn't mean I agree with others' attitudes about where they have a right to be and what they have a right to take for themselves."

"What exactly do you not agree with?" asked Shayla. There was less challenge to her statement this time, as if she was as curious as I was.

"I guess you could say that the biggest point of contention amongst those of the Underworld is our relegation to that realm without access to the Here and Now, and more particularly, to the humans."

"Access as in ... what?" I was totally confused.

"Well, as you know - or perhaps you do not - the creatures of the Underworld, regardless of what race they were a part of in the Here and Now, have a thirst for human energy. It is quite potent, that energy, and it creates a need in us that is nearly impossible to ignore. When you have lived with lack - complete lack, as we are wont to do in the Underworld - the draw of this energy can be maddening. All demons crave it, and it is part of our punishment to crave that which we cannot have."

"Wow. I wonder how stressed humans would be if they knew there was a whole realm of demons wanting to get out and suck out their souls." I shivered at the thought of a legion of Torries coming after me and all my friends back at school. There were a few teachers and a Vice Principal I wouldn't mind feeding to them, but for the most part, no one I used to know as a human deserved that kind of awfulness. Maybe Brad Powers, but that was it. *Oh, and Samantha, too.*

"Let us just say what the humans do not know cannot hurt them," he said, smiling humorlessly. "Regardless, some demons, having grown quite powerful using the negative energy from the fae world which they *do* have limited access to, made the decision to actively seek a way to breach the space between the realms in order to get back to the Here and Now on a more permanent basis. Once here, it is clear they intend to take the humans and their energy for their own selfish purposes."

"They are breaching the Gray," said Shayla, matter-of-factly.

"Yes. They apparently have caused a tear or tears in the veil, and are making their way here, albeit in smaller numbers than they are planning to eventually bring over."

"I don't get it," I said. "You yourself crave this energy but you don't agree with coming over here and taking it?"

"Yes. You see, I have other, stronger motivating forces that help me balance out those needs."

"Like what?" I asked, noticing him trying not to look at Shayla.

"My punishment was to live with lack so that I might earn the right to come back to the Here and Now once more and prove myself worthy of the Overworld. To *have*, as it were. If I give in to my baser instincts, I will not earn my place here. I will not earn the right to have anything. And I really, truly want the opportunity to prove myself again." It was clear that his last statement was for Shayla. "I do not agree with changing the Order of Things and forcing my way into the Here and Now to take whatever I want. I believe that just beyond chaos lies nothing - a void. And that would be worse than anything I have experienced in the Underworld."

Shayla was refusing to acknowledge his statement, but I could see she wasn't unaffected. Her throat moved up and down as she swallowed several times in quick succession. She had to clear her throat before she spoke again.

"We in the Overworld do not feed off the humans. We share our light with them, but have only done it in times of great need. Many years ago, we stopped doing so, and agreed after certain events to remain apart from the human and fae worlds. The fae have taken over our positions, offering their light to the humans when necessary."

"Why would you do that?" I asked, flabbergasted to find that the angels had abandoned us. "Humans and fae need you guys."

She shrugged. "That may or may not be so. But it was not our decision to argue. The fae did what they felt was best at the time, and we continued our existence while respecting their wishes. It appears as if the Underworld did not accept their decision so easily."

"You could say that," said Garrett, sounding bitter.

"So what's this big decision?" I asked. "I'm sorry to be so dense, but none of this is making any sense to me."

Shayla looked at Garrett. "Should we tell her?"

"I do not know that it is our place."

"Um, hello? I'm sitting right here."

"Perhaps it is not our place, but she is their Mother. I cannot believe that she does not have the authority to weigh in on any future decisions they might make."

"That is true. But again, I ask if it is our place to share. Perhaps there are others in your realm who might make that decision."

"Hey!" I yelled, getting up. "I'm standing right here! Stop talking about all this mysterious shit like I'm not right in front of you!" I hated that I felt like a child just then.

Shayla looked at me. "Forgive us for wanting to protect you."

"Oh, shut up," I said, glaring at her, refusing to fall victim to her guilt trip.

That earned me some raised eyebrows, but I continued. "I've been stumbling around in the dark since I got here a few months ago as a human, and let me tell you, I'm friggin tired of it. *Sick* and tired of it. Do you know how much better I could get along with people if I knew what the hell was up? I could stop making so damn many mistakes, for one. I could make good decisions instead of stupid ones. I could make people proud instead of angry ... " I was willing to continue, but I was interrupted.

"But what would be the fun of that?" asked Shayla, expressionless.

"Fun? What the hell are you talking about? Life isn't meant to be *fun*."

"Well, sure it is. It is meant to be exactly that. Growth is fun. Learning is fun. Challenges and the rising above them is fun. If you knew all the answers, would you even bother with questions anymore?"

"Stop getting philosophical on me," I said, not really sure where she was going, but I felt a lesson coming.

"It is not philosophy so much as common sense," said Garrett, joining the fray. "You are in the Here and Now to discover things for and about yourself. If you already know everything there is to know, and you never make mistakes trying to find the truth, how will you ever get to *really* know who you are and what you are capable of? How will you ever be challenged to grow beyond that which you were when you arrived as a squalling babe?"

I sighed loudly. These particular angels and demons were quickly becoming a pain in my ass. "Okay, listen ... I get the whole life lesson bullcrap. Really, I do. And I appreciate the fact that according to your information here, I've got a lot of super-evolving to look forward to, since I seem to go from one epic fuck-up to another, pretty much on a daily basis it seems. That's good. That's great! But right now, I'd rather know a little more, so I can screw up in a good way, you know? I don't mind learning from my mistakes, but I kind of hate it when my mistakes hurt others."

"Especially those who you are close to," said Shayla.

"Yes. Especially them." Finally, she was getting me.

"And yet, when someone you love is damaged, and sometimes even must sacrifice his or her life, you learn the hardest and most valuable lessons of all."

I was ready to cry with frustration. "Please, Shayla ... Garrett ... I don't want anyone else to die over this shit. I really don't. And if you tell me that my Tony has to ... " I couldn't finish the words. The thought of Tony leaving this realm was too much. I choked on a sob.

Garrett put his hand on my arm. "Calm down, young Jayne. There is no need for you to get yourself upset over this hypothetical discussion we are having." He frowned at Shayla. "Neither of us knows who will live through the coming days and who will not. That is above our pay-grade, as they say in the human world. All we know is just what we have experienced from our own history and what we know from our realms. And neither of us is so evolved that we have even come close to the Ascended Masters. We are nearly as in the dark as you."

"Garrett is right. Take a deep breath and just ask us the questions that plague you. We will do what we can to answer them for you."

# Chapter Twenty-One

BEFORE I COULD BEGIN ASKING my questions, I heard a familiar buzzing getting closer.

"Hey, guys, before he gets here, I wanted to mention that a baby pixie is about to show up. He's the son of my roommate and very good friend, so don't swat him or anything, as tempting as it might be after you meet him."

"And you do not fear pixelation?" asked Garrett curiously, watching Willy's drunken approach.

"No. These pixies are cool."

Garrett shrugged his shoulders at Shayla, and she did the same in return.

"Hello, Lellamental!" said Willy, hiccuping and smashing into my shoulder. He fell down into the grass.

"What's the matter with you, Baby Bee?" I asked, picking him up gently out of the tall weeds and dried flower remnants.

"Nothin'," he said, sitting up in my hand, looking around. "Whooooo-weeeee, what's thaaaaaat?" he asked, looking in Shayla's direction.

She had stood and backed up into the sun, her wings on full display again. She fluffed them out once, immediately sending

Willy into spasms of delight.

"Ooh! Oooh! *Oooh!* Giant momma pixie! Giant big pretty momma pixiiieeeee!" he squealed, reaching his arms out towards her. But then he stopped suddenly, getting a confused look on his face, dropping his arms and holding his stomach with both hands.

"What's the matter?" I asked, all of a sudden worried. He didn't look good at all. His skin had gone kind of greenish.

"I don't feel so good," said Willy, looking up at me with a sick expression on his face.

"What's the matter? Did you eat something out there?"

"Just some ... " He hiccuped and coughed once. Then he barfed into my hand. I nearly ralphed too, feeling the warm splat hit my skin.

Shayla giggled.

"Oh, my *word*, that is *quite* disgusting," said Garrett, staring at the pixie in fascination. "But I cannot seem to look away. How curious."

I looked down at the pixie, aghast at the tragedy that had befallen my palm. "Oh, for the love of ... *Willy!* What the *fuck?!*"

"What the fuck ... ," he said weakly, stumbling to the side and then falling onto his back. His tiny uneven snores and green complexion told me he was still alive, but definitely not feeling well.

"Oh shit," I said, picturing the look on Abby's face. "I have to get this little turd back to his mother."

"Yes, you most certainly do," said Garrett. "He appears to be drunk."

"He always flies like that," I said, walking towards the spot where I knew the door to the compound would appear.

"Would you like us to accompany you?" asked Garrett.

I stopped for a moment, considering it, but then decided against it. "I think it's better that you stay out here for a while longer. I'm not sure how the council would react to having Otherworlders in the compound yet."

"We shall wait here for you," said Shayla.

"Yes, we will pass the time comparing notes about our past," said Garrett.

I didn't even have to turn around to see the scowl I was sure Shayla had for him. "You do that! I'll come back after lunch!" I shouted over my shoulder. I was nearly to the door and didn't want to waste any more time chatting with them. The quicker I could unload this damn baby the better off we'd all be. I spoke down at my hand. "I should have known better than to take you out here, you little troublemaker."

He moaned in my palm, trying to turn over.

I tipped my hand and rolled him into my other, non-barfy hand, and closed my fingers around him. "You're not going anywhere until I have you next to your mother." I bent down to wipe the pixie barf off in the grass. "Friggin babies. You guys are nothing but trouble."

"What the fuck," he whispered, his eyes still closed.

"You said it, Baby Bee. You said it."

# Chapter Twenty-Two

I MADE IT BACK TO my room without anyone catching me holding a prone, snoring baby pixie in my hand. I put him down on his parents' bed and ran to the bathroom so I could wash my hands thoroughly. I was drying them off when Tim flew in through a crack in the door.

"What's up?" he asked, making me jump.

I had been staring in the mirror at my hair, wondering if I should start trying to do something with it.

"Nothing. Just washing pixie puke off my hand."

Tim laughed. "Nice. How'd that happen? Was my boy trying his papa's famous barrel rolls?"

"Nope."

"His papa's famous double twist into a quadruple somersault?"

"Nope."

Tim frowned. "His mother's death-defying super-gravity dive?"

"No. He was eating shit out in the meadow."

"*What?!* You let him go *outside?!*"

I cringed a little. "Uh ... yeah. Is that bad? It sounds bad."

"Of course it's bad, you nincompoop! Do you have any idea how much trouble a baby pixie can get into out in a meadow?"

"I'm starting to get the idea, actually." I frowned at the frustration that was causing Tim to ruin his gorgeous hair-do.

Tim shook his head, running his fingers through his hair and scrubbing it a few times. "I'm not even going to tell Abby. I'll let her figure it out for herself. Come on ... we have to get out of here."

I abandoned the towel and pushed through the door, heading for entrance to the hallway. I felt like a delinquent. "Are you sure this is a good idea?" I whispered. "Running away like this?"

"Shhh! Just shut up and go! *Go! Go! Go!*"

I had my hand on the door when Abby's voice came to us from the garden area. "Tim? Could you please come here for a minute?"

"*Ack!* She's coming! Open the door! Let me out!"

It had only opened an inch before he made it through, disappearing into the blackness of the corridor. I looked back once at the garden but didn't see Abby or the baby, so I shrugged and stepped out too, shutting the door behind me quietly. No way was I facing her down without Tim there to back me up.

I tried not to feel guilty as I ran down the hall, putting as much distance between my bedroom and my back as I could. I caught up to the frantically flying Tim, who kept up a zig-zagging flight path in front of me.

"Why are you flying like that?" I asked breathlessly, slowing to a fast walk.

"So she can't hit me."

"Hit you? With what?"

"Pollen balls. Seeds. Wasp stingers. Whatever she gets into her crazy she-pixie mind to launch at me."

"Daaaamn. Wasp stingers? She'd do that?"

"Never underestimate the ire of a she-pixie. The Underworld hath no fury like a pissed off Abby. Trust me on this."

"I don't doubt you, believe me. I hope she's not too pissed at me."

"If you're lucky, she'll never know you were involved."

I frowned, imagining the dining hall door in my mind so it would eventually appear for us in this spelled hallway. "I'm not so sure that will be possible."

"Why?"

"Because I might have accidentally taught him some new phrases today that she will know came from me."

"Oh, goody. Do I want to know what they are?"

"No. Definitely not."

"Oh, well. If they're any good Willy will be using them when I get back. Where are we going, anyway?"

"Lunch. I'm starving."

Tim floated down and landed on my shoulder. "Goodie. I'm going to ride the mule so I can save my energy for strawberry murdering."

"I've never known you to run out of energy."

"You've never known me to get busy all night with a wild she-pixie either."

"*Ugh,* total *ew,* Tim. Please, I do not want to know what you guys are busy doing in the next room, okay? It's bad enough your baby puked on me today."

"Pixie puking can hardly be compared to pixie sex."

"Yes, it can! In the grossness department it can!" I insisted. "Now stop talking about it or I'll launch you down the hall."

Luckily the door to the dining room appeared, sparing me any more of his pixie porn talk. I forcibly turned my brain away from thoughts of his naked self and focused on the tables in front of us. My friends were already gathered at one of them, the twins noticeably absent.

"To the buffet, Mule! Heeyah! Your rider is hungry!"

I waved to my friends before going to the food line.

Tim flew off and went over to the table, yelling over his shoulder as he went. "Get me some strawberries! And make sure they're extra juicy!"

I was soon joined in line by Aidan the werewolf, standing at my elbow with a plate in hand. "Hello, Jayne. I haven't seen you in a while."

"It was just yesterday you saw me," I said smiling. For some reason he made me feel warm inside - comforted. Maybe it was because he was so strong or something. My eyes strayed for a second to his thick arms, but I looked away hurriedly as soon as I realized what I was doing, afraid he would catch me ogling him.

"Oh, yeah. It seems longer than that." He grinned back at me.

I breathed in his smell, which reminded me briefly of Chase. It wasn't exactly the same, but it had a sense of strong male associated with it that made my nose tingle. "So what's new?" I asked, trying to ignore his yumminess. "Any news from the council?"

"Nothing from the council, but word on the street is you've a big fight on your hands."

"You probably know more about it than I do," I said, spooning some fruit onto my plate.

"All I know is that it's tomorrow and the fae are all placing their bets," he said, stabbing a giant forkful of meats to add to his plate. They were the kind I always avoided - the wiggly ones.

"Are you serious?" My hand froze over the tongs for the salad. I shook my head. "That's just ... wrong."

"My money's on you," he said. "In fact, most of the money's on the elementals. If Maléna wins, there will be a few fae who will take enough tokens from the rest of us to retire."

"Do fae even retire?"

"Nah, it's just an expression. But they'd be able to lord their victory over a hell of a lot of fae if they win."

"So the odds are in my favor."

"Weellll, not exactly."

I turned to face him fully. "Out with it, Aidan."

He wasn't smiling. He looked uncomfortable, his expression almost apologetic. "The betting is split between the three of you - not just elementals against silver elf."

"So people can bet *for* Ben and *against* me?"

"Yeah. Pretty much."

"Where's your money?" I didn't mean to test him, but his answer was important to me for some reason.

He grinned. "It's all on you, babe. No pressure."

His confidence in me warmed me to the bone, as did his handsome smile.

"I appreciate your vote."

He shrugged. "What can I say? I've always been a fan of the underdog."

I shoved him lightly before going back to the food. "You're a jerk."

"Nooo, come on," he said, nudging me back. "It's all in good fun. Ben wouldn't let you get hurt."

I looked over at the table with my friends, trying to find him, confused when I didn't see his familiar face there.

"You looking for him? For Ben?" asked Aidan softly.

"Yeah. Isn't he here?"

"Yeah, he's here. But not with your friends. He's over there." Aidan gestured with his elbow to the table that Ben had wanted me to sit at before - the one at the front of the room.

He was there, but he wasn't alone. He was sitting with someone else. A girl.

My blood started to boil when I realized who it was. "What the fuck is *she* doing sitting there with him?" I gave them both a death stare, but neither of them were paying any attention to me, so it was wasted on them. But I noticed other people looking at me and cringing.

"Well, the rumor is that you weren't interested in what Ben was offering. I guess she is."

I turned away from them, trying to focus on the food again, but I'd suddenly lost my appetite and wanted nothing to do with the things I had already chosen.

"I'm done here. See you later, Aidan."

"Yeah. I'll catch up with you later," he said.

I could tell from his tone that he was feeling sorry for me, and that only made it worse. *What do I care if Ben wants to be with that ho-bag? They're a perfect match. A couple of jerks who think they own the world and think they can make decisions for everyone else.*

I got to my friends' table and took the empty seat next to Becky and Scrum.

Becky smiled at me brightly - maybe a bit too brightly. "So! Jayne! What have you been up to today?!"

"Ease up on the manic, Becks. I'm not in the mood."

"Hey, Jayne," said Scrum, smiling warmly. "Long time no see."

"Yeah. Hey." He was too cheerful as usual. Sitting between him and Becky was like being stuck in a friggin happy-sandwich.

"Don't be jealous-a-them," Finn said, glancing meaningfully

over at Ben. "It don't mean nothin'. He didn't invite her there or anythin'. She just went over there, brazen as hell, and took the chair."

I shrugged, trying not to look at them, but unable to stop myself. I felt like barfing when she leaned into him and laughed. He smiled back at her, making my stomach churn. "What do I care what he does? He and Samantha can go screw each other silly for all I care."

"Jayne," scolded Becky, "don't say that. You two are bound. He's not going to screw her or anybody else for that matter."

"I wouldn't be too sure 'bout that if I were you," said Finn, still looking over at them, now with his eyebrows raised.

I didn't want to look but couldn't help myself again.

She had her hand on his arm, and he was patting it while he smiled.

"Fuck me," I said under my breath, tearing my eyes away and jabbing my fork into a piece of melon.

"Hey! Watch what you're doing up there, Gigantor! I'm trying to eat here too," said Tim's annoyed voice from down at the table. He was wiping off a squirt of juice that had hit him in the cheek.

"Sorry," I mumbled, forcing the melon into my mouth even though I had no taste for it. I was going to try and pretend that it wasn't pissing me off to see the guy I had no interest in, cuddling up to a girl I hated with every fiber of my being.

"Seriously, Jayne. Let it go. Things are going to work out, you'll see," said Becky, rubbing my back.

"Whatever. I have other things to worry about. Things more important than what Ben decides to do behind closed doors."

"Or right out here in the open," said Finn, still staring at them, frowning.

"Shush, Finn!" urged Becky, slapping him on the arm. "You are not helping!"

"Oh, sorry. I'll shut up now." He looked down at his plate, but kept sneaking glances over at the other table.

"So, I talked to an angel and a demon a few minutes ago," I said casually, looking down at my food.

Several utensils dropped onto plates and the table around me, causing everyone from the nearby area to look our way.

"Whaaat?!" said Becky, leaning her face over my plate. "Jayne, you are *joking*. I know you are. You didn't go back into a dream again, did you? Cuz that seems too dangerous if you ask me. I think you should avoid doing that, like, ever again."

"I feel like I'm completely out of the loop right now," said Scrum. "I haven't seen you in a while, but geez. Angels and demons? What did I miss?"

I smiled ruefully at my daemon friend, patting him on the arm. "Sorry, Scrum. Shit's hit the fan again. Wish you could have been there to see it."

"Maybe I should be in the future. I was reassigned, but if you need me, I can be with you whenever you want. I'm sure they'd understand."

"Nothing you could do would help me right now, I'm afraid. But thanks for the offer."

"So what's this about more demons and angels?" asked Spike. "Last time I saw you, you were outside Tony's door waiting for him."

"Yeah, well, when you *abandoned* me there, I was waiting. But I decided to go hang out in the meadow while he was with the girls, and I met up with them then. And they told me all kinds of crazy shit that we need to discuss. But not here," I said, looking around. I didn't trust that there weren't listening spells in every corner of this space, and I'd already revealed enough to get me in trouble.

"Meet me in my room after lunch," I said. "We can talk about it then. I need some help getting the pieces all put together."

"Maybe we should go to Tony's room," said Tim, munching on a strawberry seed. "Then we can avoid Abby too."

"Good idea. Tim suggested we meet in Tony's room. That way he can participate."

"I think we'd better plan that for after dinner. According to what I heard, you're supposed to be fighting the good fight tomorrow. You're supposed to work with Ben today," said Scrum. "There're about ten daemon being called in for extra protection, me included."

"Seriously? What do they think is going to happen that they'd need that kind of squad there?"

He shrugged. "Our two elementals in training for a power fight? One of them ... uh ... a bit inexperienced? Who knows what could happen? We're just being cautious."

I sighed. "Okay. I get it. Better wear your anti-coma gear."

"We already planned to," he said, smiling. "Witches hooked us up."

I stuck my tongue out at him and stood. "Well, I'm going to go talk to Ben. Wish me luck."

Becky grabbed my wrist as I turned to walk away. "Jayne ... be nice."

I shook her off. "Fuck that." I walked over to where Ben was sitting, stopping in front of his table.

He lifted his eyes as I approached, a haughty but guarded expression on his face.

I refused to even acknowledge Samantha's presence. "Hello,

Ben."

He nodded his head once. "Jayne."

"I hear we're supposed to train together today."

"Yes. At the green elf training grounds. After lunch."

"What time?"

"Two o'clock. Bring your weapon."

"Hello, Jayne," said Samantha, her voice dripping with saccharine sweetness.

I turned my head slowly and looked at her, saying nothing. I simply stared her down.

"Thanks for choosing to sit elsewhere. Ben's a fun guy to hang with."

"I guess you've moved on from Jared. Fickle, aren't you?"

Her smile became a frown. "Shut up, Jayne. You have no idea what you're talking about. As usual."

"Of course I do, cousin. Way more than you realize."

I walked away but not before I heard Samantha say, "What the hell is that supposed to mean? Why did she call me that?"

I smiled, happy to find that I actually knew something she didn't. Every time I interacted with her, it seemed to be that I was suffering the result of one of her awesome spells. It was nice to have the upper hand just this one time.

I left the lunchroom, happy to sense Tim arriving to ride my shoulder just as I left the room.

# Chapter Twenty-Three

"WHAT THE HECK JUST HAPPENED over there?" asked Tim, facing behind me. "Samantha looks maaaad."

"Good. I hope she is."

"You sure about that?" he asked, turning around to face forward while holding onto a hunk of my hair for balance. "She's a crazy-talented witch. It never hurts to have one of them on our side."

"Yeah, well, I can manage. I have Maggie." I pulled open the door and stepped through into the hallway beyond, letting it shut on its own behind us.

Tim snorted. "You might *think* you have Maggie, but I wouldn't bet the farm on that one."

"Do you even know what a farm is?" I asked, making my way to the door that would lead me back to the meadow.

"Of course I do. I spent three months on one as a dragonfly. It had cows, pigs, horses, chickens, dogs, cats, tractors, electric bug zappers ... the works."

"What were you doing there?" This was one of the few times Tim had offered me a glimpse of his life interacting with humans.

"I was on a mission."

"For whom? Doing what?"

"Spy stuff. Top secret. I can't tell you or I'd have to pixelate you."

"Are you serious?" I asked, stopping.

"That's for me to know and you to ... always wonder about," he said, jumping off my shoulder to do some barrel rolls out in front of me.

"You are a serious pain in the ass, you know that? I can see where your son gets it."

"Someone who will insult a man's child, is in desperate need of finding criticism."

"Who are you, Confucius? Shut up and come over here so I can flick you in the ass."

"No way, your breath is rank today. I'll be keeping my distance, thank you very much."

I shook my head, grabbing onto the door handle leading to the Infinity Meadow. "Whatever. There's an angel and a demon vampire out here, so you may want to stay inside."

"Whoa, Nelly, what'd you just say?" asked Tim, hovering in the doorway, a look of fear on his face.

"I *said*, there's an angel and a demon out here, so if you're afraid, you may want to get back inside like a good pixie."

Tim put his hands on his hips. "I'll have you know that I've been thrice recognized for my bravery in the field, young lady, and I have never shied away from danger!"

"Except when it comes in the form of your wife."

He dropped his arms. "Well, of course. The Underworld hath no fury, remember?"

"Oh, yes. I'd forgotten. So are you coming or not?"

"Lead on, Magellan!" he said, flying out the door Superman-style.

I shut the door behind us and trudged through the heather. I found my two friends waiting for us under the tree. Upon seeing Tim, Garrett backed up a few paces.

"He's with me," I said. "Don't worry about him pixying you or anything."

Tim flew up to hover in between Shayla and Garrett. "I shall permit you to share my airspace so long as you do not threaten me or Jayne," he announced, crossing his hands over his chest.

I noticed they were standing closer to one anther than they had been before when I was around. I tried to read their expressions, but they were giving nothing away. I was curious whether their closeness was based on shared pixie-caution or maybe the fact that they'd reached some sort of agreement about their past.

"So. What'd you guys figure out while I was gone?" I asked.

Tim cleared his throat. "A-*hem*, Jayne? Some introductions, perhaps?"

"Oh, yeah," I said, holding up my hands in a halting gesture. "I forgot to introduce you guys."

"Make sure you add the good stuff," said Tim, speaking behind his hand in a stage-whisper.

I frowned not sure what he was talking about. I shook my head and continued. "Garret and Shayla, this is Tim. Tim this is..."

"No!" yelled Tim. "That's not the good way. Do it the good way. With style! Put a little pizzaz on it!" He did a somersault for effect.

I sighed and started again, putting zero inflection into my voice just to piss Tim off. "What I meant was, Shayla and Garrett, behold. This is Tim the Pixie of ... awesomeness. Winner of three medals for bravery or something cool like that. Pixelator of guardian angels." I gestured towards Shayla. "Tim, this is Shayla the dragonslayer." I swept my arm towards Garrett. "And this is Garrett the dragonslayer."

I dropped my arm down to my thigh. "Is everyone happy now? Can we move on?"

Shayla bowed respectfully to Tim. "Sir Tim. It is my privilege and honor to make your acquaintance."

My draw dropped open.

Garrett was next, bowing down almost to his knees. "Tim the Brave. I am at your service, good sir."

Tim was nodding regally. "Now that's what I'm talkin' about."

I laughed to myself, not sure if they were just shining him on or if he actually had a reputation out there in the fae world as some sort of superhero. But I had other more pressing issues to deal with, so I let that thought float out of my head and steered the topic towards our former conversation.

"I've invited my friends to talk to you. Any chance I can convince you to meet with us in my friend's room in the compound? It's not that big, so it might be a little crowded, but I know they'd like to hear what you have to say."

"Why can't they meet us out here?" asked Shayla, fluffing her wings once.

"One of them is sick. He's my friend who's recovering from the Gray incident."

"Ah, yes. Well, it isn't a problem for me," said Shayla, looking over at Garrett.

He shrugged. "Nor I. Although ... I am concerned that I have once again become quite hungry."

Tim flew up high above my head, yelling, "Run for the

compound, Jayne! Hungry vampire on the loose!"

I laughed. "Relax, Tim. He's not going to attack you."

Tim slowly lowered himself down, never taking his eyes off of Garrett. "Don't be so sure about that. He's a demon. Never forget that about him."

"You can have another sip of my blood if you want," I said, rolling up my sleeve.

Shayla stepped towards me suddenly, grabbing my arm. "Are you *mad*? Why would you offer such a thing?" She looked down at the marks on my arm left over from his earlier meal and gasped.

"Uh, because he needs it?"

Shayla was outraged. "Tell me you did not take blood from her without discussing the sacrifice!" she demanded of Garrett.

His lips thinned and he shrugged. "There wasn't time, as I recall."

"The hell there wasn't!" she said, pulling the dragon fang out of her sheath.

I grabbed her arm, stopping her. "Hey, relax! Nothing happened. He took a sip and I was fine. See?" I held up the arm that he'd drank from before. Two black circles remained where he had bitten me. I frowned, not noticing before how ugly they were. *Ew. That's kind of gross.*

"Tell her!" demanded Shayla. "Tell her right this instant, or I shall burn you all the way back to the Underworld. *And* I will make it my eternal mission to ensure you never see the light of the Here and Now ever again."

Her oath had my throat closing with fear. *What could possibly be so bad that she'd go that far on my behalf? What have I done now?*

Garrett sighed and took a few steps closer to me, but Shayla's weapon coming out and pointing at his heart made him stop in his tracks.

"Jayne. Please allow me to explain. I apologize for not doing this before, but as you will recall, we were in somewhat of an emergency situation."

I nodded. "I do recall that. I'm not angry at you. Not yet, anyway. Go ahead."

"Thank you. Well, what I should tell you before you offer to feed me again, is that blood-letting by a member of the Underworld upon a member of the Here and Now can place a taint on the soul of that fae or human."

"A taint?" I asked, my voice lacking its usual volume.

"Yes. A taint. It is but a smudge. But too many of those smudges can equal a swath of evil that is quite hard to move beyond, in one's daily existence."

"I have no idea what you just said." I looked to Shayla. "Translation?"

"What he's dancing around saying, is that if he drinks from you enough, he will turn your insides black and cause you to become a permanent member of the Underworld, even though you might still be present in this realm ... in the Here and Now. All the decisions you make will be tainted with this blackness. You will, in effect, be evil personified."

"You'd turn me bad?" I asked, feeling more than a little betrayed.

"In a manner of speaking, that could happen. But I would not allow it. I would never take that much from you."

"As if you could control your need," scoffed Shayla.

"I *can* control my need!" shouted Garrett. "I have had a thousand years to learn how! Believe me, it was a difficult lesson, but one I have mastered quite fully, no thanks to you or anyone else."

"Me?! You are blaming *me* for your fall? Of all the nerve ... "

"Hey! Lovers quarreling! Do you mind? We don't have time for this crap. This guy is hungry and I have blood, so unless any of you have another idea about how to feed him, I'm going to give him a small taste." I jerked up my sleeve. "Garrett, if you turn my soul even a tiny bit black, I will stick my weapon right into your heart and take you with me into darkness, do you understand me?"

"Very clearly," he said, taking my wrist in his.

"Jayne, you do not need to do this," said Shayla, looking a little sick.

"I know. I'm a big girl, and I need Garrett and what he knows. I can't let him die or whatever happens to guys like him out here when they starve."

"We turn to ash. Our souls extinguish, never to walk any of the realms ever again." He looked directly at Shayla.

I saw a tear in her eye before she turned away from us.

"Go ahead then. Do what you must, but don't take too much." I pulled my weapon out of its sheath just in case.

Garrett leaned down and took my wrist into his mouth, biting down hard enough to break the skin with his fangs.

"Mother*fucker*," I said. "Ooooh, *shit* that hurts."

Shayla slowly turned around, studying my face. "It hurts?"

Garrett raised an eyebrow but kept his mouth in place, sucking hard on my vein.

"Holy shit, yes." I hissed with the ache, unable to stop myself. I held my elbow up with my other hand, trying to support it better, hoping that would help the pain. But it did nothing. "Hurry up, Garrett, it feels like my arm's on fire."

Shayla walked over. "Are you certain? Perhaps the euphoria

is manifesting in strange ways for you."

"Euphoria? Are you friggin kidding me?" I started bouncing up and down on the balls of my feet. "Okay, okay, okay, Garrett, that's enough. Fuck, that's *enough!*" I yelled, hitting him on the head with my weapon. A little wisp of smoke rose up from his scalp.

He pulled away, licking my wrist once and then his lips as he straightened. "Wow. That was ... something unexpected." He reached up and patted the top of his head gingerly, looking up at the smudge of soot on his hand left from his blackened hair, frowning but saying nothing further.

Shayla was scowling at him. "She said it didn't feel good."

He shrugged. "Well, either I must live with the fact that my talents as a vampire are more than sub-par, or consider an alternative."

"Being ...?"

"Being that perhaps because her blood is not like the others, the effects of our blood-letting might also be different."

"Can we do an x-ray of my soul or something?" I asked, holding my wrist against my tunic. "Maybe I won't have any black marks at all."

Garrett reached over and put his thumb over the two puncture marks and held my hand above my head. "Direct pressure, above the heart. Remember from last time?"

"Oh, yeah. Sorry, I forgot."

"Consider my mind blown right now," said Tim, coming to stand on my shoulder. "I never would have thought I'd see that in my lifetime."

"What?" I asked, irritated at the stinging that wouldn't go away.

"Vampire bites hurting and possible immunity from black marks. We need a witch to look you over."

"Tim says a witch needs to check me out."

"Better a wrathe," said Shayla.

"I know just the guy," I said weakly. "But I've got to go. I have an appointment with an elemental in just a little while, and he'll be pissed if I'm late."

"Shall we go with you?" asked Shayla.

"No. I don't want him to know about you. He's a pain in the ass and bossy as hell. I'm sure he'll decide he's the boss of you too and start telling you what to do if he sees you."

"He could try," said Shayla, smiling serenely.

"Ha! Yeah. I'd like to see that match-up," said Tim. "Maybe they should come."

"No. Just us. Come on, Tim the Awesome. I need you to watch my back."

"You know it, Lellamental. Ride on, oh mulish one."

I pulled my arm out of Garrett's strong grip. "I hope that will tide you over for a while," I said, pulling a little of The Green into me to help me over the hump of tiredness I was suddenly feeling. It rushed into me, spreading its warmth and strength into my system. I couldn't help but smile. "I'll see you tonight right here. Either I or someone will come and get you for the meeting in our friend's room."

"We shall await your summons," said Shayla, nodding to me and bowing slightly to Tim.

I shook my head at her formality where Tim was concerned. As I walked to the door, I said, "One day you're going to tell me all your dirty little secrets, Tim. I'm serious."

"I can start with one right now if you'd like."

"Okay, shoot," I said, pulling the door open, hoping I'd hear about his medals of honor.

"I'm not wearing underwear. The beast is unleashed!"

I laughed despite the horrible images of pixie packages that his admission created in my mind. "You're a sick little pixieman, you know that?"

"You said dirty secrets, and I served one up hot and fresh, so you can hardly complain," he said haughtily, flying out ahead of me in the hallway, going towards the door that would lead us to the green elf training grounds.

"Whatever." I let my mind wander from Tim's dirty secret over to my training with Ben. I was nervous on many levels, not the least of which being that this would be the first opportunity he would have to ask me why I'd pulled him into my dream and put his face on my nightmares.

# Chapter Twenty-Four

I ARRIVED AT THE TRAINING ground to find a whole crew of daemon guardians, Ben, and Samantha waiting for me.

"It's about time," said Samantha, turning her back to me and walking over to stand closer to Ben. Her cape swirled out behind her, making her witchy status impossible to ignore. My lip curled with disgust at her arrogance.

Ben glanced at her but said nothing. I noticed he didn't move away either. *Stupid jerk.*

I looked over at Scrum and nodded. He smiled and waved back, never one to be reserved or cool. The familiarity of his openness gave me a little boost of courage just when I was needing it, so I smiled back gratefully.

"Let the games begin," said Tim quietly in my ear.

"You said it," I whispered back.

"Witch bitch, coming at ya, two o'clock," hissed Tim.

I didn't think about it, I just did it. I pulled the Green into me and threw up a shield between Samantha and me. Whatever spell she'd tried to throw at me bounced off and hit her in the gut, throwing her backwards to land on her ass.

Tim started singing off-key. "I'm rubbeeerrrrr and you're

gluuuueee, whatever spell you throw at me will bounce back to youuuuuu!"

I laughed. "You rock the party, you know that, Tim?"

"You know it, Lellamental. Don't let that bitch get away with that shit."

"Careful with the potty-mouth, Tim. I don't want Abby climbing all up in my ass over your descent into madness."

"Yeah, you're right. Consider my act cleaned up. Go get that Jezebel and show her who the red-headed step-child of the Blackthorn family *really* is."

"On second thought, I think it's more effective when you use swear words."

"Yeah. You're right. Let's bag that bitch."

Samantha was standing again, poised and ready to hurl something else at me. Ben held up his hand to stop her, but I ignored his attempt at making peace. Samantha was here without an invitation, deliberately trying to mess with me, and I meant to show her that it was a mistake to piss me off like that. *This is my house!* I used the spell that Maggie had inadvertently taught me, sending a message out to a nearby tree, hoping it had legs under Samantha's feet.

It didn't disappoint. Big, gnarly roots burst out of the ground and wrapped themselves around her feet and calves, rooting her to the spot. I pictured some vines coming out of the brush to tie her hands together, and they raced to do my bidding. Within five seconds, she was trussed up tight, unable to move her hands or her legs. I slowly lowered the power shield between us, but didn't let my hold on the Green go. I had no idea what she was capable of on a good day or in a good mood; and now she was what Finn would describe as madder than a wet hen.

"Let me out of this, Jayne!" she spat, struggling against her bonds.

"You started it," I said. "Don't think I didn't sense you winding up to throw something else at me. I can feel you in the Green, Samantha." I'd never really thought about it too hard before, but as I said it, the feeling came in so crystal clear that I almost surprised myself with it. I *could* feel her there. Even when she wasn't near me, I could get a sense of her presence. I cocked my head, staring at her, wondering if it was because we were related or if it was something else. I'd done it with the green elves before, but they were so connected to the energy in the forest, it had been easy.

"Let her go, Jayne," sighed Ben. "She's not here to cause any trouble. She's here to help us."

"*Shuh.* Yeah, right." I laughed bitterly. "That's all she's ever done, right? Tried to help?"

"Exactly," he said. "Let her go." He was getting angry now. I could tell not only by his tone but by the heat I could sense coming from him.

"She has no business here with us. This is *my* training, not hers." As soon as the words were out of my mouth I regretted them, but only because they sounded petulant. I had wanted to sound confident and sure of myself, but I'd chosen the wrong words or something. I shifted my weight from one foot to the other, not sure how to get out of the situation with any dignity.

"We have only one day to train. She can help us short-cut the process. She offered to be here, okay? We need to accept whatever assistance anyone is willing to give."

"If you can vouch that she'll keep her dirty spells off me, I'll let her go," I said, lifting my chin.

"My spells aren't dirty!" screeched Samantha.

"That's a matter of perspective," said Tim quietly in my ear.

"Word, pixieman," I said, holding up my index finger for a high-one. His tiny little hand made contact and I smiled, knowing Tim had my back.

"I will vouch for Samantha that she will do nothing to harm you today."

I tilted my head to the side, unable to stop the snide remark from coming out. "Isn't that sweet?" I looked over at Samantha, wanting to gouge her eyes out at the satisfaction I saw there. "Don't get too excited," I said to her. "His emotions come and go like the wind he commands. Trust me on this."

"That's *enough*, Jayne," warned Ben.

I asked the trees and vines to let Samantha go as I walked towards the two of them. *"Is* it? Says who, Ben? You? Are you in charge of *me* now, too? Maléna, the council, all the fae in the Green Forest, and now me too?"

"Uhhh, Jayne? Are you sure you want to go there?" asked Tim, sounding nervous.

I didn't care what Tim or anyone else thought about me just then. All I knew was that I felt like a total fool, letting myself get hitched to Ben the way I had. I'd fallen for a stupid kiss and a cute face, and now for the rest of my life I was going to be bossed around by this pig of a guy who couldn't keep his hands off the one person in the entire universe I couldn't stand to be around without wanting to strangle her.

Samantha took two steps back as I got closer, looking nervously from me to Ben.

"Stop, Jayne," said Ben, holding out his hands.

I pulled the Green fully up into me and then asked Water to join the Earth's power that was humming through my body. I had snapped, I knew that now, but the freedom from reason felt amazing. I'd held the power at bay for too long, trying to be responsible and nice and mature and everything else everyone expected of me. *Not anymore!* I shrieked in my own head. I felt a crazy laugh bubbling up from within me and I let it out, reveling in the madness of it.

Ben pulled his Fire and Wind into him in less than a second, letting it swirl around in a miniature cyclone of power. Samantha ran away to join the daemon guardians, who I noticed were backing well out of our way, mingling in with the trees.

"Back down!" yelled Ben.

"Go to hell!" I yelled back, shooting out a ray of Green power into his gut, hoping to blow him across the field at the very least.

He took the punch to his middle, bending over for a moment before he stood straight up again and roared. His body stood a full foot taller, his entire form ablaze with fire. The wind whipped leaves and grass and even small branches around us, but none of it could touch me in my power bubble.

I laughed maniacally, feeling high with the energy, deciding to go completely nuts and throw some Water at him. I never played with that element, not feeling as confident with it, but today, in this moment, I totally didn't care. I opened my mouth and felt the water coming from me, up through the ground and into my body and out of my jaws to drown Ben and his fire.

A tidal wave of my anger hit him full in the face, extinguishing his flames in an instant and sending him under a bubbling blue cover where he floated, a shocked look frozen on his face. The wind died down to nothing, and the only sound I could hear now was the roar of the oceans I commanded and the hum of the Green in me, the cracking of its energy surrounding us.

"Jayne!" came a tiny voice through the pulsing din. "Jayne! You're killing him!" It was Tim, and he sounded scared.

I tried to ignore it, but he was so damn persistent.

"Jayne! Stop! It's the taint! It's the taint! The vampire! Let him go!"

I was confused for a second. *What in the hell is he talking about? Taint? What taint?* I looked down at my wrist, which had suddenly started to tingle so badly it itched. I scratched at it absently and flinched when my nail caught the open wound. *Black. It's black.* Four puncture marks surrounded by rotten-looking flesh. *Ew. What happened to my arm?*

The voice came again. "Jayne! Let Ben go!"

I looked up and saw Ben's eyes starting to go blank in the water. A bubble escaped his lips and floated up. *What the hell?* "Ben? What are you doing in there?" I asked. I looked around, but I couldn't see anything but greens and blues swirling in the space surrounding me. It was just Ben and me now, both of us captured in this elemental storm.

It finally penetrated my brain that I was killing the guy who was supposed to be helping me. I shook my head to clear it and then quickly let the elements drop back into the earth.

After they left, I was suddenly overwhelmed with fatigue. I sank to the ground in a heap, flinching at the squelching sounds my body made as it landed in the wetness around me.

Tim came over and buzzed in front of me, alternatively snapping his fingers and clapping his hands. "Hey, hey! Jayne! Wake up, crazy person! You need to get your butt over there and heal your boyfriend or it's lights out for the Father, you get my drift?"

"What?" I asked, totally confused. His words made absolutely no sense to me.

Tim flew in close and slapped me in the face. Then he zoomed up and poked me in the eye.

"Ow, *shit*, Tim! That hurt!" I yelled, clapping my hand over my now throbbing eyeball.

"Good! Because you need to wake the hell up! Go over to Ben right now and heal his sorry ass or we're all doomed! Doomed, I say!"

I looked over with my one good eye and saw Ben lying in a soggy heap on the ground about ten feet away. I gasped, shocked at finding him looking so helpless and ragged-out. *Oh shit. I did that.* I crawled over on my hands and knees, too tired and my limbs too heavy to do any better than that.

I got to his side and pushed weakly on his shoulder. "Ben! Get up!"

He didn't respond.

"Ben! Come on, get up!" I grabbed his tunic in my fist and shook him as hard as I could. His body rocked back and forth and some water leaked out of his mouth, but no breath or words followed. His sightless eyes continued to stare up at the sky.

"Holy shit," I whispered, feeling sick to my stomach. "I killed him!"

"Heal him with the Green," said Scrum, running up to kneel at my side. He took me by the shoulders and leaned me into his chest. "I've got ya. Now do it. Send him some of the Green. Leave Water out of it. I think it's toxic to his Fire."

"Ya think?" I asked, laughing bitterly as I reached out for the Green and asked it, begged it, to heal the Father of the fae. I cried, watching the green glow crawl over him, not knowing if it was going to do any good.

"Shhh, it's going to be okay," said Scrum, rocking me a little and petting my head awkwardly.

I felt someone else come over to my other side. When she dropped down to her knees I could see it was Samantha. She wasn't crying like I expected her to be.

"Let me help," she said, staring at Ben intently.

"Do whatever you can," I said, waving at his unmoving body with a weak gesture.

She grabbed my hand and squeezed it between her two, mumbling some words and closing her eyes.

"What the fu..." I started to say, when I felt a tingling in my fingers. A not uncomfortable warmth came from her hands into mine, and lingered at my wrist. I watched in fascination as the black wounds on my arm turned angry red and then slowly healed over and faded to plain white scars.

"Whoaaaa," said Scrum, also watching.

Samantha opened her eyes and glanced down at my wrists. "You were under the influence, weren't you?"

"I have no friggin idea," I said, watching her face, lost for any other words.

She dropped my hands and gestured over at Ben with a nod. "He's coming back."

My head jerked towards Ben, and my heart leaped when his lids closed and then opened back up again to reveal his normal eyes, no longer staring sightless up at the heavens.

I pushed out of Scrum's arms and crawled over to Ben, falling down on my stomach in the mud next to him. I reached up and put my hand on his forehead, smoothing the hair away from his face and leaving ugly brown streaks of mud on his skin behind. "I'm so, so sorry I just did that. Will you please forgive me?"

Ben just blinked, saying nothing.

"I promise, I'll never do it again." I was crying, thinking how close I'd come to snuffing out his fire forever. I didn't care how much of an ass he could be, he definitely didn't deserve that.

Ben sat up slowly, looking around him in a daze. "Where am I?" he finally asked.

Samantha stood and walked over to him, holding out her hand to help him up. "You're at the green elf training grounds."

Ben stood and looked down in confusion at his muddy clothes. "What happened?"

"She happened," said Samantha, not even looking at me.

I used Scrum's strong hand and arm to get up, standing in front of Ben. "It was me. I did it. But I didn't do it on purpose."

"Yes you did," challenged Samantha.

"Okay, maybe I did, but I didn't mean to hurt you, Ben!"

"Of course you did," said Samantha, getting all bitchy now. "What else do you call it when you use your elements to snuff his out and drown him?"

My mouth opened but no excuse would come out. Because there wasn't one. I hung my head in shame.

Ben slowly walked away, not even looking at me.

My heart was breaking over the pain. I could feel the beating muscle shriveling in my chest. I watched his back disappear into the trees, Samantha at his side.

*What have I done? What have I done?!*

Tim came over and landed on my shoulder. First he sighed heavily. Then he said, "Come on, kid. Let's go home."

If he had said anything else, I probably would have handled it without a problem, but the fact that he got all parenty and papa-like on me was too much to bear. I started crying like a baby, my shoulders slouching into my body, making me feel like I was collapsing in on myself.

Scrum came over and propped me up. He acted as my crutch all the way back to my room, leaving me at the bathroom entrance to shower myself off.

"I'll be right in your room here when you're done. Just get yourself cleaned up a little first."

I stepped mindlessly into the shower and turned on the hot water, drenching myself and my clothes in the element that had nearly killed my life partner and had probably made him my enemy for all eternity.

# Chapter Twenty-Five

I STOOD IN THE SHOWER for as long as I could take it, but I wasn't feeling entirely comfortable with the Water element, having so recently used it to almost kill Ben. I stripped off my wet clothes and wrapped a towel around me, walking back into my room to get something dry to put on.

Scrum was sitting in a chair in the corner of the room. "Feel better?" he asked.

"No," I said, going through my drawers and picking things out.

I went back in the bathroom and got dressed, leaving my towel on the floor when I walked out. I almost wanted Netter to get mad at me. I felt like I deserved for everyone to hate me, even my brownie.

Scrum stood when I came out. "I think you should lie down for a while. We have some time before our meeting in Tony's room."

"You heard about the meeting? How?"

"Tim flew up to my ear and filled me in."

I looked around the room, realizing it was too quiet. "Where is he?" My voice hitched as I considered the fact that Tim might have decided I was too much of an asshole to live with.

"I think he went to tell everyone what happened."

"Is that what he said?"

"Well, yeah. He also said something about calling in the troops, but I wasn't sure what he meant by that."

"I'd be surprised if any troops would bother to come if they knew it was for me."

Scrum stood and walked over to me, patting me on the shoulder. "You're being too hard on yourself, as usual, Jayne. Just relax, okay? It's not as bad as you think."

I looked up at him with tears in my eyes. "You were there, right Scrum? You saw what I did?" My throat was burning really bad from the sorrow that was choking me.

"Yeah, I saw. And I also saw some weird stuff with Samantha, with her attacking you first, and then her doing something to your arm. Tim says you were bitten by a vampire." He frowned. "How is that even possible? Vampires? They aren't fae, right?"

I shook my head. "It's a long story."

"Yeah, well Tim says we're going to figure it all out tonight. He said he's calling in some favors and everything. And he also said not to let you get all whiney-baby either."

I laughed absently, impressed that he could annoy me by proxy so effectively, and wondering who he had to con to get a favor owed. I shuffled over to the bed, no longer caring about the meeting or the fight with Maléna. Maybe she'd win and put me out of my misery.

"Where are you going?" asked Scrum.

"I'm taking a nap, like you told me to. Wake me when it's all over." I pulled down the covers and crawled in under them, drawing them up over my head and enveloping myself in darkness.

# Clash of the Otherworlds: Book One

I had just started to drift off, the haze of a not very happy dream starting to overtake me, when I heard voices. They pulled me out of the fantasy and back into reality, annoying me immensely. I tried to tune them out and go back into the gray world that beckoned, but it became impossible when the bed moved. Someone was getting in with me.

"Whoever you are, get the hell away from me or I'll drown you, too."

"It's me," said Spike, "and I'm not going anywhere."

I felt a rush of cold air when he lifted the covers to get in.

"Fuck off, Spike."

"Mmmm, don't mind if I do," he said, now fully under with me and leaning in towards my neck.

I was half-ready to cry and half-ready to scream, so I did what came natural to me and gave life to both emotions.

"Leave me alone! Can't you see I'm dying in here! I want to be *alone!*" I was sobbing and shaking, hating myself and anyone else who was going to try and make me feel okay about attempted murder.

Spike shoved one arm under me and put the other over me, enveloping me in a giant, under-the-covers bear hug. "Shhhh, you're going crazy on us, Jaynie. You need to just calm down and let that shit out, already. You're going to self-destruct if you keep it up." He kept making soothing sounds near my ear and alternated between squeezing me and rubbing my arm and back.

I struggled to get him away from me, not interested in his pity. "Just leave, Spike. Don't you get it? I don't *want* you here."

"Your mouth says no, but your heart says yes."

"Spike," I said with a lot less volume, "that sounds an awful lot like a rapist talking, don't you think?"

"In other circumstances, maybe. But here? No. I can feel your need, Jayne. You know I love you. Let me help you heal."

"Get your healing nonsense away from me," I said, no longer crying, almost laughing at the ridiculousness of an incubus flirting with me at a time like this.

"Okaaay. If you prefer, I could call the twins in. They're a little tired from helping Tony, and I can't vouch for their control when they're like that, but I'll get them if you want."

"*Ew*, no. They can keep their grubby hands *and* their hooters away from me." I struggled again to free myself, but Spike wasn't having it. Messing with him wasn't helping me forget, but it was at least keeping my mind off the crying. My struggles were decidedly weaker now.

"Just kiss me once. If you don't like what happens with it, I'll go away. No harm, no foul. And you've got Scrum out there keeping an eye on things, so you know I won't hurt you."

"Don't you understand?" I whispered, no longer fighting him but nearly begging now.

"No, I don't," he whispered back. "Explain it to me." He forced me to turn and look at him. It was dark under the covers, but the red swirling light in his eyes was visible, making him seem like a creepy monster. But he was one monster I didn't fear, because no matter how strong his need, I knew he was a friend. And he had forgiven the unforgivable on more than one occasion.

"I don't deserve this."

"This what?"

"This ... friendship. This understanding. This kindness," I said, crying again.

"Why not? Jesus, you're a good person, Jayne. You try really hard. You've changed a lot since we first came here, and as far as

I'm concerned, you just keep getting more awesome."

"A good person doesn't try to kill the Father of the fae," I said, ashamed to even hear the words come out of my mouth.

"She does if he's a flaming asshat," growled Spike.

I tried to shove him but he was holding me too close. "Shut up," I said. "I'm serious."

"So am I. Come on, let's be honest. You were forced into marrying the guy when everyone knew you were in love with Chase. Or me. I mean, we both know you still have the hots for me, and who can blame you? And suddenly everyone expects you to have all the answers. Shit, you didn't even know the effects of a vampire bite, so give yourself a break, would ya? I have to tell you ... all the self-pity just isn't doing it for me. You're much cuter when you're fighting the good fight."

"Spike, I told you before. I love you but not in that way."

"Kiss me and prove it, then. If you only like me as a friend, you'll be able to resist my charms."

I was tempted. For the first time in a long time I was. "That's not fair to you."

"Don't worry about what's fair. Let's just worry about what's fun."

He tickled me a little, making me giggle. I could practically feel the challenge in his voice.

"I'm going to kiss you now," he whispered.

I could feel the heat of his breath on my face.

And then our lips touched. Tentatively at first, but then gradually we were consumed by such a strong need that we pulled each other in tightly, our tongues moving together in a rhythm neither of us was setting but both of us just somehow knew how to follow.

"Jayne, you're so beautiful," he said between kissing my mouth and neck. "Let me do this for you."

"No sex," I said, not even sure I meant it.

"No sex," he assured me. "Just look in my eyes and open your mouth."

I did as he instructed and instantly felt the connection settle between us. Something inside of me was coming out - something that felt heavy and sad, alien and dark. I pressed into Spike's body, yearning for the lightness of spirit he was causing in me. His arms tightened their hold, and I could feel every inch of him against my body. My heart soared with the heady rush it brought.

I heard a throat being cleared in the distance, and the feeling of Spike's incubus passion began to fade in response. Scrum was asserting himself, just as things were getting interesting.

*Dammit.* I whimpered a little, gripping onto Spike's shoulders, begging him without words to stay and never stop.

But he ignored my pleas and kissed me once softly on the lips, closing my jaw for me with the pressure of his mouth and a gentle hand at my chin.

"We're done," he said softly, hugging me once hard before withdrawing.

"Where are you going?" I asked.

"I think I'd better go now. But you're going to be okay, Jayne. I promise." He left the bed before I could protest again.

I threw the covers down to yell at him for leaving, but the only one left in the room with me was Scrum. "What the hell? Where did he go?"

Scrum shrugged. "He flew out of here in a blur."

I sat up, breathing in and out a few times. I felt lighter. Not as depressed. The nap that had sounded like such a good idea before, now seemed like a horrendous waste of time.

"Looks like it worked," said Scrum.

"What worked?"

"The healing. Whatever he did to you. I'm not sure what it's called, actually."

I put my hand on my chest, no longer feeling a heaviness there. "Wow, you're right. I do feel a lot better." I threw the covers all the way off my feet and got out of bed. "Come on, Scrum."

"Where are we going?"

"To go see Tony."

"Shouldn't we wait for Tim?"

"Nope. We'll leave him a message."

Scrum frowned in confusion but followed me out of my room.

"Baby Beeeee!" I yelled out towards the garden.

"I'm in here," said a grumpy voice from the pixie bedroom.

"Well, come over here, I need to talk to you," I said from the hallway door.

"I'm not allowed."

I walked over to the pixie table and peered down into his little house. Willy was sitting cross-legged on his parents' bed, rolling a little yellow tennis-ball-looking thing on the covers in front of him.

"What's the matter, Willy?"

He didn't look up at me; he just kept rolling the ball. "Momma says I'm in a time *out* and I'm nodallowed to fly at *all* today. I'm *grounded.*"

"Oh, man. That sucks, Baby Bee. I'm sorry." I play-frowned at him to show him how bad I felt. I could imagine how much it must suck to be a hyperactive pixie and not be allowed to fly.

"Momma says I have a potty-mouth and if I say *what the fuck* again she's gonna wash my mouth out with ladybug pee."

My eyes bugged out a little at that, wondering if it might actually qualify as some kind of pixie child abuse. "Damn, Baby Bee, your momma's not messing around."

"My momma is *mean*. I want a *new* momma." He looked up all of sudden, a smile breaking out across his face. "Hey! *You* can be my new momma! That's a good idea, right?"

I panicked. "Uhhh, no, that's a terrible idea!"

His face screwed up and a tear slid down his fat little cheek. "It is?" he asked pitifully.

"Yeah, but that's because you're so *awesome!*"

"I am?" he asked, now looking confused.

"Yeah, of course! See awesome baby pixies need to be with mean mommas. That's the rule."

"Who said?" he demanded.

"Uhhh, this guy named Ben. He's the boss of stuff like that, and he said only the awesome baby pixies get mean mommas. He's kind of a jerk but we have to do what he says."

"Maybe I can *not* be so awesome and then you can be my momma, though. How 'bout that idea?"

"No, you're Tim's boy. So that makes you awesome by birth. You're stuck with it. But the good news is that you'll be the best flyer and the best spinner and the best of all the things."

"Even pollen eating?"

"Yeah. Pollen eating, booger eating, the works."

Willy sighed heavily. "Okay. Bye, Jayne." He waved half-heartedly and slouched down again, rolling his ball.

"Willy, will you do me a favor? It's very, very important. It would be like spider nakie stuff."

"Okay!" he said brightly, jumping up on the bed and bouncing a few times.

## Clash of the Otherworlds: Book One

"Careful! No flying!"

"I'm noooot!" he yelled. "I'm just jumping!"

"Tell your papa that I'm in Tony's room, okay?"

"Okay! And then what?"

"And then ... uh ... tell him it's top secret spy stuff. And to bring his best weapons."

"Okay! I'll tell him, Jayne. Spider nakies to the rescuuuuuee!" He started stripping his clothes off and throwing them onto the top of the table.

I stepped back a few paces and then ran to the door before he could recruit me into the game.

"What did he say?" asked Scrum, coming up next to me in the hall.

"He's going to strip off all his clothes and then tell Tim where we are.

"Why is he taking off his clothes?"

"Apparently baby pixies like that shit, I don't know." I hurried down the hallway, now anxious to talk to Tony not only about all the angels and demons but about that awesome incubus stuff. I wondered if it was the same for him and the twins.

I reached his door and knocked, pushing it open when I heard a voice inside. It swung open, and I froze in mid-stride, halfway in and halfway out. "Uhhhhh ... sorry. I didn't realized I was interrupting."

## Chapter Twenty-Six

TONY SMILED LAZILY FROM THE bed. "Come on in, Jayne. You're not interrupting anything." Felicia lay curled up next to him. Theresa was nowhere in sight.

I frowned. "Are you sure? Because I kind of feel like I'm intruding on something private."

Scrum peered over my shoulder. "Hey, guys! What's up?"

"Hey, Scrum," said Tony, waving his arm. "Come on in. We're just hanging out."

I slowly stepped the rest of the way in, staring at Felicia. She just lay there acting like nothing weird was going on. After a few seconds it got to me.

I put my hands on my hips, trying rein in my irritation at her but not having a lot of luck. My toe started tapping rapidly on the floor. "So what's the deal, Felicia? I think maybe you're overstaying your welcome in here."

She smiled serenely. "I don't think I am. Am I, Tony?" She turned her head to look at him, and he smiled back down at her, mirroring the expression on her face. They looked like lovers.

"No, not at all. You can stay as long as you like."

I whipped around to face Scrum, dropping my arms stiffly to

my sides and halting the toe-tapping. "Are you okay with this? Shouldn't she be getting a daemon bear hug or something?"

He shrugged. "She's not taking him down. They're just ... cuddling. He's not in any danger, Jayne."

"Humph," I said, looking back at them. I didn't know what to think now. *Are they dating? In love? Is he mesmerized? Am I upset he looks so happy?* I shook my head once to clear it. Nothing was making sense anymore. "Well. I don't know what to say, I guess." I just could not get over the sight of my best friend in bed with this soul-sucking, super-model cheerleader and looking so comfortable and happy. It just wasn't like Tony at all. He should have been stammering and turning red and nearly puking on himself with nervousness.

Scrum leaned in and whispered in my ear. "I think they ... you know ... did it."

I whacked Scrum in the arm. "Ya think?!" I nearly screeched at him.

He frowned, rubbing his shoulder. "Ow."

The door opened and Finn and Becky came in, laughing at something they'd been talking about out in the hallway.

Finn stopped short upon seeing Tony and his girlfriend. "Whoops. Dang me. Didn't know ya'll were havin' a private party in here. I'll just be outside when yer ready." Becky was in his way, so he stopped in the middle of his exit, doing a shuffle to try and get around her.

Becky craned her neck to see past him. "Hey, guys! Whatcha doin' over there? Cuddle time? Awww, look! They're so sweet together!"

Finn put his hands on her upper arms, pushing her back out of the doorway. "Come on, water girl. We ain't supposed to be interruptin' the lovebird session."

"Jayne's here," she protested. "I want to stay too." She disappeared and reappeared on the other side of the room.

Finn fell forward when the object he was pushing against suddenly wasn't there anymore. "Dang it, Becky! We agreed! No more disappearin' in my presence unless I say it's okay!"

I raised an eyebrow at that. "Finn's in charge of you now?"

Becky snorted. "As if. He's just bitter."

"Hey! You'd be bitter too if the love of your life took you on a ride through hell and back with zero warnin'!"

Becky disappeared and reappeared at Finn's side, wrapping her arms around his neck. "Did you just say I'm the love of your life?" She kissed him loudly on the cheek.

"No." He looked confused.

"I'm pretty sure you did," she said, grinning like a fool.

"Slip o' the tongue. Didn't mean nothin'."

She slapped his face lightly and let him go. "Too late. You're my love-slave now. Come on in and cop a squat. The meeting is gonna start soon."

Spike and Theresa came from the hallway and squeezed into the doorway without hesitating.

"Hey, guys," said Theresa, going over to the bed and sitting at the bottom by her sister's feet. "Hey, Handsome," she said, smiling and grabbing Tony's toes, shaking them gently.

"Hey," he said, grinning back at her.

I could tell by the dazed look on his face that his wiener and his brain were still in succubus la-la land. I shook my head with disgust. *Guys are so damn easy.* I glanced over at Spike, but he was looking at the ground. I stared at him for a while, but he wouldn't look up. I couldn't tell if it were deliberate or not, but a sound at the door interrupted my thoughts and I forgot to worry about it anymore.

Aidan was the next one in. "What's up, everyone?" He nodded around the room at the mumbled responses he got, a serious expression on his face. When his eyes lighted on me he winked, still not smiling. I wondered if my friends knew him, but none of them looked confused about seeing him here, so I said nothing.

The door opened again and Jared stepped in. Aidan moved over so he was farther into the room, making space at the entrance.

"Jared!" squealed Becky. She ran over, pushing through the bigger bodies to get to the daemon, giving him a big hug when she finally reached his side.

I walked over and held my hand out. "Hey, Jared. Nice to see you again. It's been, like, forever." He was the daemon who'd pulled me into this whole crazy life, tricking me into thinking he was a homeless teen in Miami, giving Tony and me a place to stay before luring us into taking the changeling test. I'd hated him for a while over that until I was finally ready to admit he'd done me a huge favor. Even now, after all this mess I'd gotten into, I was still grateful for it.

He pushed my offered hand aside and pulled me into a strong hug. Display of affection was a rare thing for Jared; I'd never seen him even touch another fae. So I was stiff with surprise at first, but then I couldn't deny the warmth of friendship and support that he was offering. I melted into him just a little and enjoyed the kindness he was sharing with me.

"Good to see you, Mother. I've missed you." He pulled away and stared into my eyes. "Looks like you've bitten off more than a mouthful this time, haven't you?"

I smiled ruefully. "Yeah. You could say that."

He rubbed my arms a couple times before dropping his hands. "Nothing to worry about. We'll just come up with a game plan and execute. Just like we always do."

"I wish it were that simple," I said, taking a step away. He was such a magnetic personality, it felt wrong to hog him all to myself. I put the distance between us so the others could share his presence.

Jared looked around. "Is everyone here?"

"No. We're missing Tim. And the other two. Did anyone go get them?" I asked.

"Go get who?" asked Aidan.

"Tim did," said Scrum. "He said to wait for him and he'd be back with your two meadow visitors. They might be the troops he was talking about, I don't know. It was a little hard to understand him."

"Who went with Tim? He can't open the doors himself," I said.

"Gregale," answered Scrum. "At least, that's who he told me he planned to use."

No sooner had the words left Scrum's mouth than the door opened and I heard, "Have no fear, Tim is here!"

I was shoved to the side by Jared, right before he jumped on Garrett as he walked in the door.

Gregale fell back out of the doorway and into the hallway with a gasp, inadvertently taking Shayla with him. The door shut behind them.

"Vampire!" warned Jared, wrestling him to the ground. I caught the shocked look on Garrett's face before he disappeared under Jared's arms.

The door opened again and Gregale and Shayla stepped through. Shayla had her weapon drawn and was looking for someone to stab with it.

"Stop!" I yelled. "He's with us!"

Jared held him in a headlock, keeping Garrett's head pointed at the ground. He looked up at me, his face beet-red from the exertion. "What?!"

"Let him go, I said! He's with us! I asked him to come in here, along with the angel you see standing there behind you with a dragon fang pointed at your head."

Gregale looked like he was about to faint, his shaking hand fluttering up to rest on his chest. His eyes darted around the room, taking in all the fae and other creatures standing less than ten feet away from him.

Jared's gaze followed my pointing finger. He gradually stood, loosening his hold on Garrett.

When he was nearly straight again, Garrett shoved Jared's arm off of him and immediately set about putting himself to rights. "Of all the rude greetings I have ever suffered ... that has to be the very worst," he huffed, trying to smooth his hair. A clump on top refused to lie down, making his attempts at seeming sophisticated almost comical.

"I'm sorry, vampire, I didn't know that you were invited."

"My name is not vampire, daemon. It's Garrett."

Jared held out his hand. "Nice to meet you."

Garrett stared at the offer of peace for a few seconds before finally accepting it. "And may I say it is a unique pleasure, having met you ...? I'm sorry, I didn't get your name."

"It's Jared." He looked over at Shayla. "Welcome."

"Thank you. I am Shayla of Blackthorn."

Jared looked from her to me. "She is of your line."

"Yes, she is."

He looked at her again, studying her closely. "You are the dragon slayer," he said finally, sounding surprised at his own conclusion.

"Yes. As is Garrett." Shayla nodded her head towards the very proud-looking vampire standing next to her.

"Forgive me, Garrett. I had no idea," said Jared, nodding his head in deference.

"It's quite all right. I do not walk around with a sign around my neck announcing my past deeds."

The now mostly-recovered Gregale half-bowed from the doorway as well. "It is an honor to meet you both." His eyes were shining as he stared at them, and I could practically see the wheels spinning in his head. He wanted to question them about every event they'd ever seen in the last three thousand years so he could analyze it until the day he died.

Garrett and Shayla seemed even more impressive to me now, knowing that Jared and Gregale held them in such high esteem. Gregale was brilliant and Jared was nothing if not loyal and dedicated to all faekind. I knew that even if I couldn't trust him to do what was best for me personally, he'd always do what was best for the fae. He had a kind of singular purpose that I envied.

Tim interrupted my self-analysis and review of the status of those before me with typical Tim style. "Wow, it's hot in here, and there's no circulation *at all*. I hope no one has gas today. Were there beans on the buffet? Does anyone remember?"

I cleared my throat, grateful that no one but me could hear him. "So, I guess we'd better get started talking about what's going on, since I think we only have about an hour's worth of oxygen in this room.

That earned me a few laughs.

"Where is Ben? Shouldn't he be here?" asked Jared.

"Maybe not for this meeting," I said. "We've had some incidents lately, and I think he's probably in recovery somewhere right now, anyway." I ignored the twinge of guilt I felt tweaking my heart.

"Recovery?" he asked.

"I'll tell you later. Anyway, I wanted all of you here to talk to these two, Garrett and Shayla, and see if we can figure out what's going on and what we can bring to the council."

"Why us?" asked Becky. "I mean, I appreciate the vote of confidence and all, but why not bring these guys right to the council directly?"

I wasn't sure I even knew the entire answer myself, and since I didn't think they'd buy the I'm-going-on-instinct answer, I pulled some stuff out of my butt. "The council gave me the job of finding out how the demons were getting through to our realm and told me to go talk to Maggie and stuff. And when I did that, I found Garrett. And then I found Shayla. So I'm just doing what I was told. But I don't want to go back there with half an answer, and since all of you are from different races, I figured you'd have as much input as any of those dodes on the council." I cringed and looked over at Jared and Aidan. "Not including you guys, of course. You're not dodes."

Aidan smiled. "Of course."

Jared said nothing. He just studied my face, and I tried not to let it freak me out. He could be so intense sometimes.

I looked at him sideways, wondering if he were going to call me on my bullshit, but when he said nothing, I continued. "So here's the nutshell version of what we're looking at: the demons are getting through to our realm using a tear in the Gray. That's the space dividing our realm from the Underworld. Because of that tear, Shayla got through too ... something to do with our connection and being related or whatever. Garrett got through when Maggie messed around with some spell at her house. I happened to be visiting when it all went down. Tony was in the Gray recently, and he has some stuff to add to my story." I glanced over at him, receiving a nod before I continued. "I also had a dream the other night, and during the dream I pulled Torrie the demon and Leck the wrathe in with me. Then I called Ben and he came in. I'm not sure what that means, or how these things are connected, but I'm open to hearing what you think. Especially if you have ideas about making that dream stuff never happen again, because it pretty much sucked the major honkiss."

"What can you tell us?" Jared asked Garrett and Shayla both.

Shayla spoke first. "As you know, the portals were closed a thousand years ago, give or take a decade. The Overworlders ended their influence in the Here and Now as requested by the fae. We have respected that request and will continue to do so until or unless the portals are opened again."

"That cannot happen," said Aidan.

Garrett spoke up. "You might not have a choice. The demons are coming. Their determination grows stronger with each breach. They have tasted the freedom of this realm, and all it has done is increased their thirst. They have found a way in. And not only do you have no guardians at the gate, you risk the fall of the Gray entirely."

Aidan gasped, and it sounded spooky as hell coming from such a strong guy. "You cannot be serious!" he said, his last word turning into a growl.

I thought my eyes were deceiving me when I saw him grow

taller and some hair sprout out of his face.

Jared took a step towards him and yelled, "Control the shift, Wolf!" Jared's arm was angled back towards me, stiff, as if keeping me away from Aidan. Or Aidan away from me.

Aidan growled loudly and then craned his neck out really far, the sounds of cracking bones making me jump in fear and disgust. But then, a second later, Aidan shook himself hard and was suddenly back to his normal self, but now looking chagrined. "Sorry," he said, shaking his head again, "but that was a little shocking, you must admit."

Jared ran his fingers through his hair. "Yeah, you're right. I don't blame you. If I were a shifter I'd be covered in fur right now too."

Aidan laughed.

I just stood there, mystified, looking around at my changeling friends. They all had the same expression as I did. *Good. I'd hate to be the only clueless one in the room.*

Tim came over and settled on my shoulder. "Wow. The doo-doo is really gonna hit the fan. And in my lifetime. How unlucky can a pixie be?"

"What are they talking about?" I asked quietly.

Jared interrupted Tim's response. "Tony ... tell us what you saw in the Gray."

Tony cleared his throat and sat up straighter in bed. His color was back to its normal pink, but all his acne was suddenly gone. He was handsomer than I ever remembered him being, which was weird because I never even noticed that stuff about him anymore. He was always just ... Tony. Now suddenly he was a cute guy. *Weird. Maybe the end of the world really is coming.*

"I was in the Gray, checking out some strange vibes in there when I found a space that just seemed ... off."

"Off?" asked Jared.

"Yeah. That's the only way I can describe it. I was trying to figure out what it was, when I encountered some beings there who didn't belong."

"And who were they?" asked Jared.

"And *what* were they?" asked Aidan.

"I believe they were Torrie, the demon, and some of his friends. They were definitely from the Underworld and not the regular souls I usually see and feel there. And they were in solid form, not the spirit form I also usually see."

"What about Leck?" I asked. "Wasn't he supposed to be in there with you?"

"Yes. He was there and then suddenly he wasn't. First Torrie disappeared and then Leck did. I didn't know what happened to him until you mentioned pulling him into your dream. I think you pulled them both out of the Gray and into your head or whatever."

"I wish I knew exactly when everything rolled out," I said, mostly to myself. Leck wasn't off the hook in my mind. I was going to have to confront him someday about it, but right now I was more worried about this falling Gray thing.

"You really believe the Gray could fall?" asked Jared.

Shayla nodded her head. "Yes. And so does Garrett. We've discussed it at length. You know the Gray was never meant to be a two-way egress. It's being abused right now, and no one knows what could happen if the abuse were to continue for too long."

Jared nodded, his expression grave. "We need to bring this to the council immediately."

"What exactly would we be bringing to them?" I asked. "I'm sorry to sound so ignorant, but I'm kind of lost again. What's this

# Elle Casey

about portals? And the falling of the Gray?"

"Yeah, sorry, y'all, but I'm a little lost myself," said Finn.

Becky raised her hand. "Me three."

"I expect all of you changelings to be lost," said Jared. "This was definitely not included in your training."

"We had no reason to think it needed to be," said Gregale. "This is just ... inconceivable."

"Never doubt the determination of a demon with a taste for human light," said Garrett, looking every inch the scary vampire.

I rubbed my wrist, glancing down at the scars that remained white. If they started turning black again, I was going to have a party in Samantha's honor and invite Spike over for a three-way, so they could both work their healing magic on me again. No way did I ever want to feel that shitty again. I narrowed my eyes at Garrett, wondering now how much I could trust a guy who'd put a smudge on my soul like that just because he was hungry. I ignored the part about his survival and the whole ashes to ashes thing, not sure it warranted being so sneaky.

Garrett looked over at me, the darkness in his eyes lightening as he straightened his features. "I am sorry, elemental. I did not wish to cause you harm."

All eyes in the room turned towards me.

"Never mind. It won't happen again. The blood bank is closed."

Jared's eyes grew wide. "Please tell me I misunderstand."

"Oh, you don't," said Tim, flying up in front of Jared's face. "He was, like, 'Oh, I'm so hungry, why don't you let me sip a little of your blood, it won't hurt at all, just a little smudge, yadda yadda yadda' ... and she was, like, 'Okay, go ahead handsome demon,' ... and he was, like, 'Grrrr, nom nom, black mark on your soul, nom

nom nom ..."'

I leaned over and waved Tim away from Jared's airspace. "It's over with, Jared. I've learned my lesson, and I'm fine, see?" I held out my wrist for his inspection.

He took it in his hand and studied the marks, looking up at Garrett with accusation in his eyes. "You've let her blood twice."

"Yes."

"You knew the danger."

"Yes. She was informed."

"Only the second time," said Shayla, challenging Garrett to argue with a lift of her eyebrow.

Garrett merely nodded. "Shayla speaks the truth."

"He didn't have time to tell me the first time," I said, yanking my arm back and pulling my sleeve down, "and the second time was a mistake on my part. I knew exactly what I was getting into. But I won't do it again, trust me." I looked at Garrett. "Sorry, dude. If you get hungry you're just going to have to blow away in the wind, because I'm done with that shit."

He bowed once. "As you wish."

Shayla's jaw tightened, and I saw a flash of fear in her eye before she schooled her features to appear unconcerned again.

Jared shook his head in disgust and then turned to Aidan. "You are on the council. What are your thoughts?"

Aidan remained silent for a full minute, the only sounds in the room that of people breathing and shifting around. Then a tiny squeak from Tim's butt.

"Sorry," Tim said, before flying to the corner of the room, giggling as he went.

"I think we have two problems of immediate concern, and I am honestly at a loss as to which must be dealt with first."

"I know of one," said Jared.

"You have been gone a while," said Aidan, sighing. "We have a power challenge, issued by Maléna against Ben and Jayne. They are to meet tomorrow to resolve the issue."

"That is a problem," said Jared looking at me. "Are you ready?"

I laughed bitterly. "Uh, no. Not really. I was supposed to train with Ben today and that didn't really work out."

"She killed him," said Scrum. "Then she brought him back to life. It was kind of shocking, really. I was a little afraid for my own life too, which doesn't happen often."

"Scrum!" I exclaimed, feeling a little sold out.

"Oh, sorry. Did I say that out loud? I meant to keep it in my brain."

"Stupid gnome-head," said Tim, flying down near me again. "Don't listen to him. He hasn't shampooed in weeks. All that nastiness is seeping into his gray matter."

"Well, that's not a good sign," said Jared. "What caused all of this to happen? Wasn't he there to help you?"

I felt my face getting red. The heat was burning my ears, too. "Well, Samantha showed up and threw a couple spells at me. And she was lording her Ben crap over me. And with all that vampire shit going on inside me, I guess I kind of ... lost my temper." I looked down at the floor, unable to meet his eyes. He was totally channeling Dardennes, and I felt like I was facing down the most powerful dad of all time.

"You call killing an elemental losing your temper?" he asked.

"Yeah. I'd call it that." I looked up at him. "Unless you have a better name for it."

Jared's mouth quirked up in the corner. "I'd call it kicking some serious ass, if it were me."

I felt my mouth stretching up to match the look on his. "You would?"

He put his hand out for me to take.

I shook it hard.

"You don't need his help to do what you need to do, Jayne. Believe in yourself. I do."

My throat closed up with emotion. I couldn't speak, so I just nodded. I wasn't proud that I'd nearly killed Ben, but now I didn't feel quite so guilty that I had the power to do it.

"That's right, bitches! And she's my roommate, so step aside!" yelled Tim, zooming around the room in circles, causing several of the onlookers to have to duck.

"I don't mean to be a wet blanket here, but I feel as though the voice of reason should weigh in," said Gregale.

"By all means," said Jared, gesturing for him to continue.

Gregale cleared his throat and then spoke. "It appears to me that the demons who are trying to breach into our realm find their purposes plainly served by our two elementals fighting for power over the council's control. I must wonder why anyone would feel the need to instigate such a struggle when we have such bigger issues to manage. I was not privy to the council event that fostered this challenge, so perhaps one of you members could shed some light on it for me."

Aidan frowned. "I guess it was pretty simple, from what I remember. Maléna asserted the council's right to direct the activities of the elementals. Ben rejected her claim, and she challenged him."

"Did it appear ... deliberate to you?" asked Gregale.

I was starting to get a little tickle of misgiving running up my spine. Maléna had seemed a little over-excited about the idea of us knuckling under to what almost seemed like her rule at the time, and not necessarily the council's.

"I'm not sure. What do you think, Jayne? You were there."

My mouth dropped open before I was ready to speak, so I stood there like a dummy for a few seconds before I could collect my thoughts enough to put them in order. "Uhhh ... I'm not sure. She did seem kind of nutty about it. Like, aggressive. But I don't know if that's how she normally is or not."

"Normally, she's pretty level-headed, actually," said Aidan. "At least when she's happy she is."

"What are you suggesting, Gregale?" asked Jared.

"I am not certain that this even rises to the level of suggestion; but might we consider that if you are kept busy fighting amongst yourselves on the council, you might be too preoccupied to notice other matters of import going on in the background."

"As in, Maléna's causing a distraction and letting the demons sneak in while we're turned the other way?" asked Tony. "It would be a brilliant move, really," he said, respect lacing his words. "The classic distractor technique. I'd use it, if it were me."

"Oh, fuck-a-duck," I said, letting their words sink in. "That would be ... I mean ... holy shit." I couldn't put into words the feeling of betrayal that was flooding into my heart and brain. I shouldn't have been surprised, being that it was Maléna; but part of me always wanted to believe that no matter what, we all had our best interests at heart. And letting demons into our world could never be good for any of us, Light or Dark fae.

"I don't think you should jump to any conclusions," said Garrett. "Anyone could have been recruited over to their side, given promises in exchange for aid. And the traitor wouldn't necessarily be obvious about it or be an obvious choice."

Everyone in the room looked around at each other. I knew that I, for one, was wondering if there might be a traitor amongst us here in the room.

"Is he serious?" asked Scrum.

"Nah, he don't mean us," said Finn, punching him in the shoulder. "We're the good guys."

"It could be *anyone*," said Shayla. "He is right. But you cannot run around your world accusing everyone and trusting no one. That will help them reach their goals faster than any use of an agent of darkness."

"Agent of darkness?" asked Becky meekly, now practically whispering. "Like a spy for the Devil?"

"In a manner of speaking," said Gregale. "And so, based on the limited information we have before us today, at this moment in time, I would encourage those of you on the council to gather for an emergency meeting and sort this out."

"And do not hesitate," said Garrett. "The end is coming. The veil will fall and then all will be lost."

"Part of it has already fallen," said Tony.

All eyes turned to him. "That's what was feeling so strange to me in there. There was this piece of the Gray just ... missing. Like it had fallen and created a door."

Gregale's face went white. He lifted his trembling fingers to his mouth. "Mother and Father, save us all," he whispered.

I had to cough hard to get my heart pumping again.

Jared grabbed my arm. "Come with me, Jayne. Aidan! Let's go!" He shoved past the couple of fae near the door and opened it up. "Garrett and Shayla, please come with us."

Tim came buzzing over to land on my shoulder. "Giddy-up,

mule. We've got a realm to save!"

"Don't we need our cloaks?" I asked.

Jared stopped. "Yes. Run! I'll meet you in the phi room."

Jared and Aidan wasted no time, running in the opposite direction.

I focused on a vision of my room so the door would appear and ran as fast as I could down the hall.

"If you guys wear those cloaks I'll be shut out!" yelled Tim in my ear as my feet slapped rapidly on the stone floor.

"I'm sorry! Be we can't risk anyone listening in!"

I reached my bedroom door and yanked it open.

"Tim!" screeched Abby from their table. "Get your sorry buns over here right this instant!"

I ran past her and into my room, yanking the cloak off the back of my door and throwing it over my shoulders. I could hear Tim whining in the other room.

"But I have to go save the realm, Abby! I don't have time for this right now!"

"You don't have time for ... are you *kidding* me?! This is our *son*, I'm talking about!"

"Yes, but ... "

"No buts! You're not going anywhere until we find him!"

"But Jayne needs me!" he roared in the toughest voice I've ever heard him use.

I hesitated at the door wondering if he was going with me.

"*Jayne* needs you? No, Tim! *I* need you! I. Need. You. And so does your son. You leave, and you will never come back to me again. Do you hear me? *Never!*"

I stopped breathing for a second, hoping he'd make the right choice. I sighed in relief when I heard his whipped puppy voice say, "Yes, dear. I guess I'll just have to let the entire universe fall into the hands of demons so we can go play hide and seek in the garden with our wayward child."

"Thank you. Now get out there and find him."

I ran out into the hallway, thinking about going right past Ben's door. But I came to a skidding halt when I realized that he needed to be at the meeting too, much as I might like to avoid him right now. I took a deep breath and knocked on the door.

# Chapter Twenty-Seven

HE DIDN'T ANSWER. I HAD no idea if he was even in, but I knew that we needed him at the council meeting, and he'd just suffered a pretty bad injury. If I let him sleep through this meeting, I knew there'd be no forgiveness for me. I knocked again, louder this time. *Come on, butthead, answer the damn door.*

When no one responded, I decided to try going in. I pushed on the handle, and it offered no resistance. The door swung open, revealing the dark interior. I craned my neck around trying to see the sitting room. I couldn't get a view of all of it from where I was, but it was clear that Ben wasn't there. I was just about to turn and leave when I spied the door on the other side of the room.

*Of course if he's sick he's going to be in there, not out here drinking that green stuff, whatever it is.* I sighed heavily, stepping into the room, reluctant to see him but knowing it was one of those must-do kind of things.

I walked across the floor, praying I wouldn't find him in bed with Samantha. I couldn't figure out why it was that I found that idea so distasteful. I didn't want him, and I sure didn't have any interest in her ... so why did I care about what they did? *I don't care. I don't. Focus, Jayne. Get Ben, and get the hell out of here. Everyone's waiting.*

I reached the door and tapped on it gently. When I received no response, I turned the handle and pushed it open, taking a few steps into the room. A lamp lit the space with a warm light, and the large bed that was up on a platform looked like it had recently been used, but there was no one in it now.

A sense of relief flooded my heart as I backed out of the room, pulling the door closed softly in front of me. I was glad that I hadn't found him there. Now no one could blame me if he wasn't at the meeting; I'd done everything I could. I was just getting ready to turn around when the sounds of movement coming from behind me froze my breath in my lungs and my feet in their tracks. *Busted!*

I regained my ability to move and breathe while my brain quickly started formulating excuses for being in his bedroom. I turned around quickly to explain. "I was just ... "

I stopped in mid-sentence, as soon as I realized that the room was empty. I'd been so sure Ben would be standing there, I didn't know what to think now. I frowned, still holding onto the door handle behind me, sure the noise hadn't been a figment of my imagination.

"Umm ... hello?"

No response came.

I let go of the handle and stepped to the side, bending over to peek under the couch that was across the room, wondering if someone might be hiding underneath it. But there were no legs there or other signs that someone was on the other side of the furniture.

My heart was hammering in my chest, making me feel like I was almost choking on the fear. I reached down slowly and took the edges of my cloak, pulling it around me. I had no idea if its magical properties would shield me from anything, but I wasn't taking any chances. I pulled the Green up into me with the plan to power-shield myself until I was out of the room, but as soon as the cloak began to shimmer with its light, the sounds came again. Only this time, I was facing them. Yet still, I saw no one and nothing there.

"Who the hell is that?!" I yelled out into the empty space. "I'm not kidding! If you don't show yourself right now I'm going to blast your ass into the Underworld!" The Green was humming in me now, answering my desperate call for protection.

"Tooooo laaate, sssss," came a voice. It was part-voice, part-hiss and probably should have scared the shit out of me, but the note of sorrow it carried made it seem less frightening. Either that, or I'd entered into another level of fear that no longer considered my mortality first before allowing my brain to be curious.

"Who is that?" I asked, moving farther into the room, one cautious step at a time. I was getting close to the table with the green liquid on it.

*Is the green stuff talking to me?* I got to the table and looked down, reaching out slowly to touch the decanter.

"Drink." The voice made me jump. My hand jerked back and went into my cloak, once more wrapping the material around me.

My eyes went left and right as my brain tried to figure out how a bottle could be talking to me. I gave up trying to find the answer in the air around me and bent down, talking to the liquid. "Are you talking to me?"

"Yessss," said the voice, but it wasn't coming from the bottle. Now that I was eye-level with it, I realized it wasn't the thing demanding I have a buggane martini.

*Phew. That's a relief. I thought I was going crazy for second there.*

I stood up straight again and spoke out into the room. "Where are you? I can't talk to you if I can't see you."

"You cannot sssseeee me until you drink," was the response.

The sparkling of the tapestry across the room caught my eye. I frowned in confusion, staring at the dragons there. I could have sworn they had been in different spots before.

I walked over to it slowly, temporarily forgetting the invisible hissing creature that was somewhere in the air around me as I tried to conjure of the memory of the tapestry as I'd seen it before.

"What the hell?" I whispered, now just four feet away from it. I held out my finger, pointing at each dragon in turn. "Black, silver, purple, red." I knew that the purple one hadn't been on the right when I was in here before, seeing Ben's room for the first time. Purple is my favorite color, so I had noticed the purple creature right away as the first dragon on the left.

"You've moved," I said softly, getting closer to the tapestry, my hand held out to touch it. It was mesmerizing the way it winked with hidden lights or sparkles, I couldn't tell which.

The hissing sounds came again, only louder, sounding like many voices instead of just one. They reminded me of snakes but then again, not snakes. There was a more human-like quality to the sound than I would have expected from a hissing reptile.

I shook my head to clear it. Even to my own mind, it seemed completely nuts, but I'd seen enough nutty things in the last few months that I really shouldn't have been questioning anything anymore.

My fingers were just inches away from the purple dragon, and now I could feel heat actually coming from it.

*It's alive!* I yelled in my head. *I'm going to touch a live friggin dragon that lives in a tapestry, and I'm pretty sure I'm not even crazy!*

# Clash of the Otherworlds: Book One

My fingers made contact, expecting to feel a rough canvas or heavy cotton material. But instead, they touched something smooth and hard, almost like metal. It was warm, and it moved beneath my hand.

"Whoooaaaaa, that is some seriously fucked-up shit," I said mostly to myself, fascinated by the fact that I was feeling some sort of creature in this picture. I refused to consider that I'd lost my mind completely.

"Drink," came the voice again. It was coming from my left. *Holy shit on a stick. One of the dragons is talking to me.* My breath was coming rapidly, a combination of fear and excitement pumping adrenaline into my system, making me want to pull Blackie out and wave it around a little, just to keep anything that might be tempted to eat me from indulging.

"You mean the green stuff?" I asked, pulling my hand away and letting it drop to my side, trying to figure out which dragon was doing the talking. I took some deep, calming breaths to control my fight-or-flight instinct. I didn't want to leave just yet, and I also didn't want to piss this creature off. Not yet anyway.

"Abssssinthe."

I looked over at the buggane martini, swallowing hard as I imagined myself trying it. I was never much for hard alcohol or even beer; it all tasted nasty to me. But then I wondered how many times in my life I'd probably have the opportunity to do a shot with a dragon, and decided to give it a whirl. "What the hell?" I said to the purple dragon. "What have I got to lose, right?"

I kept the Green flowing through me as I poured myself a glass of the green stuff - the absinthe. I raised the tumbler to my nose to give it a whiff. The smell reminded me of herbs and black licorice. *"Ew.* That's gross."

None of the creatures answered me, so I figured they weren't going to peer pressure me anymore than they already had. I plugged my nose and lifted the glass in their direction, smiling, excited - probably stupidly - about the prospect of partying with a bunch of dragons. I told myself the council meeting could wait five minutes while I had a little drink with a mystical beast from some of my favorite books.

"Cheers, dragons!" I made sure I couldn't breathe through my nose and therefore smell or taste anything, and then threw the stuff in the glass back, taking three large gulps and downing the contents completely before letting my nostrils go.

My tastebuds registered how horrible it was within half a second. The entire stomachful tried to come back up, but I forced it to stay down, dropping the glass with the effort of controlling my gag reflex.

I was finally able to breathe normally again about ten seconds later.

"*Gah!* That was *terrible!* How does anyone drink that shit?" I scrubbed my bottom lip and tongue with the sleeve of my tunic, trying to get the bitterness and the taste out of my mouth. "Holy gagballs, that stuff should be banned from the earth." I scowled at the offending bottle, tempted to pour it all down Ben's toilet.

"Oh, shit-on-a-stick," I gasped, suddenly remembering why I was there in the first place. *"Ben.* I have to get out of here." I was going to miss the meeting. The reason for drinking the gagworthy liquor didn't seem as important as it had less than a minute ago, as I imagined walking into the meeting and every fae there waiting for me, scowls on their faces.

I took a step towards the door, but faltered, the room having started moving in strange ways. "Whoopsy," I said, bumping into a small side-table and laughing a little at the tickling sensation the tilting room caused in my stomach. "Stop moving, room." I blinked my eyes a few times hard, trying to clear my vision. Things were swimming around, even the chairs refusing to sit still.

I looked up at the tapestry and was shocked at what I saw there. The dragons weren't flat anymore. They were in three dimensions now, their eyes blinking, their heads moving around atop their long scaly necks, and their wings snapping out and drawing back in, floating on invisible air currents. I saw the claws of the black one opening and closing, like he wanted to grab something and squeeze the hell out of it.

"Hoooollly pixie parts," I said, stumbling over to get a closer look, heedless of any danger tapestry dragons might pose to my person. But my legs didn't want to function properly, sending me diagonally towards the black dragon instead of the purple one. I flinched back when it opened its mouth and hissed loudly at me. The red one next to it hissed too, baring some seriously sharp-looking fangs. I looked again at the black one and realized it didn't have any of the longer teeth the red one had.

My hand moved down to my thigh, pulling Blackie from its sheath at my leg. I slowly held it up in front of the black dragon, my hand swaying a little with the weight of it. "Missing one of these, aren't you?"

I huge burst of fire flew out of its mouth, hitting me full in the face.

"Aaaaaahhhh!" I screamed, ducking behind my forearm, certain I was going to have melted skin or at the very least, singed eyebrows. I remained crouched over, my arm over my head, waiting for the pain that didn't come. *Maybe the martini has numbing powers along with room-tilting powers.*

A voice came to my ears after the fire finally stopped washing over me. "You are uninjured, sssstand elemental."

I wiggled my eyebrows and noticed my face felt fine. I was pretty sure all my hair was still there, too. I lowered my arm and stood cautiously, waiting for another blast from the furnace that I feared was coming. It hadn't hurt, but the heat was there. Sweat droplets beaded above my upper lip and across my forehead.

I glanced at the black dragon first. His mouth was closed now, but he eyed me with malice. I looked next at the purple dragon, the one who I thought had spoken to me. It didn't look angry or happy, no expression at all showing on its face, making it possible for my blood pressure to go down enough that I had the presence of mind to study what was in front of me a little closer.

The dragons had grown in size, but weren't what I always thought they'd be like. All of them were about as big as sheepdogs. They had scales of their predominant color but in varying shades. The purple and red dragons where boldly-hued, their scales shimmering and glistening, reflecting some light from a source I couldn't identify. The black and silver dragons had scales that looked duller, more like armor than the other two dragons'. They were also a bit bigger - largish sheepdogs compared to smallish ones.

I stepped over closer to the purple dragon. "Are you for real?" I asked, reaching my hand out again. My fingers trembled, and I was scared shitless, but I had to see how deep I'd fallen into this hallucination. The room felt like it was moving still, and the different shades of purple in the shining scales made me feel almost woozy - but in a good way.

The dragon remained motionless except for its wings that moved slowly, as if making adjustments on the wind.

## Clash of the Otherworlds: Book One

My hand made contact with the body of it, the heat coming to me instantly. It didn't burn. The skin just felt ... *alive*. "Oh my god ... you're real ... you're ... you're *living*. You're alive!"

"Of courssssse we are alive. Jussst as you are."

"Ha!" I laughed with the insanity of it, but then got instantly sober again, lost in the dragon's sparkling scales. "Why are you here? In this tapestry?" I stroked its neck and a purring-type sound came from its nostrils along with a wisp of smoke.

"It isss here that we are kept contained, as our ssservicessss are no longer needed by the fae and humanssss."

"What services?" I asked, my mind blown all over again, trying to figure out how dragons could have ever been in the service of me as a teenager in Florida. There were about ten dorks at my school who still played dragon role-playing games, who I knew would totally shit their pants right now if they could see this. I wished in that moment that I could go home and tell them they were totally right about all of it, so maybe they wouldn't be mocked so hard by everyone else for their games anymore.

"Guardianssss of the portalssss."

"I heard something about that," I said. "But why? Why don't we need you anymore?"

The black dragon hissed loudly, more flames bursting out of its huge jaws. I only ducked a little this time.

"You do need ussss. That issss the problem now. Go, elemental. Tell them. The Fall drawsss nigh."

"The Fall? Like as in Autumn? I'm confused."

Now both the red and black dragons were using their flame throwers on me, so I backed away from the tapestry, stumbling as I went. My tunic was sticking to me with my sweat, so I plucked at it to get it away from my skin. I was so distracted trying to do too many things at once, my foot caught the edge of the carpet, sending me down to my butt, making my teeth clack together uncomfortably. My cloak flew up at the same time, covering my head; and the more I tried to free myself, the worse it got tangled around my neck.

"Jesus ... fuck ... get the hell *off* me you friggin ... "

"Let me help you," came a voice - a fae voice this time.

I stopped struggling, recognizing the voice's owner immediately. As the cloak fell from my face, I gazed up into the eyes of none other than Ben.

"What are you doing in here?" he asked, a stern expression on his face.

As I looked up at him, I found myself wishing I saw anger there instead of disapproval. I hated when he got all parental on me. "I came to find you," I said, getting to my feet, ignoring the hand he held out and only falling to the side a little. "We have a very important ... *hiccup* ... meeting to attend, like, right this second." I couldn't get my mouth to open all the way and my words were coming out a little slurred. I stretched my jaw open wide and wiggled it around a little, trying to limber it up so it would work properly again.

Ben frowned at me and then leaned in close to my face. I tipped my head back as far as I could, my lower back straining with the pressure.

"Have you been drinking?" he asked.

"No," I said, defensively, "I have not. I don't drink." A hiccup escaped my mouth again, and my hand flew up to my lips of their own accord. "Excuse me," I said, moving my fingers away to keep my hands busy with straightening my cloak. "Get your cape. We have to go. Seriously, it's like, life or death or something."

"I already heard. I came to get my cloak after I ran into Jared in the hallway." He shook his head at me a couple times before leaving me to go into his bedroom.

I patted myself all over madly, trying to get my tunic to stop looking like I'd entered and won a wet t-shirt contest. I still had the Green linked up and the turquoise swirls in the cloak were making me queasy. Try as I might, I couldn't get my connection to go completely away. I took some deep breaths, trying to center myself. *Fine, Green. Stay if you must. Maybe I'll get lucky and get kicked out of the meeting so I can go sleep this shit off.*

Ben came back out about thirty seconds later with his cloak over his arm. "Come on. Let's go."

I noticed that he glanced at the dragon tapestry on the way out, but the dragons had all gone back to their regular positions, and none of them were hissing or throwing flames anymore. As I left the room, I wondered if I'd imagined the whole thing. The last thing I saw before I walked out the door was the deep red eyes of the black dragon, staring out into the room. He still looked pretty cranky to me.

# Chapter Twenty-Eight

BEN AND I WERE THE last ones to arrive at the meeting. I put on my most apologetic expression, but Ben didn't bother. He looked like he didn't give two shits about everyone having to wait on us.

I nudged him in the side, trying to communicate to him that it would probably help our cause to be at least a little humble.

He just ignored me.

I frowned at his back. *You could at least fake it, jerk.* When I was done staring holes in his back, I glanced at the faces around the table. The room quieted down as Ben and I took our seats. My gaze finally fell on the silver elves at the head of the table. Both Céline and Maléna kept their eyes forward, not looking at anyone. Dardennes had a very sober expression, which struck me as appropriate but also a little bit unnerving. He usually had at least a small smile for people at meetings - but not today.

"Thank you everyone for coming on short notice," he said without preamble. "Jared, we appreciate you alerting us to the need for this meeting. I'd like to turn the chair over to you now so we can get right to the point."

Jared nodded once at Dardennes and then stood, his eyes scanning the council members' faces as he spoke. "As Anton has already said, thank you for coming on short notice. This is an emergency situation, and so while we appreciate that you have many things to attend to right now, we are quite sure you will not fault us for interrupting your work on this occasion."

Jared's eyes stopped on me, making me squirm in my seat. I felt queasy and wondered what the odds were that I might upchuck right here in the meeting. My gaze slid to the door, as I tried to gauge how quickly I could make it out of the room if my stomach lost control.

"Jayne and Tony, along with ... some others ... have brought things to my attention regarding the sudden influx of Underworld creatures we've noticed."

"Who were these others?" asked Red.

I frowned at him. Friggin old coot. He never could let anything just slip by. "Just chill, Red, and let him tell the story. Geez." The words were out before I could stop them. I seemed to have lost the break between my brain and my mouth. I smiled sheepishly, realizing I was working against myself by calling attention my way. "Or, you know, go ahead and ask your questions. Whatever." I wanted to slip down in my chair until I fell under the table. I got about halfway there before a jab from Aidan stopped me.

"What's wrong with you, elemental? Have you been drinking?" he asked softly as Jared continued talking.

I sat up straight, deciding that acting outraged was my best defense. "What? Who me? I don't drink. That's ridikalus."

"Ridikalus?" asked Aidan, laughing softly.

"You know what I meant," I growled, scowling at him.

Jared's voice made its way into my consciousness. "Based on what I just explained, I ask that you allow me to answer your question in due time, Red. I'd like to share some things we have learned first."

Red nodded once, now deliberately not looking at me.

I kept staring at him, hoping I could catch his eye so I could stick my tongue out at him or something. I wasn't sure why I felt this was my best course of action, but I focused on it with everything I had, most of Jared's words getting lost in the haze of absinthe afterglow.

A few seconds or a few minutes later, I didn't know which, Céline said, "What did you hear, Jayne?" Her voice had drawn me out of my plans for revenge against Red, making me once again the center of attention. Only now I had no idea what anyone was talking about.

"Huh? About what?"

Aidan leaned in and whispered in my ear. "Are you okay, Jayne? You seem ... a little out of it."

I shoved him away from me. "Shut up, werewolf hairy beast man. You dunno what you're talkin' 'bout." He was making everyone look at me while I was trying to be all incognito, and it was pissing me off. *How am I going to get out of this place without giving away my secret, if everyone keeps talking to me?* I'd decided that drinking swamp juice in the middle of the day was probably a bad thing to do no matter where you came from, so it quickly became my deep dark secret that I didn't want to share with anyone. Not even Tony or Tim.

"Jayne? Are you alright?" asked Céline, concern lacing her voice. If it had been anyone else asking, I probably would have gone right ahead with my plan to insult anyone who accused me of being drunk, but I couldn't do that with her. I was afraid I'd hurt her feelings and make her cry or something. She'd always been so nice to me.

"I'm just feeling a little woozy is all." I gave her a weak smile, all I was capable of at the moment. "I think I might have had something that didn't agree with me."

Red stood suddenly, followed by Celeste. "Come here, changeling," he demanded. Celeste motioned for me to come too.

I looked at both of them, pushed out my pursed lips, and shook my head. No way in hell was I going over to the crusties and letting them get a whiff of my breath. I'd be outed as an absinthe-a-holic for sure.

"Jayne, I believe they are concerned you've been spelled. Please let them check you," said Céline.

"I don't think it's a spell," said Aidan.

I whipped my head sideways to tell him to shut up, but his big smile threw me off.

"She's been drinking," he explained. "I can smell it on her breath."

My jaw dropped open. I recovered quickly and yelled, "I have *not!*" probably a little too loudly. A few council members flinched.

Ben pulled me by my cape towards him and got right in my face, his nose nearly touching my lips. "Yes, you have," he accused. "What did you drink? Who gave it to you?"

I karate-chopped his hand to get it off me. "None of your cotton-pickin-beeswax, buttwad, so hands off the merchandise." I looked up at Jared and gestured graciously, using my most mature voice. "Please, Jared. Continue. What were you saying?"

He cleared his throat, erasing whatever expression he might have had on his face to appear unaffected by the craziness around us. "As I said, it is clear to us now that something must be done to keep the Gray from collapsing, and that you might have ideas, based on some things you've heard, about some possible solutions."

Since I had no choice but to answer now, lest the conversation turn again to my little issue, I responded. Unfortunately, I couldn't quite get my brain around the words before they were already leaving my lips. "Yeah. The angel dragon slayer and the vampire guy both said the Gray is falling. Tony agreed. And then the dragons said the time draws thighs, so we're, you know, up shit's creek and all that."

The looks on the faces around me ranged from confused to shocked. I slapped my palms to my cheeks, trying to keep the heat away from them or at least from showing my embarrassment to the rest of the world. "*Gah*, this place is friggin *hot*. Can someone open a window or something?" I started snickering. "That's a joke. Get it? We don't have any stupid windows in this place." I turned my head to look at Ben, my hands still on my face, making my lips go somewhat sideways. "Can you whip up a little wind in here, elemental guy? I'm hot."

"Dragon's mead!" shouted Red from across the table. He was still standing, but now he was pointing an accusing finger in my direction.

I looked first at Ben and then Aidan. "Yo, Aidan. I think you're in trouble, dude. He's pointing at you."

Aidan was smiling like a loon. "Nope. I'm preeettty sure it's you he's pointing at. Not me."

"*Pfft*. Yeah, right." I refused to look back at the old geezer, instead focusing on Céline's face. She looked so sweet and nice and confused. I much preferred that to angry right now.

"Present yourself, changeling!" demanded Red. Several of the other fae were grumbling now, and it sounded like they agreed with him.

"She does not answer to you!" yelled Ben, standing next to me, holding his arm out in front of my face.

I shoved it way from me, sick of him thinking he could answer for me. But before I could protest to any of it, Maléna stood.

"Yes, she does. As do you! Present yourself to the council, elemental."

Aidan leaned over, looking concerned. "I think you'd better do it, Jayne."

I smiled at him serenely. I was feeling much better now. The queasiness had left and been replaced by a soaring sense of confidence. I felt like I could practically fly if I wanted to. "Don't worry, Aidan. I got this." I turned to face Maléna, smiling devilishly at her. *So you want a challenge? I'll give you a challenge you nasty demon ho.*

"First of all, you can suck it, Maléna. You don't tell me what to do *ever*. And second of all, I seem to remember you wanting to throw down today. Why don't we just start now?" I rubbed my hands together, reveling in the energy pulsing through me. It ramped up several notches without me even thinking about it, making my cloak go mad with color.

"How dare you!" she hissed.

I giggled, leaning in towards Ben. "She sounds like a dragon when she does that."

He looked at me with his eyebrows all scrunched together. "What did you just say?"

I stood back up straight. "Yeah, I dare. Come on, then. Give me your best shot, ho-bag." I tapped myself on the chest with both hands. "Need me to draw a target for you? Right here, babe. Hit me." I drew an imaginary circle around my chest.

"You are lucky one of us has self control," she growled at me.

"*Pfft.* Scared. Just like I thought."

She lifted her arm and drew it back behind her ear, like she was ready to pitch a fastball at me. I readied myself to throw up a shield, praying it would act like rubber and bounce her nasty shit right back at her, but Ben beat me to it.

I felt the heat of his element before I had time to even look at him. A wall of fire suddenly surrounded us, blocking the others from my view.

I put my hands on my hips and glared at him. "What'd you do that for?! I was getting ready to let her have it!"

"What's gotten into you, Jayne?" he asked, searching my eyes. "I'm seriously worried about you."

"Worried? Huh." I didn't see the anger I'd expected, which threw me off and calmed me down about five notches. "You're not mad at me for killing you?"

"You didn't kill me, obviously."

"Well, I did, actually; and then I un-killed you. And if you'd done that to me, I'd be super pissed at you. Like never-to-be-forgiven pissed."

"If I responded that way every time you did something to anger me, we never would have gotten to the binding ceremony."

I raised an eyebrow. "And that was such a fabulous idea, wasn't it?"

"The reasons for it have not changed. In fact, they have only grown stronger. I would have liked for it to be more than in name, but what's done is done." He shrugged. "We need to move on and do what is best for the fae."

I couldn't lie to myself; his rejection stung. He'd come out and acknowledged we weren't going to be boyfriend and girlfriend, and it pissed me off that I wasn't feeling relieved so much as dissed.

"It's my hair isn't it? It's ugly, I know. Tim's always telling me to do something with it." I reached up to tug at my ponytail.

"What? What are you talking about? No, it's not your hair." He shook his head at me.

"The face, then? Yeah, it's the face, isn't it? Samantha's prettier than me. I'm woman enough to admit that."

"Samantha is pretty, but I really don't know what that has to do with anything."

I shrugged. "I don't blame you for wanting to be with her and not me. If I were a guy, I might feel that way too." Saying it out loud, I broke my own heart a little. I couldn't believe I was being so stupid. "Jesus, I am never drinking any more of that friggin buggane martini ever again. You should flush that shit right down the drain."

Ben grabbed my upper arm. "What'd you just say?"

His grip was uncomfortably tight, so I reached up with my other hand to pry his fingers off. They were warm and strong. When I touched them, he took my hand and refused to let it go.

"Tell me," he said.

"I'd rather not," I said, not pulling my hand away. His grip felt steady and sure. My whole world was spinning out of control, so it was nice to have this anchor.

"Jayne, seriously. Just tell me. I'm not going to be mad."

"Probably you will be."

"Okay, maybe I will, but I'll get over it. I got over you murdering me, didn't I?"

"Hey! You said I didn't kill you! You can't go calling it murder now, that's not fair."

"What's not fair is you keeping secrets from me. We're bound. We live together. You can't keep secrets."

"Why not?" I asked, my chin jutting out in defiance.

"Because it makes it too difficult for me to protect you," he said simply.

My head dropped down a couple inches, the guilt soaking into my brain. "Oh." I could detect no guile or deceit in his words. He really meant what he was saying. I sighed heavily, ready to cast off the secrets and be done with getting the humiliation over with. "Okay, fine. I'll tell you." I lifted up my head and said, "Hello, my name is Jayne Sparks, and I am an absinthe-a-holic."

Ben laughed once and then looked confused. "Uhhh... what?"

"You heard me," I said, jerking my hand out of his grasp. "I drank some of that green shit in your room, I got wasted, and had some hallucinations, and then came in here and made a fool out of myself." The sobering effect of the truth was making me feel sick all over again, only this time it wasn't the drink in my stomach but the thoughts of having to face all these really smart and nice fae who'd witnessed my being an idiot. *Again.*

"You drank the dragon's mead in my room?" he asked, his tone clearly saying he didn't believe I could be that stupid.

"Yeah. But it wasn't my fault. They made me do it." When in doubt, blame the nearest scary creature. That was my motto now.

"Who made you do it?"

"The dragons."

"What dragons?" he demanded, sounding angry now, like he didn't believe me.

"The dragons in your room, dummy. What other dragons would I be talking about?"

"Jayne, stop being daft. There are no dragons in my room."

"You're the one being daft. What a stupid word, by the way. There are exactly four dragons in your room, and they told me to drink it, so it's mostly not my fault. I mean, when a dragon tells you to do something, I'm pretty sure it's a rule that you just have to do it."

"Holy shit. You're being serious."

"Holy shit, Ben. You just cussed!" I was pointing at him, my mouth hanging open in a half smile. "Ha! That's awesome!"

He grabbed my finger and held onto it, staring at me intently. "Forget that and back up a second. You're telling me you talked to dragons in my room. *Real* dragons."

"What other kinds of dragons are there?" I asked, unsuccessfully trying to get my hand back.

"Where are they now? What did they look like?" He sounded like a little kid at Christmas, guessing what his presents might be.

I couldn't figure out what kind of game he was playing. He looked at that stupid wall-hanging every day. Surely he knew there were dragons on it.

"I know you know there are dragons in there. Stop playing with my head. I'm not drunk anymore, so it's not going to work."

He grabbed me by the upper arms and shook me twice, snapping my head back and forth. "Jayne. Tell me about the dragons."

I flapped my arms a few times to get him off me. When he wouldn't let go I glared at him. "Get your dick-beaters off me, or I'm gonna blast you to kingdom come again."

He dropped his hands and waited expectantly for my answer.

"Fine. You want to play dumb? Go ahead. The dragons told me some stuff and I'm pretty sure it's important, so you'd better drop this fire wall so we can talk to those other fae out there."

"You said they talked about your thighs. How can that possibly be important?"

"I did not."

"Did too."

"Did not! I said that they said the time draws nigh!"

"That's not what you said."

"Whatever!" I yelled. "The time is coming, so drop the wall already!"

"Tell me first. Maybe we shouldn't tell them at all."

I took a step away from him. "Be careful, Ben. You're starting to sound like one of the bad guys again."

"Listen," he said, running his hands through his hair in frustration, "I don't really know what the hell is going on. After hearing what Jared said and getting knocked out for several hours by my partner ... everything's kind of ... confusing. I just want to figure things out for you and me, first, before we involve everyone else. We have to stick together."

I was tempted to go along with his idea, but then I thought about Tony and Tim and all my other friends. I didn't like the feeling that I was in a little bubble with Ben and all of them were standing outside it. That just didn't seem right to me.

"Sorry, dude. As tempting as it is to say it's you and me against the world, it's just not going to work. I can't cut my friends out like that."

"I'm not asking you to do that."

"Then explain better, because that's what it sounds like to me."

"I just want you to trust me."

"You sat with Samantha at lunch." My response sounded petty and pitiful to my own ears, but it was out before I could stop it.

"So? You didn't want to sit there. What was I supposed to do? Eat alone for the rest of my life?"

"Yes! Or come sit with me! Why her, of all people?"

He looked at me like I was nuts. "What is it with you and her anyway? Why is it such a big deal that she and I are friends?"

"Shit, I don't know. Go ahead and be her friend. Eat every meal with her. I don't care." I couldn't figure out what my problem was. He wasn't my boyfriend. I had no claim on him.

"I won't. Never again. I can see it upsets you, and I don't want that."

Now I felt like a total jerk. Samantha was going to get rejected because I was a jealous dode. "Never mind I said anything. Really. Eat with her. She needs friends."

"We all need friends," he said softly. "At least we have that, right?" He reached down and laced his fingers in mine.

It made my heart skip a beat. It was nice to think of a powerful guy like him declaring his friendship for me. This felt more real than the romance stuff had.

"Yeah. We do. So long as you don't piss me off."

He laughed, squeezing my hand once before letting it go. "Okay, fine. I'll work on that. But for now, please just one more time, tell me about the dragons."

I let go of my anger and tried to just talk to him as if he were a normal person. "The dragons in your tapestry told me to drink that green crap, and when I did they talked to me. And kind of came alive. They told me they are needed again, or something to that effect."

"Did they mention portals, by any chance?"

"Yes, they did. What do you know about them?"

"Not a lot. But the fae around this table know everything there is to know. Shall we share what you've learned with them?"

"What do you think?" I trusted his judgment right now, especially since he hadn't laughed at me for hallucinating about dragons coming off the wall.

"I think we should. Maléna is chomping at the bit to get you thrown off this council. We need to show them you have value to everyone."

"Are you serious?" I was all offended now. "She's got serious balls if she thinks she can decide whether I stay or go."

"My thoughts exactly." He nodded at the wall. "Are you going to be ready to face her when we get out of here? The challenge is going to have to start after the meeting. She's going to demand it."

"I'm ready."

"We never had time to put together our plan to fight her off," he said, worriedly.

"A demon told me to steal her wind from her and then it'd be easy."

"Since when are you friends with demons?"

"Since never. But apparently they have secrets to share, and I'm not ashamed to take advantage of that."

Ben looked at me sideways as he got ready to drop his fire wall. "Just be sure it's you that's taking advantage and not the demon."

The wall dropped and we found ourselves faced with not just Maléna, but several other fae, all of them poised, ready for a fight.

# Chapter Twenty-Nine

THE WALLS TO THE MEETING room fell away, and we were all transported to a grassy clearing somewhere outside the compound.

"What the hell?" I asked, looking around me in confusion, immediately noticing I had never been here before. I wondered how far from home we were.

"Now!" yelled Maléna, lifting her arms and bringing up huge gusts of wind to batter us.

Leaves and dead flowers flew up into our faces, dirt stinging my eyes and making it hard to see. A yellow smoke blew over into our noses. I pinched my lips closed to keep from breathing it in, but I couldn't stop inhaling through my nostrils. I caught a faint whiff of sulfur before my nose got totally stuffed up.

"Grab her wind, Ben!" I yelled when the yellow junk had dissipated from the air a bit.

I looked over at him, expecting him to be surrounded by protective flames, but he was standing still, his arms locked down at his sides. There wasn't a single lick of fire anywhere near him.

"What are you doing?!" I yelled, freaking out that I was the only one with elements in the fight.

"I can't!" he yelled. "There's some kind of spell at work here!"

I tried to see through the mix of grit and crap flying through the air. There were vague shapes in front of us, figures with robes on, but I couldn't tell who they were or what they were doing.

"You still have your Earth element!" he yelled, looking over at me. His head seemed to be the only thing that was able to move.

I looked down at my cloak and saw the colors hadn't left it. I tested my connection and found Earth more than willing to do what I wanted. I pulled more of it up into me and threw some of it up around Ben, too. I encountered a resistance, though, when I tried to use it to heal him of the spell.

"What the hell is that?" I asked. My nose was tickling, and I really needed to sneeze. My words were coming out sounding like I had a head cold.

"What?" he asked, a look of panic on his face.

"There's something ... in you. I can't get the Green in there to help you out."

"Just focus on shielding me! You need to use your other element to hold them off until this spell has worked itself out of my system!"

"Hold them off, my ass!" I yelled with my stuffed up nose. "They're pissing me off, now. I'm not just going to let them get away with this bullshit." I didn't know why the spell hadn't worked on me, but I wasn't going to wait around and give them time to get a second shot at it. I stepped over and grabbed Ben's hand. "Hold on to me for luck."

He gripped my hand firmly at his side. "You can do this, Jayne. Just focus on putting the energy out at them ... concentrate. Keep it out of your eyes."

I drew even more of the Earth power into me, the Green pulsing as it flowed almost like the heartbeat of a massive creature.

I thought of Water, rippling in the lake and present invisibly as humidity in the air around us, picturing it gathering all the droplets together to form a liquid body that I could mold into a form and use as a weapon. I channeled it into churning walls of blue, rising up gradually as standing waves to our right and left. My hair crackled with the static being created in the now overly dry air around us.

I put the shield up stronger for Ben using just a small bit of the Green power.

He squeezed my hand, and I took it as gratitude.

"Where are they?" I asked. "I can't see shit out in that storm." My chest was thrumming with the threads of power that trembled there, woven together yet separate and distinct. I had to focus on each one so I wouldn't lose control of the massive power structures around us.

"You need to pull Wind away," he said. "Without it, they have only spells, and your shield should stop them from hitting us."

"I have no idea how to do that!"

"Dammit!" he yelled, clearly frustrated with being taken out of the game. "I'd know how to do it if I had control of Wind. I hate being locked out of my link."

"Just tell me how you'd do it, and maybe it'll work with Earth or Water."

"It's hard to explain. But if I were to describe it, I'd say it's like opening up your arms and pretending you have wings, catching the wind and reining it in with them."

I looked at him sideways. "I've never seen you put out your arms or having any imaginary wings."

"I do it in my mind. Visualization is the key."

I closed my eyes, not questioning him for a second because the desperation in his voice told me he wasn't messing around. I pictured myself lifting my arms and beautiful, huge white wings like Chase's coming out from behind me to pull in the element that was battling against me now. I could almost feel the imaginary feathers ruffling, fighting against the strength of the element working to snap them into pieces, but slowly winning the battle and then moving the flow however I wished it to go.

"Jayne!" said Ben excitedly. "You're controlling Wind! I can't believe it, but you're actually controlling my element!"

I dropped his hand in my excitement over his enthusiasm, and the wind that had started to die down kicked up again full force.

"Take my hand again!" he urged. "I think you're channeling it through me."

I did as he instructed, again working on my visualization, but this time doing it with my eyes open. It was harder, but soon the results began to show. The wind seemed to almost pause, as if waiting for my order.

"Push it back. Make it leave us."

"How?!" I yelled, panicked at the idea of controlling three elements now. I could feel my eyes burning with the effort.

"Watch it, Jayne. You're losing focus. You have three channels now, keep them separate.

"Okayokayokay," I chanted, taking deep breaths through my mouth since my nose was completely blocked now, trying to keep out the deafening sounds and crazy swirling tree parts that would have surely knocked us on our asses if the shield hadn't been there to protect us. *Don't fuck this up, don't fuck this up, don't fuck this up.*

The wind gradually died down under my constant litany of cussing chants. They helped me stay focused and centered, when I knew that it could be so easy for me to lose myself into one of those elements. Working three was nothing like working two. They fought to override one another while also stretching and yearning to combine in a way that made them seem almost human or fae.

"That's it. Keep doing that."

Figures came into focus as the maelstrom dissipated. Maléna stood in front of a group of fae, one of them Leck who was just behind her and to her right. If I were a betting fae, I'd say they were all witches, save him.

"That motherfucker," I said, anger burning my face. I probably would have sounded a lot more threatening if my nose hadn't been so stuffed up.

"Do you have a cold?" asked Ben.

"I think I must have an allergy to something out here. I was fine in the meeting."

"What is he doing out here?" Ben asked, apparently seeing Leck for the first time.

"Good question. Whenever I have a severe pain in my ass he seems to be standing around.

Maléna screeched over her shoulder at one of her cohorts. "Work your spell, witch!"

The witch I didn't recognize and who I knew wasn't on the council yelled back, "I already have!"

"Well, why is he controlling Wind then?"

"He's not," said Leck, staring me down. "She is."

Maléna's head whipped over in my direction. "That's impossible. She doesn't control Wind."

"Apparently, today she does," he said, clearly unhappy at the idea.

The walls of water had gone down in size as I'd put my attention into controlling the wind around us. I let them stay at that height, remaining as a threat to the ones they surrounded. I could see two of the four witches looking at them nervously.

"Do something!" Maléna hissed at them.

"We have done everything we can," said one of them, taking a few steps back. "You said you could deliver our spells, but you have failed."

Maléna gestured to Ben. "As you can see, I have not failed to deliver your spells. He is incapacitated."

"Well *she* isn't. We're leaving," the witch nearest Maléna said, backing away, too. Then the witch turned to look at me. "We would like to leave now. We ask that you permit us through your water shield."

I looked at her incredulously. "You've got to be fucking kidding me."

The witch got a nervous expression on her face, but straightened her shoulders and tried to look tough. "You have no quarrel with us as we have none with you. We were under orders from the silver elf."

"Traitor!" yelled Maléna.

"Don't worry about it, Maléna. I'm not buying her bullshit anyway." I looked at the witch again, making sure my gaze skimmed over all of them before stopping on her. "Orders to hurt me or Ben should have been ignored. Now you pay the price."

I could feel something tickling my back. A quick look over my shoulder revealed nothing, so I closed my eyes, focusing on the three elements I was commanding.

"No!" someone screamed.

"Easy, Jayne, not too much," came Ben's steadying voice.

And then I felt the fire. The one that warmed me but did not burn.

# Chapter Thirty

SCREAMS RENT THE AIR. I refused to open my eyes, all of my concentration taken by controlling the four elements that rushed into and out of every part of me. Ben was trying to pull his hand out of my grasp, but I held on tighter, using the Green to bind us together.

"I'm not ready to let you go yet, Ben."

"Jayne, it's too much! You cannot use all four elements! It will destroy you!"

I ignored his warnings. The power was seething, neither good nor evil, just pure everything. I saw them coming together in one awesome ball of color and light. The reds and oranges of Fire tangled in with the silver and black of Wind, the blues and greens making varying shades of turquoise as Earth and Water danced together. Strands of each wound around the other making a kaleidoscope of rainbows and shattered, splintered lights sparking out in every direction. My vision was completely obscured by the show.

I pictured the water washing away the witches who'd conspired to end Ben and me.

Ben's grip nearly crushed my knuckles and his voice was

shouting in my ear, but I disregarded all of it.

Next came Leck, who I pictured being swallowed up by the Earth, and left to feel the pressure of the creatures who walked above it, pressing down on him until no more breath could reach his lungs.

Last came Maléna. I laughed maniacally as I pictured her engulfed in flames, her face melting away from her skull, the fire turning her from fae to ash in a slow and painful torture I designed just for her. I felt nothing as her traitorous black demon-screwing soul disappeared from this realm.

# Chapter Thirty-One

BEN'S HAND LEFT MINE AND his elements followed a moment later. Then the pressure of his mouth was on my lips, and I couldn't think about the destruction or hatred of those who'd acted against me any longer. I felt myself enveloped in warmth again, but it was different this time. Now it felt like healing and sanctuary instead of like an angry mess lashing out against the world for the wrongs done to me and my friends.

His lips left my mouth, and he rested his forehead on mine. "Let your elements go, Jayne. We need to figure out what's going on."

"But they're going to kill us."

"No, they're not. I'll protect you."

"How can you do that if you're paralyzed?"

"I'm not anymore. I'm fine. Open your eyes and look at me."

I didn't want to, so I resisted at first. But his refusal to take no for an answer and his increasing pressure on my upper arms as he squeezed them made me respond. As my eyes opened and let the light in, focusing on the space around us, I realized we were no longer out in the middle of a strange meadow. We were in his room, and it was just the two of us.

I stepped back away from him, looking around in confusion. "What the hell just happened, Ben? Did I just imagine that entire thing? How did we get here?"

"The battle with Maléna and her cronies? No. Unless we were both part of the same nightmare, I believe it was entirely too real."

"We were in a meeting before, though, right? With the council?"

"Yes."

I wiped my hand under my nose, taking another step back from him as I tried to gather my thoughts and memories into a cohesive frame of reference. "Thank the universe, because I was starting to wonder if I'd suffered some permanent brain damage from that green shit."

Ben's eyes flicked over to his crystal decanter. "You drank the absinthe for real?"

"Yes. And before you get all pissy about it, I just want to say that I'm sorry and I'll never do it again. I'm pretty sure I'm suffering an allergic reaction to it right now as punishment."

A banging on the door interrupted our conversation.

Ben loped over, throwing it open to reveal Dardennes, Céline, and Jared. Tim came flying in over their heads.

"Jayne!" he yelled zooming over and hovering two inches from my face. "Talk to me, Goose. Tell me you're okay!" He came up to my eyeball, reaching out as if to take my eyelashes in his hands.

I leaned back. "Get away, lunatic. I'm fine."

"*Phew-ey*, what is that *smell*?" he said, waving his hands rapidly in front of his face. "I haven't smelled that odor since ... " He gasped and froze in midair, dropping a couple feet almost to the ground before his wings started working again and brought him back up to my eye level. "No! You didn't!" he yelled, buzzing over to the decanter. He landed on the table next to it and walked around it, eyeing the offending liquid carefully.

Before he could report back that he noticed some of the disgusting drink missing, the rest of the group entered the room and began speaking all at the same time.

Ben held up his hands for quiet and everyone immediately settled down. "We know you must have a lot of questions, as do we. May I suggest we sit and relax while we figure this out?" He gestured towards his conversation area, which was way too close to his alcohol stash for my comfort, but before I could complain and offer another option, they moved to comply.

I took a space on the chair directly in front of the decanter, deciding a body-block was my best bet at distracting anyone from looking at it.

Another knock at the door came and Ben went over to let Red and Niles in. I noticed Ivar with them too, but the ogre took up a position outside the door and refused Ben's invitation to come inside.

"What did we miss?" growled Niles, moving his stubby legs over in our direction so fast they were nearly a blur. I worked hard not to laugh.

"Nothing. We've just arrived," said Céline. She turned her attention to me. "Are you okay? We were so worried."

"I'm fine," I said, my stuffy nose making me sound ridiculous. "Other than seriously messed up sinuses."

"I don't recall you being sick in the meeting," she said. "I'm sorry for not noticing sooner. Perhaps we can find some herbs to help you."

"She wasn't sick earlier," said Ben, staring at me. "She got that way while we battled Maléna and her pack of traitors."

"Tell us," prompted Dardennes. "We had no idea where you all disappeared to. We've been searching the compound and exterior high and low. We'd already come for you here once, but didn't find you the first time. It was Tim who alerted us to your presence."

Tim flew over and stood on the arm of my chair. "Heard ya in here. I was going to knock but then decided reinforcements might be a good idea."

"Good thinking, Tim," I said. If he'd been caught up in that shit storm earlier, he'd be dead right now. I was grateful for his caution. If I'd killed him by accident I'd never be able to live with myself. Even the passing thought of it made me get a little choked up. I cleared my throat a couple times so I wouldn't embarrass myself.

"We were transported out of the meeting by one of Maléna's witch friends. They had some sort of spell planned for us that Maléna was supposed to deliver on the wind. But something happened they weren't expecting, and it didn't affect Jayne like it did me."

"What did it do to you?" asked Red.

"I was paralyzed and cut off from my elements."

Even Niles looked a little bit shocked at that.

"I cannot believe she would do such a thing," said Céline. "I am ashamed to call her my sister."

Dardennes patted her on the hand. "Don't say that. We don't know what exactly is happening yet. Let's wait to judge until after we hear everything."

Céline sniffed, her eyes suspiciously wet as they looked at me. I could practically feel the apology beaming out of them.

Ben continued. "Jayne was fine, although her nose got very

stuffed up," he looked at me, a faint smile playing on his lips, "and she just took over for both of us. She used her elements as shields and then, believe it or not, took my elements and used them too."

"That is not possible," said Niles, banging his hand down on the couch cushion he was standing next to.

"Apparently it is. It only worked when we were physically touching, but it was she who commanded Wind and Fire, not me. I was as helpless as a babe."

"That is an interesting way of wording your condition," said Red, a look of extreme concentration on his face. "There is a very ancient spell, one I have not seen used in a very long time. It renders the victim helpless - as a babe, so it has been described." He looked over at me. "And yet it did nothing to you. How curious."

"It made my nose all stuffed up. That's not nothing. It's kind of irritating, if you must know." I could feel a tickling coming from deep in my sinuses. "Does anyone have any tissue. I'm about to sneeze, and I'm almost afraid of what's going to happen when I do." I'd had too much dragon's whatever to drink, I'd just annihilated at least five fae after inhaling some toxic fumes, and I still had no idea where the hell I'd been or how I'd gotten there and back. I could sneeze and blow up the compound at this rate.

"Did he say that the spell was sent to you on the wind?" asked Tim, now up near my ear.

"Yeah. It was like a yellow smoke."

Tim flew up into my face, making me go cross-eyed he was so close again.

"Get away, spaz. I'm trying to listen."

Red was talking about the spell again, but I couldn't concentrate on what he was saying because of Tim's antics.

"I just need to look at something," he insisted, flying by my mouth now, laying horizontally on his back and zooming back and forth under my nose. He looked ridiculous.

"Seriously. Go away or I'm going to make you my badminton birdie."

"I'll be right back," he said, flying up into a corner of the room. I couldn't believe it when I saw him disappear into a crack in the stone.

*Why, you sneaky little bastard. You have a tunnel from Ben's room to mine.* My face blanched as I wondered how much spying that little turd had done not only here but wherever else he had his little hidey holes. My eyes narrowed as I thought about his secrets. He was so going down the next time I got my hands on him. *Roommates' honor code, my ass.*

When I was focused back on the meeting, Ben was filling them in on the fight.

"I couldn't see anything other than the elements. You'll have to ask Jayne what exactly happened."

All eyes turned on me, making my face get warm with embarrassment. I wondered briefly if I were going to be prosecuted, and if self-defense was a valid law in the fae world.

"Jayne, please tell us what happened. We are not here to judge you. We know you are not a vicious person," said Céline.

*Ha, ha. Don't bet on it.* I thought about the angry visions I conjured while I sniffed a couple times, trying to breathe around the blockage in my nose, giving up when it didn't work right away. I ignored the tickling that grew more intense with each minute and prayed they wouldn't decide I needed a one-way ticket to the Underworld for what I'd done.

"Well, I didn't see what *actually* happened … only what I

wanted to have happen."

"How is that?" asked Red.

"I use visualization to control the elements. That's the key you know." I looked over at Ben and he winked at me, encouraging me to keep going. "So I pictured the elements kicking their asses, basically. I'm not sure if I killed them or not, but just so you all know, it was totally self-defense. They were going to kill us, I'm pretty sure."

"No one is accusing you of anything," said Dardennes. "The rules of engagement in this type of situation are quite clear. Maléna knew the risks when she issued the challenge."

"*Pfft.* Do those rules allow for sneak-attacks?"

Dardennes smiled. "Not generally, no."

"She's a cheater. Why am I not surprised." I was feeling less and less guilty the more I learned.

"What I don't understand is why the spell didn't affect Jayne," said Red. "If it is the spell I am thinking of, it is powerful and foolproof. Neither she nor Ben should be here right now."

"Do you mean ... ?" said Céline, shock in her expression.

"They should be dead," he said simply. "It's meant to incapacitate so the death blow can be delivered. It has been used effectively against all manner of creatures in the past. Perhaps you have heard the tales of Nightshade's Lullaby."

"No!" gasped Céline.

Dardennes just shook his head, looking supremely disappointed.

Even Niles looked disturbed. It was one of the few times I'd seen him looking anything other than pissed off.

"What's that?" I asked. "It sounds badass, whatever it is."

I noticed some movement up in the corner of the room, and

out of the hole in the wall came not only Tim but Abby and Willy, too. Tim had Willy by the hand and was dragging him behind in the air. Willy didn't look very happy. He kept trying to reach up and disengage himself from his dad's grip, but Tim wasn't having it.

"Did I just hear Nightshade's Lullaby?" he asked, landing with Willy on the table next to the decanter.

I had to turn around to see him. I shot him scolding looks and jerked my head to the side, trying to signal him to move so he wouldn't attract so much attention to the absinthe, but he ignored me. I gave up and brought him into the conversation.

"Yes, they said Nightshade's Lullaby. I guess it was the spell they used against us."

Tim let out a low whistle. Abby's hand went up to her mouth, and she shook her head slowly.

"I take it this is a bad thing," I said, reaching up to rub my nose. My eyes were starting to water with the terrible twinges I was getting up high in my nasal cavity, almost near my forehead.

Willy kept tugging on his dad's hand, but his eyes were on me. He would not stop staring at my face.

I reached over and nudged him gently on the butt so he'd quit it, but it didn't do any good.

He grabbed ahold of my finger and tried to use it as leverage to get away from his father.

"Stop it, Willy, or I'll give you a spanking," threatened Tim.

"You'll do no such thing," said Abby, frowning at him.

"I. Want. My. *Polly balls!*" yelled Willy, ignoring the threats from his father and the protective measures coming from his mother.

I was completely mystified as to what they were doing in here with their baby. It seemed kind of like this meeting had some R-rated stuff going on, what with me talking about killing off bad-guy fae and all. I was no parent, but it seemed like maybe they should have left him in the other room.

Dardennes reached into a bag at his waist and pulled out a handkerchief, handing it to Céline and gesturing at me.

I leaned over and took it gratefully from her, wiping under my nose, trying to keep the dripping at bay. No way was I going to honk the schnoz right here in front of everyone, but at least I could keep stuff from running down my face. I nodded at Dardennes in appreciation.

"Polly ba-ha-haalllls!" wailed Willy. "I want my polly baaaalllss!" He went from distraught to angry and back again, obviously in full freak-out mode over his toys.

No one else could hear him but me and his parents, but it was so distracting I could barely pay attention to the conversation going on around me. Red was explaining exactly how the spell worked, and Jared was commenting on the last time he'd seen it used, but I missed everything Dardennes and Céline said because they were turned away from me and Willy had gone ballistic over his stupid toys again.

"Polly balls! Polly balls! I. Want. My. Polly balls. Right. *Now!* They're *mine!* They're *mine!*" He turned his face up at me, beet red, with tears running down his cheeks and snot dripping off his nose. "Gimme my *polly balls*, Lellamental!"

"Jesus, Tim, give the damn kid his polly balls, for shit's sake!"

All conversation in the room stopped. Everyone stared at me.

"What?" I asked innocently. "The kid wants his polly balls." I had no idea what a polly ball was, but they seemed important to him; and I for one was all about shutting his loud ass up, no matter what the cost.

"*You* give them to me!" he screeched, giving me the meanest face I think a baby pixie is capable of making. He was glaring at me.

I pointed at my chest. "Me?"

"Yes!" he said, crying and stomping his foot.

My nose started itching uncontrollably. I put the handkerchief up to my nose, ready to go ahead and blow, willing to risk sounding like a deranged moose in favor of fighting the tickling any further.

"Noooo!!!" yelled Willy, breaking free of his father's grip. He flew up into the air as I folded the cloth over the top of my nose, taking a deep breath in so I could blow out.

Willy flew straight at me, making a beeline for my face.

I blew my nose as hard as I could, trusting he'd change course in time to avoid a face plant into my skull.

As I blew, I felt something come loose, high up in my sinuses. I cringed as the sounds of disgusting things leaving my nose and going into poor Dardennes' monogrammed handkerchief echoed across the room.

I was afraid to pull the cloth away when I was finished, knowing the chances that it was a clean blow were slim. Shit was sure to be dangling from my nose. No way was I getting out of this without total humiliation. This was karma, kicking my ass once again.

Willy landed on the front of the cloth as it hung from my nose.

"Baby Bee, what the hell are you doing?" I screeched from behind it.

"Getting my polly balls!" he shouted, full of self-righteous indignation and full-on you-ain't-stoppin'-me-for-nothing determination. He climbed down to the bottom of the handkerchief, sending me into a panic.

"Get off, Baby Bee! Go away!" I shook my head back and forth, trying to dislodge him, but he was having none of it.

"They are *my* polly balls, Lellamental. *Mine!*"

He'd reached the bottom of the cloth and was climbing up inside it.

"Tim!" I yelled. "Get your little freak off me!"

Tim was already halfway there, having recovered from the shock of seeing his child headed for my nose. "Willy get your tiny buns over here, son!"

"My polly balls, my polly balls, my polly balls," was all I could hear coming from inside the handkerchief.

I turned my back on the fae in the room and pulled the handkerchief away from my nose, praying I wasn't going to squish him and equally praying I didn't have any boogs hanging off my face. I breathed in once experimentally, wiggling my nose around, relieved to find I could inhale through it again.

I cringed inwardly at the faint smell of sulfur that rose up from the cloth in my hand. I looked down, unable to see Willy at first; but I could feel him wiging around in there, so I cautiously opened up the booger-soaked rag, feeling a little sick the entire time, fearing what I was going to find.

Tim arrived on my shoulder, out of breath. "What happened? Is he okay?"

I said nothing, just stared down at the train wreck in my hands, speechless.

"What's wrong?" asked Ben.

"Stay back!" I screamed, finding my voice just in the nick of time. I calmed myself and turned my head around partway, my features carefully schooled to look natural. I was still afraid of giving them a full view, knowing for sure there was something nasty on my face, but the last thing I wanted was anyone coming over for a good look at what I held in my hands. "Just give us a minute, okay?"

Tim was stuttering. "Uhhh... huh, huh ... that ... uh ... that is ... uh ..."

"Tim," I said, not sure if I should be disgusted, amazed, or just throwing up, "that has to be the most fucked up thing I've ever seen in my entire life."

"Baby Bee?" Tim asked hesitantly, his wife flying up to stand next to him, gasping at what she saw below her. "What are you doing?"

The baby pixie glared up at us, busy walking through my snot, gathering up little yellow balls of I didn't even want know what.

"I'm taking my polly balls back!"

"What is a polly ball, Tim?" I asked in a whisper.

"Oh. My. Goodness," whispered Abby. "I think I know what they are."

"I do too," said Tim. A snort escaped his nose.

"What's so funny?" I asked, suspiciously.

"Ummmm," Tim said in a falsetto voice, just barely holding back massive hysterical laughter, "I believe a polly ball is a ball of pollen. Sticky stuff. Apparently easy to hide in the nasal passages of lellamentals."

My jaw popped open and slanted off to the side as I contemplated the awfulness of what I was seeing. When I could again, I spoke. "Are you telling me ... that your evil child ... was storing pollen balls in my *nose?!*"

I heard a snicker behind me and whipped around to see who

had done it. Everyone stared back at me with blank expressions, but Red's looked a little too perfect. I watched as a tear escaped his eye and rolled down his face. A smile quirked up at the corner of his mouth, and his chin quivered ever so slightly.

Céline giggled.

I glared at her, but then Dardennes covered his mouth and dipped his head down, shaking with silent mirth, making it impossible for me to know who to give the death stare to.

"Pixies," said Niles with disgust in his voice. "Pesky varmints. I don't know how you abide 'em."

Jared let out a hearty guffaw that shocked me in its enthusiasm.

When Ben finally joined in, I could do nothing but sputter.

"Are you ... you've gottta be fucking kidding ... Tim, your kid ... dammit! Tim! Your kid shoved pollen up my nose while I *slept!*"

"I believe a thank-you is in order," said Dardennes, clearing his throat loudly several times before continuing.

"Please tell me you're joking," I said, incredulous that he would even suggest such a thing.

"No, I'm not. It appears as if those sticky pollen balls packed into your nostrils kept the contents of the spell from reaching your brain. If it weren't for the small pixie's penchant for collecting pollen balls and storing in them in such a ... safe place ... you would no longer be among us. Nor would Ben."

Everyone turned to look at the little baby pixie who was now flying up in the air, his arms full of booger-covered polly balls, glaring at me in accusation.

# Chapter Thirty-Two

IT TOOK A LONG TIME for the laughter in the room to die down. I finally got over myself enough to thank the little turd for saving my life, but I wasn't sure he appreciated what I had to say. I was probably never going to be able to count on polly balls to save my life again, since I apparently did a terrible job of taking care of them.

Abby took Willy and his polly balls from the room, but Tim stayed behind.

"Much as I appreciate the levity provided by your son, Tim, I must ask that we all get back to the subject of our earlier discussion. Our problem with the Gray. I believe you have more to share, Jayne." Dardennes looked at me and then meaningfully at the tapestry.

*Dammit! How does he know?* I tried to act innocent, but he frowned at me and gave me a very slight shake of his head. He was using his awesome parental guilt trip powers on me again, knowing I was helpless against them.

"Okay, yeah. So there's some stuff I have to tell you."

"This should be interesting," said Red out of the corner of his mouth.

"Hey, old man. Watch it, or you're gonna get kicked out," I threatened, only partially in jest.

He held up his hands in surrender.

I couldn't help but smile as I realized that somehow, as a result of bringing out the contents of my nose, we'd turned a corner in our relationship. It made me feel all warm inside to know I might have just an ounce of respect coming from the crusty old dude.

"I was here in Ben's room looking for him before our meeting and took a little drink of the green stuff there and had a few hallucinations."

"Why do I feel we're getting an abbreviated version of events?" asked Red sarcastically.

"Because the details aren't important," I said, frustrated.

"Please allow us to make those determinations," said Dardennes.

"Details, changeling," demanded Niles, just a tad of his gruffness missing.

"Fine. So I was going to leave without Ben and I heard a noise in the room. When I tried to find out who it was, a voice told me to take a drink."

"Who was it?" asked Céline, clearly fascinated.

"I'm getting to that. So anyway, I took a few gulps of the absinthe ... "

"A few gulps?" asked Red. He looked over at Dardennes. "She cannot be serious."

"Can I tell my story, please?"

"By all means," said Dardennes, sharing a look with Red.

The look probably meant I was a lunatic, but whatever. I kept talking, anxious now to get it over with. "So I took the drink and then all of those dragons over there came out of the tapestry and started talking to me."

"No, they did not!" yelled Red.

"Yes, they did too! Shit, first you want me to tell you the story, and then you accuse me of lying. Do you want to hear it or not?"

"Yes, we do. Please, Jayne," said Céline, sounding like she was almost begging. She'd moved to the edge of her seat, like she was watching a really fascinating movie.

"Okay, so the dragons came out, and I touched the purple one. It was warm. I messed with the black one a little, which was probably not very smart in hindsight, but at the time I wasn't really in control of myself, because that green shit is seriously strong."

"One sip of the absinthe would have been enough," snorted out Red. "You took enough for an army."

"Well, I'm sorry! But I didn't see a dosage label on the bottle, so whatever."

"I'm just wondering what you mean by messing with the black dragon," said Jared, admiration in his voice. The fact that he wasn't being critical encouraged me to elaborate.

"Well, I noticed it didn't have the fangs like the purple one, so I pulled my weapon out and asked him if he was missing something."

Jared's mouth dropped open.

"The Great Spirit bless us, she could have brought the entire realm down with her sadly misguided attempts at humor," whispered Niles. It was the only time I'd ever seen him look afraid.

"Oh, get off it, Niles. It wasn't that big a deal. He took it ... pretty well, all things considered."

"What did he do?" asked Céline, smiling brightly. She was apparently pleased as punch that I almost killed her and her whole family.

"He flamed me a little." I chuckled. "I kind of thought I was going to get a melted face or at least some singed eyebrows from it, but it just got a little warm."

Red's head was shaking. "I cannot fathom what has happened today. Nothing in our near history has prepared me to consider anything of this magnitude."

"Your memory has holes in it, old man," said a voice from the doorway.

"Oh, boy," said Tim. "Hold on to your knickers, Jayne. Here she comes."

I smiled in recognition. "Thank goodness you're here," I said. "Shayla, could you come in here and explain to everyone what you and Garrett said, please? I'm sure they won't believe me if I tell it."

# Chapter Thirty-Three

SHAYLA CAME IN, AND SHE wasn't alone. Another angel came in after her, his wings folded but fully visible, and I was taken aback with how cute he was. I was totally jealous that she had such a hot boyfriend. *Man the Overworld must be awesome. You get to fly and have hot guys to hang with.* I looked over at Ben. *Okay, so the Here and Now isn't bad for the hot guys part. But I haven't been able to fly yet...*

Behind the second angel came Garrett, his face a mask of seriousness. He nodded to everyone in the room, but stayed near the door.

"Who are these ... creatures?" asked Red, standing in a defensive posture. His eyes kept scanning back and forth between Shayla and Garrett. For some reason, he ignored the younger-looking angel.

I didn't have that kind of internal fortitude. I couldn't stop staring at him. I could have walked past a guy just like him in high school, he looked so ... normal. Except for the wings of course and the level nine hotness he had going on - that was kind of rare outside of Hollywood, at least in my experience. He stared back at me, not embarrassed at all about his boldness, neither smiling nor frowning. I wondered if he knew Chase.

"Come now, Red. You know me," said Shayla, taking a few steps closer to him.

"It cannot be ... ," he whispered, almost to himself, his face going white.

"Let us just say it *should* not be. And yet it is. And that is the crux of the problem, is it not?" She turned to Dardennes. "Anton, it is nice to see you and Céline again."

He bowed his head. "Shayla. It has been a long time."

"About a thousand years, if memory serves. But let us not talk about time and the ravages it has wrought upon your countenance. I believe we have a more urgent matter to discuss."

My mouth dropped open in admiration of her skill at slamming the old folks in the room. I could see they weren't unaffected by Shayla's barbs. But she was right about one thing; whatever bad blood or memories they had between them could be discussed later.

"So, good news, Shayla," I said. "Maléna lost the challenge."

"Don't be so sure about that," said Shayla, her words striking fear into my heart. "Her little games with you and your partner did a nice job of creating a distraction, keeping all of you busy long enough not to notice several creatures sneaking into your realm from the Underworld *and* the Overworld."

"What are you saying?" demanded Red.

"I don't like the sound of this," said Niles.

Jared remained silent, watching each of the room's occupants carefully, especially the silent angel who wouldn't stop staring at me.

My eyes darted all over the place, my brain working like some kind of super computer trying to put all the pieces together.

Tim flew over to my shoulder and whispered in my ear. "Remember that secret I had for you. Get ready for the big reveal."

His words send shivers of apprehension down my arms and legs. Goosebumps broke out everywhere as Shayla's words came out and sank into my brain.

"I am saying that the Gray has fallen. Or a piece of it has. The demons are coming; some of them are already here. Overworlders are also arriving, many of whom are standing just outside your compound now. You must prepare for a fight and find a way to seal the tear in the veil before it is too late and all humanity is lost."

"There cannot even *be* a tear in the veil so how do you expect us to seal it?!" yelled Red.

"You can deny the truth all you want. That does not make the truth cease to exist for the rest of the world," she said in a mocking tone. "We suggest you open the portals and put the guardians in place once again. It is the only way to lessen the stress you have placed on the Gray and allow it to heal."

"We cannot," said Céline. "The decision was made over a thousand years ago. The dragons were defeated. You and the other dragon slayer made sure of that."

"Does someone want to fill me in here? Because I'm totally in the weeds," I said.

Shayla turned to me. "The passageways to the Otherworlds used to lie behind portals that were guarded by dragon guardians. One dragon pair for each portal, one to the Underworld and one to the Overworld. When the fae decided to seal the portals for good, the only way to do so was to banish the guardians to the Otherworlds. Garrett and I were sent to dispatch the guardians and see to the sealing of the portals, which we did."

"And it cannot be undone," said Red. "The guardians cannot

be resurrected. There are no more guardians, and the portals would be merely swinging doors without them."

"How many dragons did you kill?" I asked, impressed all over again with my ancestor's ass-kicking abilities. I wondered if she'd have any spare time when all this craziness was over to give me some tips.

"I killed one, and Garrett killed the other."

I looked around at all the adults in the room, but none of them had the lightbulb on over their heads like I did. I felt supremely stupid thinking I'd misunderstood, but I couldn't help but speak up.

"Listen, I'm no math wiz or anything ... but if you only killed two dragons, what's the problem, exactly?"

Red dropped his head and shook it, making my face go hot with embarrassment.

"Never mind," I said, turning to go sit down.

"She is right," said Ben, grabbing onto my hand and pulling me over to his side.

I looked over at the angel for some reason and caught him frowning before he cleared his expression again. I wondered if I imagined it, and if I hadn't, why he was doing that when Ben touched me.

"You only killed the guardians. You did not kill their mates," Ben explained.

"But their mates went with them into the Otherworlds," said Shayla. She didn't sound like she was arguing - more like probing for more information.

"Yes, but that isn't resurrection to bring a creature back from the Otherworlds who entered without death."

I frowned at Ben. *How does he know all this shit about being dead and stuff?* I pulled my hand away gently, not sure I wanted to be snuggling up to a zombie expert.

"He could be right," said Dardennes. "I had not considered that aspect."

Shayla turned to Garrett. "What do you think, vampire? Can we bring the mates of the guardians to the portals and operate them once again?"

I noticed Niles and Céline cringing at the vampire title. Dardennes and Jared seemed unaffected. Ben took a step closer to me, but I moved away, trying not to seem obvious about it. I had nothing to fear from Garrett. I was certain of it. Ben, I wasn't so sure of. He had too many secrets and too much power. The fact that he had the guardians trapped in a tapestry in his bedroom was kind of freaking me out right now.

"I believe it is possible," answered Garrett. "What do we know about them? Has anyone here gotten any information from any creatures coming over about the status of the guardians?" His gaze moved over to the tapestry behind him. "Surely someone has learned something of value."

The rest of the people in the room looked at me.

"Yeah, okay," I admitted, wishing I'd known more about this stuff when I was wasted on the absinthe so I could have asked the dragons better questions. "So I talked to the dragons. And they said the time is nigh. That the veil is falling and we need them."

# Chapter Thirty-Four

A BANGING CAME AT THE door as soon as the last word left my mouth. Ivar's head came in through the entrance.

"I am sorry to interrupt your meeting. But there appears to be a situation outside the compound, Anton."

"What is the problem, Ivar?"

"The green elves report several orcs and vampires at entrances to the compound. They have taken some casualties already."

My heart drummed hard in my chest, and I got an instant stress headache.

Shayla's hand moved to her dragon fang weapon, pulling it out of its sheath. "Come with me, Beau. Let's go see what we can do to help the green elves."

The mystery angel shifted his gaze away from me and followed Shayla to the door, his wings fluttering a little and then coming back in tight to his back. No way could he fit through the door with them open even a little.

"What do you recommend we do?" asked Dardennes, speaking to Shayla's back. It was seriously freaky to hear him asking for guidance and sounding a little lost. It scared me probably more than anything I'd seen all week, and I'd had a pretty shitty week.

She stopped at the doorway, now both her fang and her sword drawn. "Get your people together. Make the decision you must about the portals. Work with your witches and wrathes to get that veil fixed. And ready yourselves for the journey."

"What journey?" I asked, my mouth working ahead of my brain. I felt like the world was dropping out from beneath my feet when she answered.

"Your journey to the Otherworlds, Jayne. You don't think those dragons are just going to come when you call them, do you?" She winked at me and gave me a cocky smile. "See you on the other side."

The angel named Beau locked eyes with me one more time before he turned and disappeared out the door behind her.

# Hate Cliffhangers?

Not to worry! Just go to Amazon, find the next book in the series, click on the "Look Inside" cover of the book, and you'll be able to read the first several chapters of the next book for free. I know, I know ... cliffhangers make you crazy, right? Sorry. I just can't seem to help myself. :)

# Other Books by Elle Casey

War of the Fae: Book One, The Changelings
War of the Fae: Book Two, Call to Arms
War of the Fae: Book Three, Darkness & Light
War of the Fae: Book Four, New World Order

Clash of the Otherworlds: Book 1, After the Fall
Clash of the Otherworlds: Book 2, Between the Realms
Clash of the Otherworlds: Book 3, Portal Guardians

Apocalypsis: Book 1, Kahayatle
Apocalypsis: Book 2, Warpaint
Apocalypsis: Book 3, Exodus
Apocalypsis: Book 4, Haven

My Vampire Summer
My Vampire Fall

Wrecked
Reckless

# About the Author

Elle Casey is an American writer who lives in Southern France with her husband, three kids, Hercules the wonder poodle, and Monie the bouvier. In her spare time she writes young adult novels.

# A personal note from Elle ...

If you enjoyed this book, please consider leaving feedback on Amazon.com, Goodreads.com, or any book blogs you participate in. More positive feedback means I can spend more time writing! Oh, and I love interacting with my readers, so if you feel like shooting the breeze or talking about books, please visit me. You can find me at ...

www.ElleCasey.com
www.Facebook.com/ellecaseytheauthor
www.Twitter.com/ellecasey
www.Shelfari.com/ellecasey

# Acknowledgments

None of my books makes it to my readers without a lot of support. First, of course, to my readers: I give thanks to you because you are the reason I write! Every day I search my inbox, Facebook, and Amazon pages for your comments. They inspire me to keep going through it all. Thank you for taking time out of your busy lives to share your kind words and thoughts with me!

To my friends in France and elsewhere, thank you for your support and for all the fun you share with me when I'm not banging away like a possessed madwoman at the keyboard. Super hugs in no particular order to my France-friends: the Wild-Teim family, the Beplates, the Munnés, the Robinson/Caylas, the Wurths, the Buissons, and the Bayles. You make living in Southern France an absolute dream.

Always to my husband and kids. Even when we are separated by thousands of miles (ahem, baby boy), it is still all of you who lift me up, the wind beneath my wings.

On the technical side of things, thank you to Claudia at Phatpuppyart for my cover. Thanks to Amazon for giving me the platform to publish my work. To my betas, Theresa V, Amy J, Margaret R, and Craig C ... thank you so, so much!!!! You all add to my final product, and I couldn't be more grateful. And to all the websites that work with me to remove pirated copies of my work from the Internet, know that without your support, I would stop writing entirely. Every time I find someone stealing my work, it takes a little piece of me away, so thank you for all you (and others) do to help eradicate the problem of Internet piracy.

Made in the USA
Middletown, DE
14 December 2016